A RELUCTANT SEAMAN

Also by Leslie Scrase:

Days in the Sun (children's stories, with Jean Head)
In Travellings Often
Booklet on Anglican/Methodist Conversations
Some Sussex and Surrey Scrases
Diamond Parents
Coping With Death
The Sunlight Glances Through (poetry)
Some Ancestors of Humanism
An Evacuee
Conversations (on Matthew's Gospel)
        between an Atheist and a Christian
A Prized Pupil!

A Reluctant Seaman

Leslie Scrase

UNITED WRITERS
Cornwall

UNITED WRITERS PUBLICATIONS LTD
Ailsa, Castle Gate, Penzance, Cornwall.

British Library Cataloguing in Publication Data:
A catalogue record for this book is
available from the British Library.

ISBN 1 85200 101 1

Printed in Great Britain by
United Writers Publications Ltd
Cornwall.

To the grateful memory of:
Uncle Stan and Auntie (see 'Who's Who').
Lieutenant Commander Burge RN.
George Fink and Roy Mays of Alpha Cars,
and also Barbara Miller.

Of the living, David Allen, Bernard Davies,
John Edwards and Raymond Trewin
may discover how easy it is to confuse
fiction and factual memory!

Acknowledgements

I owe an immense debt of gratitude to my publisher, Malcolm Sheppard of United Writers Publications Ltd. But for him, I doubt whether *An Evacuee* would ever have been published.

It took the publication of that book plus the ceaseless encouragement of Wendy my wife, and of my brother Aubs, to drive me on to write *A Prized Pupil!*, and once again it was Malcolm Sheppard who gave the ultimate encouragement of publication which in turn led me to complete the trilogy.

Neither of us has made a fortune, but thanks to the recording system of the Library Service we know that thousands of people have read these books. For me, that is a wonderful reward.

Who's Who

Like its predecessors *An Evacuee* and *A Prized Pupil!*, this book is largely autobiographical. As a result people who knew me in my Navy days may also look for themselves and the part they played in my life. They will be relieved to find that though there are incidents in which they were involved, the characters in the book do not depict any of them – except . . .

Ah! This time there are a few exceptions.

Bernard Davies might recognise the fine cross country runner who became such a good friend during training and then disappeared from my life for ever. I suppose we all have a few friends from the past with whom we wish we had kept in touch. For me there are Keith Patterson from my childhood and youth; Rex Hook who was a close friend during evacuation for just one year before we were separated.

But I have also included one or two real people in this book – Billy Graham for one. Uncle Stan and Auntie were also real people. Auntie was Miss Crawford, Uncle Stan's marvellous and aged cockney housekeeper.

Uncle Stan was Stanley Foot of the famous west country Foot family. His brother Isaac is still remembered throughout Devon and Cornwall. He served twice as a Liberal MP, the second time becoming a minister in Ramsey MacDonald's National Government. Both a Liberal and a Methodist, he became vice-president of the Methodist Conference. Three of his seven children became well-known in their own right: Dingle became solicitor general in the 1960s; Hugh ended up as Lord Caradan after a distinguished diplomatic career in which he returned colonies to independence (notably Ceylon) and in which he served as Ambassador to the United Nations; and Michael who was unfortunate enough to lead the Labour Party when its fortunes were at their lowest ebb. He is perhaps the last great Socialist, a man with an incisive mind, a genuine compassion and a passion for peace. He is also a director and life-long supporter of Plymouth Argyle – we all have our weaknesses and failings don't we?

As the pages of this book will show, Stanley Foot was far less visible than some members of the family but his work was no less valuable.

Strangely enough, just as this book was about to be sent to my publisher, I was asked to conduct the funeral of Michael Foot's sister Jennifer. She was another member of the family who kept out of the limelight. But she had the same strong and practical concern for the underdog and she showed the same hospitality to all who came to Weekhayn farm.

For me it was a privilege to know 'Uncle Stan' and another privilege to meet Jennifer's family.

John Bilson is the other real person in this book. I met him at Uncle Stan's. He was Nigerian and must be linked with Godfrey Sintim Misa, a Ghanaian I met at University. Looking at multi-cultural England today, it seems hardly possible that it was not until I was almost in my twenties that I met people from Africa. These were the first two. They were men of real quality and captured my affection, respect and admiration. They taught me to respect people for their worth rather than for their nationality.

Contents

1

Harvest Camp

It was a strange summer that year of 1949 when he left Perspins College. It was a summer of waiting: waiting for his Higher School Certificate results and waiting for his call-up into the Navy.

He wandered aimlessly in the countryside near his home in Surrey. He listened to his father's music and put all the records into a proper alphabetical order by composers' names. It was a waste of time of course. Order and neatness were his mother's virtues. His father had no understanding of order at all.

His brother Gerry saw his aimlessness and invited him to join him at a harvest camp for a week. They set out on their bikes but they had only got to Mitcham when Gerry had a puncture. Roger was astonished to find that Gerry didn't know how to mend a puncture.

"I'll do it," he said. "You watch."

He took off Gerry's tyre and worked his way carefully round the inner tube until he found the hole. He took his puncture repair outfit and found a patch that would adequately cover the hole. He glued the inner tube and the patch, waited a little while and then stuck on the patch, smoothing it carefully and holding it on firmly.

Gerry watched but while he watched he ate his way steadily through the sandwiches his mother had prepared. He wasn't really very conscious of what he was doing.

Roger took some white powder and shook it around the patch generously. Then he rubbed it around making sure that it covered

13

the whole area.

"Why are you doing that?" asked Gerry with his mouth full.

"So that none of the glue sticks to the tyre."

"Oh right. Is that it then?"

"I'll just pump it up a bit to see that it's OK."

It was. He put the tyre back on, carefully protecting his repair as he did so. Then he pumped the tyre up properly.

"There," he said proudly. "All done." He rubbed his hands on a rag as Gerry finished his sandwich. "Here, give me one of those."

Gerry turned to the sandwich box. "Strewth," he said. "It's empty."

"You swine! You've eaten all my sandwiches."

"I'm sorry. I didn't realise. We'd better get on or we'll get to the camp too late for dinner."

He mounted his bike and a rather disgruntled Roger followed. They still had a long way to go. It was seventy miles to the harvest camp in Hertfordshire and they had only done about fifteen.

Thirty miles further on, Gerry stopped at a small shop. He came out with a couple of bottles of pop and two Mars bars. "That'll make up for me eating your sandwiches," he said.

Roger was still sulking. He thanked Gerry with no real gratitude and drank his pop. They continued on their journey, chewing their Mars bars and peddling on in the burning sunshine until at last they arrived at the camp.

Bell tents stood on either side of a marquee, one side for boys and one side for girls. They made their way to the marquee and signed on. Each of them was given a straw palliasse for a mattress and three old army blankets for their bed. Then they were directed to one of the line of bell tents.

By the time they had settled in it was time to eat in the marquee. Thick slices of corned beef, boiled potatoes and baked beans were served on enamel plates. They ate quickly and then washed their plates ready for the prunes and custard that followed. Roger didn't really feel full when he had eaten but his spirits began to rise all the same. Unlike Gerry, he had never been to harvest camp before. It could be fun.

By midday the following day he had changed his mind. He spent a restless night on the straw palliasse. It was difficult to persuade the straw to give in the right places. In the morning they washed with cold water in buckets brought from the farm. And then they breakfasted on stodgy porridge made the night before in great billy-cans and heated up over open fires. But worse was to come. Roger found himself on potato-peeling duty. Mountains of potatoes kept the team going all morning.

At lunch-time they took huge piles of doorstep cheese sandwiches and apples out to the workers in the fields and then they joined them. For the whole of the rest of that week Roger was out in the sun-drenched fields.

At a previous camp the reaper and binder had been at work cutting and tossing out sheaves ready tied. Campers had picked up the sheaves, banging them together and mingling the heavy heads of corn. They had leaned them together with others in stooks of six to eight sheaves standing upright to dry, safe from the damp and mildew of the stubble.

Now it was time to carry the sheaves to the stack-yard. Tractors and trailers, horses and trailers, both were there for the campers to load. Roger spent his week on trailer after trailer. Two pitchers with pitchforks tossed the sheaves up to Roger and another lad called Stephen. Dust and mice flew everywhere and thistles tore at sun-burned skin.

Roger and Stephen began to build their load. It had to be done with care and organisation. Each sheaf had to fit in its place in the sides of the load. As one was being fitted in place another was flying through the air. Roger and Stephen found themselves rising higher and higher.

At last the pitchers had to stop. They could no longer reach the top. They roped the load down and Roger and Stephen slithered down the side on the long drop to the ground before sending the load on its way.

While they climbed onto another trailer to begin all over again, their load was taken to the yard where another team tossed the sheaves onto the elevator. At the top of the elevator more campers took the sheaves and fed them butt end first to the farm hand who was an experienced stacker. His was skilled work.

He worked around the outside of the stack getting the sides vertical. He created a rectangle gently sloping from the centre to the sides to prevent the rain from getting through. Up it grew almost like a loaf of bread rising. And then he began to bring the sheaves in little by little to make the roof, thatching the top to complete the job.

They worked on until about seven in the evening. Roger felt as if he had been scratched by thistles and bitten by bugs from one end of his weary body to the other. His hair, his clothes, the very pores of his body, were full of dust. The pain in his shoulders and arms was such that he wished he could take them off. He bathed in refreshing cold water, changed into clean clothes and went to the marquee for a good, solid meal and mug after mug of water. Others drank tea.

After they had eaten, some of them went off to the nearest pub. Gerry and Roger went with them. There was nothing else to do but both of them had been brought up to be teetotallers. Roger didn't feel comfortable. Besides romances were blossoming and he felt that there was no point for him. He'd be in the Navy in a few weeks. He had no interest in starting up friendships that would have no future. Feelings returned to him that he had had as an evacuee and again at boarding school. He felt that he was part of a group to which he didn't belong. He always seemed to get on well with people but he never seemed to fit anywhere precisely.

Because of evacuation and boarding school he felt like a stranger when he was at home. At his rural boarding school he had never *quite* fitted with the country lads but because of evacuation he wasn't quite a townie either. He always had plenty of friends, always felt he was welcome but he was never quite one of the inner circle. He never quite belonged. He wondered if that was what it was going to be like in the Navy – a conscript amongst regulars.

Watching other relationships blossom he found himself thinking about Gladys who had been so good to him at Perspins. He wondered how she was getting on in her new job at the hotel in Beddingford. One evening he stayed away from the pub and wrote her a letter:

Dear Gladys, I'm at a harvest camp. There are girls here and a lot of them have already paired off with boys. But I haven't. I think about you a lot.

How are you getting on in your new job? I hope you are enjoying it. It's daft me asking you questions because you won't be able to write back. I haven't got an address to give you. I'll be in the Navy in a few weeks.

That's all I've got to tell you. Thank you for . . . he paused. How could he put it? Eventually he just wrote, *all you did for me at school. You know what I mean.*

And then he had the problem of how to sign off. 'Yours Sincerely' or 'Yours Truly' sounded too formal but he didn't think it would be wise to mention the word 'love'. And he certainly wasn't going to go in for any of those silly groups of letters like 'SWALK', 'sealed with a loving kiss'.

And yet, after he had finally settled on *Yours Affectionately* and sealed the envelope, that was precisely what he did before he posted it.

One way and another the week passed quickly. He had never worked so hard in his life. There were only short breaks during the day for a snack or a drink. Drinks were what they craved most of all.

2
Call-up

When they arrived home from harvest camp Roger's call-up papers were waiting. He had time to spend a week with his parents and with his sister Margaret on their summer holidays and then the fateful day came.

He made his way with a small suitcase to Paddington station, The platform was littered with eighteen year olds, Roger stood back a bit, feeling shy and awkward. Many of these lads already seemed to know one another and to have become mates.

The train came in and he watched as they all climbed on board. None of them had made for the very front of the train. He did. He found an empty compartment where he could be alone with a book and with his thoughts. Oddly enough, now that he was a conscript, he was reading John Stuart Mill 'On Liberty'.

But he couldn't concentrate. His emotions were too powerful, full of anxious uncertainty. He wasn't at all sure how he was going to cope with being in the Navy, at the bottom of the pile.

They arrived at Corsham station, piled out of the train, and began to drift towards two smartly dressed petty officers. At once the shouting began.

"Naval recruits over here. MOVE yourselves. Line up in threes. That's three lines one behind the other. God what a shower. Know your left hand from your right do you? Then let's have all your suitcases in your left hands. And if you're not wearing them, drape your burberries over your left arm. Burberries? Raincoats. No. Not like that. God. Here give it to me."

He took one of their raincoats.

"Hold it like so." Nobody moved. "Go on then. Do as I do." So they held their raincoats as he was holding the one in his hands. "Fold it like so." They folded. "Place over the arm like so. Now, lift your suitcases."

They all did as they were told and he returned the raincoat to its owner.

"That's better." His voice was heavy with sarcasm. "We are going to march to the ship and to do it as smartly as we can. Know how to march do we? Yes?"

Nobody spoke.

"If you think you know how to march you are wrong. Watch. The army marches like so." He marched up and down in front of them, arms going like pistons and rising until they were at right angles to the body. "Robots," he said. "Bloody robots, that's what they are. As for the Brylcreem boys of the RAF, we don't need to bother with them. They try to copy the army but they can't. They're just a bloody shower. So what about us? You're in the Navy, the Senior Service, and don't you bloody forget it. We march like MEN. Watch."

Again he marched up and down in front of them. "Watch my arms." They only rose half way to the horizontal. "See what I mean? Like MEN, not machines. NOW, stand to attention. Heels together, toes apart at forty-five degrees.

"When I say 'Right turn', your right heel stays where it is, your right toe turns and your left foot joins your right foot. Understood? Good.

"Recruits! Wait for it, wait for it. Recruits, 'ight harn."

They did their best.

"What a shower. God. What A shower. NOW: When I say 'By the left, quick march', that means that you put your left foot forward first. Got it?

"Bay the lift . . . wait for it. Wait for it. Bay the lift, QUI-ICK MARCH. Left, right, left, right. What A shower. What A bloody shower. Ift, igh, ift, igh. We'll make something of you I suppose. Keep in step there. Ift, igh, ift, igh . . ."

They marched through the gates of HMS *Royal Arthur*.

How daft, thought Roger. Fancy calling it a ship here in the middle of Wiltshire.

"Heads up. Shoulders back. The Duke of Edinburgh trained

19

here. Smarten yourselves up for God's sake. Ift, igh, ift, igh."

Nissen hut windows flew open as they marched past. Jeers greeted them, cat-calls: "Go home, your mothers want you. What A shower. What A bloody shower."

The petty officer who had been marching them roared, "Recruits. Recruits SHOW!" pronounced as in 'ow'.

They stumbled to a full stop crumpling into one another like the crashed carriages of a railway train.

"Stand up damn you. What's the matter with you all? Stand to attention. Recruits . . . Recruits, ri-ight harn."

Once again they did their best and came to rest facing a Nissen hut.

"When I say, 'Stind at ace' your left foot leaves your right foot and comes to ground close to your neighbour's right foot. Ready? Recruits . . . Recruits, STIND-AT . . . ACE. Oh my God.'

He paused in despair. "The next command is 'stind acy'. On the command 'stind acy' you keep your feet where they are but your body can relax. Understood? Recruits . . . Recruits, STIND ACY.

" 'air cuts first. Then the issue of uniforms. We wancher caps ter fit yer 'eads don't we?"

They began to file into the Nissen hut. Roger wasn't bothered. School hair cuts had prepared him for this. But some of the men were upset to be losing prized locks. A few tried pleading with the barber. When the others saw the results of their pleading they stayed quiet.

A lad with a fine head of thick black hair took his turn. The clippers ran through it as if they were cutting hay at harvest time. Soon there was a broad furrow. Suddenly the barber stopped.

"Get out of my chair and report to the sick bay. You've got nits."

The lad lived with the humiliation of half a head of hair until the next hair cut session. Another lad took his place and whisked off his wig to reveal a completely bald top. Diphtheria when he was a child had left him bald.

"Too much hair on that wig. Don't wear it with your uniforms. Understood?"

Kit issue came next. First came a huge kit-bag. A quick glance was enough by way of measurement and then came their clothing issued in quick succession and all stuffed into the kit-bag. A small canvas bag came with the kit.

"That's your housewife," said the leading-seaman issuing the kit. "No, don't stop to look at it. Put it in with the rest."

It proved to be needles and thread, scissors and thimble – everything they would need for darning their socks and mending their clothes. For as long as they were in training they would wash their own clothes with soap and a scrubbing brush, and keep them in proper repair.

Last of all they were issued with a hammock. Kit-bag over one shoulder, hammock over the other, they set off for their own Nissen huts to find their bunks and billets. Roger watched other lads sling their kit-bags and hammocks over their shoulders with apparent ease. He couldn't manage it. Eventually he hoisted both onto a table, side by side. He leaned back into them, took hold of each of them with his hands over his shoulders, leaned forward and struggled away. What the hell was the point of giving them hammocks when they were sleeping in bunks?

In the Nissen hut he made up his bed on a top bunk. Then he noticed that the lad below him hadn't a clue. He was folding his blankets in a neat pile with no tucks around the edges or at the bottom. The poor chap had probably never made a bed in his life.

"Not like that," he said. "Your blankets will all fall off and you'll freeze. And you need at least one underneath you. What's underneath gives you just as much warmth as what's on top."

"Thanks. I've never been away from home before. My name's James."

"You'd better forget that for a start," said Roger. "No one here will call you James. It sounds too posh. You'd better get used to being 'Jim'. Roger's my name so I expect I'll get 'Roj'."

"Can I . . . I mean . . . It sounds a bit wet but would you mind sort of, well, being my friend?"

Roger wasn't at all sure that he wanted to determine who his close friends would be so quickly but the lad was obviously in a pretty bad way – nervous and lost and fearful. Roger was feeling pretty lost himself but he was damned if the Navy was going to beat him.

"Of course I don't mind," he said. "We all need friends don't we?"

That night at lights out, James knelt by his bed to say his prayers. At once there were hoots of laughter and jeers of derision. Roger got out of his bunk and knelt beside his friend and whispered:

"I wouldn't do this if I were you. It only draws attention to yourself. If you want to say your prayers, say them in bed where no one will notice. Otherwise they'll all give you hell."

The two got off their knees and climbed into their bunks. But the cat-calls continued. Suddenly the lights went on and there was silence. Their petty officer was standing in the doorway.

"No talking after lights out. You'll be up early so get to sleep."

He switched off the lights and a voice said, "Fuck off, bloody little Hitler."

On went the lights.

"Everybody out. Full kit including greatcoats and gas masks. In two minutes I want you all fell in in threes outside."

Roger and James dressed in silence while all around them there were grumbles, oaths, curses. They fell in outside.

"It has taken you three minutes, twenty three seconds. Not good enough. You'll do an extra five minutes for that. Eft turn. By the left, qui-ick march."

He marched them to the foot of a dust track up a long gradient.

"When I give the word, you will run up that hill at the double. At the end of the hill you will turn and run back keeping in your rows of three. When you get back here you will run up the hill again and continue until I stop you. Anyone who falls out will do double time. UNDERSTOOD?" He paused. "Right," he said. "Gas masks on."

They fumbled in their gas mask cases, pulled out their gas masks and put them on.

"At the double, qui-ick march."

They began to run. It was stifling inside their gas-masks. And with full kit, including great coats, they were soon sweating profusely. They kicked up the dust from the track, felt stifled and stumbled on, up the track and down again, up the track and down again, on and on. As Roger heard the groans and curses all around him he was very thankful that he was so fit. If Perspins College had done nothing else for him, it had left him as fit as a fiddle. In spite of the dust and the heat he knew that he would manage this punishment with far less trouble than his companions. They ran on for a full twenty minutes and were then sent back to their bunks. No opportunity to wash. And sweat filled clothing was the clothing they would wear in the morning.

It would be drill tomorrow – all day. Their group was going to smell pretty awful by the day's end Roger thought. Perhaps it was the smell of the Navy that had defeated the Spanish Armada when those westerly winds got up. Roger giggled silently before he went to sleep. If this was what the Navy was like, he was glad he only had to do eighteen months.

3

Part One Training

The weeks that followed seemed to be an endless nightmare of drill and kit inspections.

"Get fell in. Tallest on the right, shortest on the left."

How thankful Roger was that he was neither tall nor short. He could hide himself somewhere in the middle and be as inconspicuous as possible. And because he mostly managed to get things right he never became the tortured butt of the petty officer. There were one or two who walked perfectly normally but went into a strange robotic mode when they tried to march, left hand going forward with left leg and right hand with right leg. The more the PO shouted and swore at them, the worse it became.

There was another fresh-faced lad who had joined the Navy as a boy-seaman and got himself into trouble fairly consistently. The PO marked him out for especially sadistic treatment. And because of his freshness of face, he was also singled out by some as a useful sex-object but it was a while before Roger became aware of that.

"By the left, quick march. Left harn. Right harn. At the double, quick march. Get 'em up. Get 'em up there. E-eft wheel. I-ight wheel. Halt. What a shower. What a bloody shower. Stind at . . . ace. Stind acy."

But never for long. Up at six in the morning, drill began as soon as breakfast and the morning inspection were over. It went on all morning and began again after lunch, lasting all afternoon. Exhausted, the class retired to their Nissen hut to work on their kit, preparing it for the morning's inspection.

Once again Roger was thankful. He had joined to work in education and so wore 'fore and aft rig' – an ordinary ill-fitting suit. He had little to bother with apart from his boots. Those who were dressed in seaman's rig with bell-bottoms seemed to have endless work to do. They bent and twisted their caps about to try to make them look more worn; they scrubbed their scarves to get the colour out of them and make them look like the clothing of experienced seamen; and they pressed their bell-bottoms again and again to achieve seven smart circular rings, razor sharp in their line.

They even worked on their boots in a way that left Roger astonished. It might have been against the regulations, but they burned the toes to bring them up to a magnificent black shine. Roger watched but couldn't be bothered to imitate. It was enough for him just to work up a reasonably decent ordinary shine. He had already determined that he would do what he had to, but no more than that.

After three weeks they were issued with khaki gaiters and rifles and a new bout of drill began, with new sadistic pleasures for the PO.

They stood 'at ease' on the parade ground. Their rifles in their right hands, angled out from them, butt on the ground. "Class. Class shOW!" Again that 'ow' compelling them to bring feet together and the rifle close to the body. "Class shoul-der ARMS. Hup two three, over two three, down two three."

As if by magic their rifles now rested on their left shoulders, butt in the palm of their left hands. It was time to march. But the PO preferred to make them march 'at the double'. Their rifles bounced up and down painfully on their shoulders. The PO watched, eagerly shouting orders all the time:

" 'Ight WHEEL. Mark time. Knees up. Keep 'em up, Keep 'em up. At the double, qui-ick MARCH. Ift, igh, ift, igh, ift, igh. Smarten up there. Eft WHEEL. EFT you fuckin' stupid bastard. Class shOW. Some of you still don't know your left from your right. Turn your rifles over. That's it bolt downwards. Now we are going to learn which is our left and which is our right. Class. At the double, qui-ick march."

The old 303 was a heavy weapon. As it bounced on their shoulders the bolt rammed into them again and again. They grunted with pain and ran on. The bruising lasted long after they

25

b

learned to pad out their shoulders with handkerchieves.

And then came a division of the class between those who had signed on as regulars and those who were only conscripts. The regulars were marched off to the rifle range to learn to fire their guns. But the government couldn't afford the ammunition for conscripts to do the same. So Roger and his reduced number of companions simply went on drilling: "Shoul-der Arms: Hup, two three; over, two three; down, two three."

There was never any let up until the day of the class cross country run. It was the first break in the monotony though few besides Roger welcomed it. He soon found that most of his companions had never been on a cross country run in their lives. In no time at all he was out in front and on his own. Every few hundred yards there were men acting as markers, directing them along the course. He ran the four miles as if he were on a training run; came in first and was sent to the showers with his PO's congratulations.

The following day, just before lunch the class was told that with the exception of three of them it would be drill as usual in the afternoon. But the first three runners in the previous day's race would be running the same course again, this time in competition with the best runners of all the other new intake classes.

Roger was delighted: another afternoon free from drill.

He soon found himself in the leading group of runners. Among them was a tall, gangling lad with an easy running style that seemed effortless. Before long there were just four of them in the leading group. They stayed together for the first three miles, introducing themselves to one another and chatting about how lucky they were not to be on the parade ground. Soon after the three mile mark, the tall lad, Dave, stretched his legs and left the other three standing.

"That really is running," said one of the others enviously.

"Why don't we all come in together?" panted another.

"In threes. Tallest on the right, shortest on the left," gasped Roger and they all giggled.

As they headed for the finishing line, the few men watching urged them on to race one another for the honour of their separate classes but they straightened their line and ran in joint second. At once a Chief Petty Officer barked an order at them and marched them to the Lieutenant in charge.

"These three trainee ratings have just come in joint second sir. Trying to take the micky sir." He looked at the three with disgust. They were scum – conscripts all of them.

The officer looked at them with amusement. "You do realise that you have just been taking part in a race and that the honour of your class was at stake?"

They stood in silence.

"Answer the officer when he speaks to you," bellowed the CPO.

"Yes sir."

"Speak up!"

"YES sir."

The officer could hardly contain his amusement. "I've a good mind to make you run the course again but for reasons of which you are unaware at present, that might not be a good idea. Let there be no further behaviour of this kind. Is that understood?"

"Yes sir."

"Dismiss them please chief."

"Sir. Trainees, wait for it, WAIT for it . . . Trainees, Right Turn. At the double, QUI-ICK March. Eft. Igh. Eft. Igh. He ran alongside them. "Halt. Right turn. To the showers, Dis-miss."

Another day was over and it was back to drill the following morning. Roger was finding the combination of drill and running fairly punishing on his legs. So he wasn't quite so excited when he was singled out again before lunch. He was to run for the new intake against the ship's company and this time it would be a seven-mile course. He had never run seven miles before. Nor did it seem fair that they would be running for the third day in a row against men who were fresh.

He needn't have worried. Few of the members of the ship's company team were real runners. Three of them soon led the field followed by a larger group containing Roger, Dave and their two companions of the previous day.

Slowly the second group spread with the four conscripts at its head, just about keeping in touch with the front group of three.

"I've never run this far before," gasped Roger.

"Nor me."

"Nor me neither."

But Dave had. "Don't worry about it. If you can run four miles you can run seven. Just keep it nice and steady."

The four ran on together with hardly a word passing between them. And always, on ahead, they could see the three runners from the ship's company team. After about five and a half miles Dave said, "Just keep it going like this. You're doing fine. I'm going after those three."

For the second time in two days he stretched his legs and left them standing. Enviously they followed, struggling to increase their own pace just a little. Before long Roger found that he was drawing slightly ahead of his two companions and actually making up ground on those ahead. He pushed himself and the other two pushed themselves after him.

They saw Dave overtake the leading runners with apparent ease and it encouraged them. Shortly before the end of the course they caught and passed one of the three and then, with the end in sight Roger was suddenly struck with cramp in his left leg. The pain was cruel and his leg felt like lead. It stopped him in his tracks. He dared not stop now. He limped on, overtaken at the last by his two companions and the third runner of the ship's company. He struggled across the finishing line and fell to the ground in agony. Two men worked on him until the attack had passed and he was able to walk uncomfortably to the showers.

When he heard that the new intake had beaten the ship's company he was content. That evening his PO came into the Nissen hut.

"You." He pointed at Roger. "Strip and lay out on that table."

Roger was scared, confused. What had he done? What was going to happen to him? He dared not refuse. He stripped to his underwear and laid face down on the table.

"You did well today lad," said the PO.

Roger's relief was short-lived. The PO began to pummel his left leg, hammering away at the muscles.

"We've got to free these up," said the PO, "ready for tomorrow.'

"Tomorrow," gasped Roger, almost screaming the last syllable as the PO's massage thundered down again in sharp, chopping strokes.

"Yes. You're running for the ratings against the officers tomorrow and we've a real chance of winning."

Roger's heart sank. Cross country running was one thing, but

28

cross country RACING every day, that was something else. The PO was still talking.

"I'm going to excuse you drill tomorrow morning. It's quite unofficial of course. After breakfast you will just skulk in the hut here and make sure that no one sees you. Understood?"

"Yes sir."

"And I'll give your legs another battering tomorrow before the race."

Roger wasn't at all sure about that but he dared not say anything. It was a relief to get down off the table. Perhaps a morning off drill made it all worth-while. But when he was back on the table the following day, he wasn't convinced. The sweat poured off him. The PO's massage was agony. Nor did his legs feel up to much at the start of the race. But he set off with the usual group, hoping like hell that he wouldn't let them all down.

Once again Dave kept them company for most of the race and once again he won it. Once again the other three stayed pretty close to one another throughout the race. As it progressed Roger felt that his legs were coming back to him. The act of running seemed to take the weariness from them for a while and for most of the race he ran as easily as usual.

Towards the end, all three of them were feeling pretty done in. They were running on automatic pilot now. No word passed their lips. They had little idea or interest in who was in front and who behind. All they knew was that they must finish. To his astonishment Roger found that the other two were beginning to lag behind him, but not far. They came in 6th, 7th and 8th and were a major part of the lower deck's success that day. But it was almost a relief to get back to ordinary drill until the final passing out parade.

4

Work Ship

The morning of the passing out parade, the PO was in as usual, "Let's 'ave yer. Let's 'ave yer. Rise and shine. Rise and shine. Chop, chop." And then an unusual order, "Stand by your beds."

He walked briskly round the hut and singled out the two robotic marchers who still couldn't get things right.

"After breakfast you two report to the sick bay. You've got upset stomachs. Understood?" The last word barked at them.

"Yes sir."

"Now. We've got four of you in fore and aft rig." Roger was one and began to pay closer attention. "Four spoils the look of things. Upsets the balance. Three we can manage but four – no that would never do." He swung round on the fresh-faced lad who had been the butt of his worst sadism.

"It wouldn't Micky, would it? Looking forward to the passing out parade were we? Smartened ourselves up for it have we? Spent hours on our uniform no doubt. But you're a regular, Micky. There'll be plenty of parades for you, won't there, Micky? Mostly jankers Micky. We'll let the bleeding conscripts have their day today shall we? You'll report sick Micky, with the other two. Understood?"

"Yes sir." Micky looked sick and white with anger.

The PO passed out of the hut.

"What are jankers?" whispered James.

"Good heavens. Don't you know that yet? Punishment," answered Roger. He wondered where James had been all those past weeks of cruel initiation. Had he learned nothing?

When the parade was over the PO came into the hut in high good humour. Their class was one of two that had been given top marks for smartness in turn-out and in marching. James shared the PO's feelings of pride but Roger pointed out, "Yes but it's a fiddle isn't it? How would we have done if the men on sick parade had been with us?"

With part one training over, they were given a week-end leave pass. Roger went home, enjoyed himself and was back on board all too soon.

Then came one of those transformations so common in service life. Two POs came into their hut at 0600 on Monday morning, one of them their own. He was the one who spoke first.

"Stand by your beds. You've finished with me now." They knew better than to comment. "From now until you are transferred to your ships for part two training you'll be working ship and PO Johnson here will be in charge of you. Class. Class show." He turned about and marched smartly out of the hut and out of their lives.

PO Johnson looked at them with the usual distaste but when he spoke it was with something less than the usual parade ground roar:

"Stind at ace. Stind acy. I expect you know what 'work ship' means and if you don't you soon will. Wear your number eights from now on." (Number eights were their working dress – in Roger's case, open neck blue shirt and sturdy navy blue trousers.) "After inspection I shall give you jobs to do about the ship. This will continue every day until your transfers come through. In the evenings and through the night watches you will wear full uniform and do guard duty. When you are not on duty you will be allowed ashore . . . Silence in the ranks! . . . Any questions? No? Good. I'll see you at inspection time."

They washed, dressed, breakfasted, did their daily clean-up duties and prepared for inspection. After inspection they were given their jobs. James and Roger were given three baths to clean between them. They cleaned them and returned to the PO. He was astonished. How naïve could these conscripts be?

"Did you polish the taps? Go back and make sure they are properly polished."

They were back in no time. He looked at them in despair and separated them. Roger was sent to sweep the path to the officers' mess.

"And don't forget to salute officers when they pass. Know how to salute do we?"

"Yes sir."

"You'd better show me. Put your cap on. Stand to attention. Hm." He didn't seem to be impressed. "Sa-a-lute."

Roger brought his right hand straight up to the peak of his cap, hand sloped and back of the hand forward. Then he dropped his hand to his side.

The petty officer couldn't resist the opportunity of reciting his lesson. "That's it. Shortest road up and shortest road back, not like the Army and the RAF who take their 'ands right round in a circle. We don t waste our energies like that in the Senior Service. Understood?"

" . . . Sir." These POs are all the same thought Roger.

"And in the Army and the RAF they show their 'ands." (Blimey, he was giving it the full treatment.) Any card player knows you never show your 'and. We work so 'ard in the Senior Service that our 'ands is always grimed with honest toil so we show the back of our 'ands. Understood?"

" . . . Sir."

"But what you have forgotten is that you will be salutin' wiv a broom. Know how to salute wiv a broom do we?"

"Same as with a rifle sir?" Roger guessed.

"Right. Same as wiv a rifle." He threw a broom at Roger. Standing at attention, Roger knew he mustn't move. He resisted the urge to catch the broom. "Pick it up then, pick it up."

Roger picked it up and held it, broom end up, like a rifle.

"Recruit. Recruit, stind at ace . . . Recruit, recruit stind at atten-show. SA-a-LUTE."

Roger saluted.

"Stind at ace. Stind acy. Off you go then. What are you waiting for."

So Roger went to sweep the path to the officers' mess. It was a pain in the neck. He was constantly interrupted as officers came to and fro and he had to salute. But he finally finished his task and returned to the PO for his next assignment.

Seven times that morning the PO gave him a new job and each time Roger returned for more. The PO was sick of the sight of him. How could someone be in the Navy for a couple of months without learning the art of getting his head down?

"Report to me at the PO's mess after lunch."

"Yes sir."

The PO took him to a large shed, opened the door and gave Roger the key. It was full of garden tools and cleaning equipment and just inside the door there was a tub of soft soap.

"Every day," said the PO, "you will be here at 0900 and you will issue whatever ratings need. You will keep records of all you issue and who you issue it to. You will keep that tub full of soft soap. Know how to make soft soap do you?"

"No sir."

The PO showed him. "At 1230 you will receive all the equipment back and check it against your list. At 1400 you will issue tools and equipment again and make another list. At 1730 you will receive it all back again. Understood?"

"Yes sir. And what do I do in between sir?"

The PO didn't believe this. How thick could conscripts be? "You look after the shed of course."

It was Roger's turn to be amazed. How lucky could you get?

"Yes sir," he said. For the first time in his naval career he said it with relish.

"And what are you doing?" he asked James that evening?

"I'm the PO's runner," said James. "I wait around wherever he happens to be – the PO's mess most of the time – in case he wants to send a message to anybody. He never does, so it's sheer boredom."

"Well it's your own bloody fault." It was Micky. "You kept on going back asking for new jobs. You were supposed to make your first job last all day."

"What, washing three baths?"

"Yes. 'Work ship' doesn't actually mean work. It means 'find a quiet billet and keep out of sight'."

"And what are you doing?"

"I've been put with PO Ross. He specially asked for me because he's a bummer.

James didn't understand the significance of the remark. He didn't know what a bummer was but he soon would. It was about five weeks later, just before they were due to be transferred, that he came running into the Nissen hut, half clothed, ashen white and shaking from top to toe.

"What on earth's the matter with you?"

He almost sobbed. "It's that PO Ross that Micky works for."

"What about him?"

"He . . . Oh my God. It's too awful. I can't talk about it. Oh. It's horrible."

"Calm down."

James sat on his bunk, head in hands, convulsed with sobs and with his body shaking violently.

Roger went to sit beside him and put his arm round the lad's shoulder but thought better of it.

"Calm down and tell me what's happened."

"He . . . He ordered me to follow him and took me to his cabin. Then he told me to strip. I didn't understand but I didn't question it. Well you don't do you? So I started to strip and then he . . . oh God." He groaned. "He said he had had his eye on me and I was a nice lad and we were going to enjoy sex together. It took me a moment or two to understand what he was saying but then I just grabbed my clothes and ran. What am I going to do?"

They were quiet for a while and then Roger said, "There are only two things you can do. Either you keep your mouth shut because you know he won't try it on you again. Or you go to see the chaplain and tell him what's happened."

For a time he thought that James hadn't heard him. Slowly the sobbing and the shaking dwindled and when James finally looked up there was a firmness and an iron resolve Roger would never have dreamed he would see.

"I'm going to see the chaplain. This man must be stopped. Will you come with me?"

The immediate result was that when the rest of their class was transferred, they stayed where they were. Roger continued to look after his garden shed. James became the sky pilot's runner – the chaplain's messenger – and was issued with a bike. It almost made the long wait for the court martial case worth-while. He was very proud of that bike.

Before he was transferred, Roger took Micky to one side. "PO Ross has been fucking you hasn't he?"

"Yes," said Micky. "Everyone knows that. I get fucked by any of them who want to."

"So why don't you report it?"

"Look, my life's bad enough as it is. Just imagine what they'd all put me through if I reported someone. It's all right for you conscripts. But I'm in for seven years or more. And it's not all bad. I get privileges for being available you know."

"So you won't support Jim in his case against PO Ross?"

"No bloody fear. What do you take me for?"

It was soon clear that nobody else wanted to help either. A few who had seen James running through the camp half-dressed and one or two who had seen him in the hut and overheard his conversation with Roger were drummed into the prosecution but no other victims of the PO came forward. The chances of a successful prosecution looked pretty flimsy.

5
Thinking Things Through

During part one training Roger and James had little time or energy to get to know one another. But once they began 'work ship' they began to spend a good deal of their time ashore together. Most of their classmates headed straight for the Corsham pubs.

They often came back on board a bit the worse for wear. There were group of Hull fishermen amongst them. They seemed to be able to drink non-stop without it ever affecting them but when the rest tried to keep up they were soon in trouble. And they often came back boasting crudely of their conquests with local female talent.

"Cor. Had a bloody good fuck tonight. That blonde down at the Crown and Anchor, she's a fucking good fuck."

Roger knew it was sometimes just talk but often it was true. He lay in his bunk one night counting the swear words in a conversation – ninety to the minute. It dawned on him that swear words used like that weren't really swearing at all. They were just ordinary colloquial English as spoken between large numbers of men. He wondered if the womenfolk of those men used the same language. He also wondered what all those people, mostly chapel people, back at home would make of it all. So many of them said that National Service was good for men.

"It turns louts into disciplined young men."

They hadn't a clue.

There was discipline on the parade ground and no doubt there would be discipline in action but there was precious little anywhere else. He wondered what sort of homes his classmates came from. He had no experience of the lives many of them led. But quite of lot of them came from homes with doting mothers, homes where no one had a drink except perhaps the father and then only occasionally; homes where swearing was never heard, homes like his own; and certainly homes where sex was never mentioned. Why his mother had even ticked him off for telling someone on the telephone, "Gerry won't be long. He's just on the lavatory."

That was a word never used in polite conversation. So what would all those people think of him lying in bed listening to a crowd of drunks talking in ripe language of their even riper behaviour? Would they really think that National Service was good for him? It was certainly an eye-opener. Perhaps that was what was good about it.

Roger and James had no interest in pub-crawling. They had wandered aimlessly in Corsham and found nothing there to make them want to go again. They took the train to Bath a few times. From the very first James loved the city. They visited all the usual tourist attractions. James was thrilled: the Roman baths, the Abbey, the Royal Crescent, the Circus and other spacious, elegant areas – he loved them all.

Roger felt differently. He knew that he ought to be impressed but he wasn't. Bath did nothing for him. He just felt that it was dull, dirty and dingy and hopelessly overcrowded.

When James asked him to go with him to an evangelical meeting on a couple of Sunday evenings it proved to be the final nail in Bath's coffin. He was astonished. How could his sensitive, civilised, poetry-loving friend, go to such stuff and enjoy it, as he clearly did?

The room was crowded and noisy and they sang a lot of infantile choruses which James sang as heartily as anyone else. But although he joined in the clapping, he did seem to draw the line at the hysterical 'amens' and 'allelujahs'. Roger was offended by the prayers too. These people were so familiar with their God and so bossy, telling the Almighty exactly what he had to do for them.

After the second of these sessions, when they were on their way back to Corsham on the train, Roger said, "I'm sorry James. I've had my fill of Bath and I certainly can't do with any more of

37

that religious stuff. I won't be coming with you any more. I'd rather spend my leave time exploring the countryside. To me, half a mile of a country lane with its birds and flowers is worth more than all the wonders man has made."

James was bitterly disappointed. But it was the religious meetings that he focussed on. "I thought you were a nonconformist like me," he said.

"I was certainly brought up chapel," Roger replied, "but I've never seen anything like that before – except perhaps at a tent mission I went to once. It seems so crude and vulgar. I like my religion to have a bit of dignity and reverence and respect for God."

James's face fell. "I'm sorry you feel that way. I found those meetings exciting. They make religion come alive."

"Then don't let me stop you from going, but don't ask me to go too."

So sometimes they went their separate ways and Roger found himself spending his Sundays walking the countryside in a wide circle around Corsham. It was the countryside that drew him, the hedges and fields, the woodlands and streams. Occasionally James came too, but mostly he was on his own. He enjoyed being back in the natural world and he enjoyed having time to himself, time to think.

He had a letter from Gladys. She had sent it to his old school. It had come to him via his school and home. He sat in his shed and read it over and over again, not that there was much to read.

Dear Roger, Thank you for your letter. I'm all right and quite enjoying my new job. I've been back home once or twice and seen Mrs Petherick. I'm sure you remember her.

What's it like in the Navy? 'All the nice girls love a sailor' eh? I expect you've forgotten all about me by now and got lots of girl friends. I noticed you didn't send me any love. Never mind, I'll forgive you. I hope you are enjoying yourself and I hope this letter finds you. Love, Gladys. She added a kiss.

Roger wrote straight back.

Dear Gladys, I received your letter safely. I've put my home address at the top of this letter because I shall never know where I'm going to be.

I'm glad you are enjoying your new job. You would never guess what I'm doing, not in a million years. We've done our part one training which was all marching, marching, marching. Now we are waiting to go to another ship (they call it a ship even though it is on dry land) for part two training. And while we are waiting I've been put in charge of a garden shed. So there you are: join the Navy and see a garden shed.

It was smashing hearing from you and it meant a lot. I'm sorry I didn't put love on my last letter. I didn't know what to put. We ARE friends aren't we and we have been, well, you know. But does that mean we are in love? Love is such a complicated thing isn't it. One thing I can tell you is that I haven't got any other girl friends and I haven't wanted any. And I do think of you quite a lot. (That wasn't strictly true and he wondered whether to cross it out but he couldn't do that and he wasn't going to rewrite the whole page. He decided to finish off as generously as he dared):

So I do love you more than any other girl I know. Roger. He also added one kiss. Should he add more? Better not.

Walking in the countryside he found himself thinking about Gladys or rather about the meaning of love. It meant so many different things didn't it? There was love for parents and brothers and sisters; love for friends; love for husbands and wives; and then there was sex. Was that love? Not on its own it wasn't. And then James's crisis faced him with the question of homosexual love. What did he think about that?

The one person he couldn't ask for his thoughts on the subject was James himself. He was too upset. He would have to think things through on his own. Of course, he could remember very clearly what his old headmaster thought about it. He was prejudiced beyond words.

Certainly there was some homosexual behaviour that was both disgusting and degrading. The kind of bullying PO Ross got up to was totally wrong. But surely that didn't mean that all homosexual relationships were bad. Weren't Benjamin Britten and that tenor, Tippett was he called, weren't they lovers? And couldn't it be said that it was their love that had inspired some of Britten's most wonderful music?

Roger felt confused. Homosexuality held no attraction for him at all but that only made it more important for him to try to understand it when homosexual love seemed real. The ancient Greeks and Romans had accepted homosexual relationships between men and men and men and boys as normal. And perhaps in days before contraceptives, they were useful too! But they weren't normal were they? And certainly Roger felt that boys should not be involved.

He walked in the countryside. In the animal world sex was just a means of renewing the animal population wasn't it? He knew of no evidence that animals had single sex relationships of the human kind. So you couldn't call homosexual relationships 'natural' could you.

But were any human sex relationships 'natural'? After all, humans didn't just have sex to have children. Most of the time they had sex for pleasure, as an expression of their affection for one another, their mutual attraction. Roger was all for that, but it wasn't 'natural' in the way that sex operated in the natural world.

Or was it? He had heard of pandas in zoos rejecting the mates offered to them. He knew that in some species males had sex with a host of different partners and in others females did the same. There were no simple answers were there?

He thought back to his school-days. He remembered as a boy of about ten having cock fights with other boys when they tried to grab one another, but that was nothing was it? And then he remembered one or two incidents at school that had upset him, but nothing significant. He must try to be honest.

There was one boy at school, about two years younger than he was. He had what seemed to Roger to be the most beautiful body he had ever seen – like Michelangelo's sculpture of 'David' only with bigger balls. Roger had never wanted to do anything sexual with him but he did enjoy seeing him stripped in the washrooms or for swimming. He had wanted to gaze and gaze at the boy. Had that been wrong? He knew he had felt terrible guilt at the time. He couldn't look openly. So perhaps it was wrong, or was that just his upbringing?

It was all so complicated. Man to man friendships could be some of the best friendships of all. Look at his friendships at school with Joe and Cob, and Dave and people like that. There was nothing remotely sexual in those friendships but they were terrific friendships. He didn't feel as close to James as he had to them, but he was a decent chap too and they got on pretty well.

So what did he think about homosexuality? The church was against it wasn't it. But then, the church was just as prejudiced as his old headmaster. In fact, the church was worse. It wasn't really

40

in favour of sex at all except for what was necessary to have children. No, it was no use turning to the church for guidance. He must make up his own mind.

And in the end he did.

"I think I'm a bit prejudiced against it," he said to himself, "and I certainly don't *like* the idea of sex between two men whatever form it takes. But 'it takes all sorts to make a world' and it's not for me to pass judgement on the behaviour of other people. When it is based on mutual admiration, or love, then surely it is all right. If two men genuinely love one another in sexual ways and don't do any harm to anybody else, why shouldn't they? I might not like it, but it doesn't affect me does it?"

It was with immense relief that he finally felt that he had sorted things out in his head. But it took him almost to the time when they had to go to Portsmouth for the court martial before he did.

6

The Court Martial

James was separated from the rest of them for the journey to the court martial. Roger was put in charge of the seven witnesses, probably because he was the only one in fore and aft rig.

They marched quietly through the camp to the guard-room by the main gate. After a cursory inspection, they marched casually to the station. Roger had no intention of playing the big, noisy PO.

"Why have we got to go to Portsmouth?"

"I've no idea," answered Roger.

"Bummer Ross is Pompey based," said one of the others.

"Doesn't much matter does it? At least it gets us away for a couple of days."

It was a complicated journey to Portsmouth by rail but eventually they were standing by the guard-house having their passes inspected. They were directed to a large barrack-like building, left their kit and made their way straight to the mess.

"You're too late. Cookhouse is closed."

There were some pretty ripe remarks but Roger said, "All of you wait here. I'll see what I can do."

He returned to the guard-room. "Excuse me chief, I'm in charge of the witnesses for tomorrow's court martial. We've been travelling all day and now we're told there's no food for us."

"That's tough isn't it?" answered the chief. "You'll just have to starve then won't you?"

Roger stood his ground. "May I see the duty officer please?"

" 'May I see the duty officer please?' " sneered the CPO. "No

42

you bloody well can't. Who the hell do you think you are?"

"I'm the rating in charge sir and I insist on seeing the duty officer."

"You insist do you? Well I'm the chief in charge of the guard and if I say you can't see the duty officer, you can't see the duty officer."

"Very well chief. I shall have to put this interview into my report then won't I? May I have your name please."

"You bloody cheeky monkey. I've a good mind to lock you up for insolence."

"That would look even better on my report chief, and someone would have to go and look after my ratings."

At that moment the duty officer appeared. The chief called Roger to attention and saluted.

The officer saluted back. "All quiet chief?"

"Yes sir. There is one small problem though sir." He scowled at Roger. "This rating has brought seven witnesses for tomorrow's court martial sir. They've come from HMS *Royal Arthur* sir and there's no food available for them."

"Can't have that can we chief. Send down to the duty chef. Bacon, egg and chips do your men will it?"

"Yes sir, that would be splendid."

"Bacon, egg and chips for eight men then chief. Does that satisfy you?"

"Yes sir." Roger decided to push his luck. "I did just wonder whether we could have an evening pass until midnight sir. I doubt if any of my ratings have been to Pompey before."

"You do realise the importance of a court martial? Yes, you can have your passes, but I shall hold you personally responsible if any of the witnesses go missing. Chief, take this man's name and number."

"Sir."

So they feasted on bacon, egg and chips and then went ashore. The nearest pub was far enough for seven of them but Roger made his way to a telephone box. He had two cousins in Portsmouth. He hadn't seen either of them for ages but he remembered them as two of the most beautiful women he had ever seen – well perhaps not women. The younger one was younger than he was. He'd been quite sweet on her. If he could find them, perhaps he could spend the evening with them.

He did too. They were in the telephone directory and they weren't too far away. His older cousin was just as beautiful as he remembered her and she got him some supper which made her even more attractive. But the younger one took his breath away – petite, fresh and alive, she was just too wonderful for words.

The two of them took him to their badminton club and he spent the happiest evening he had had in a long time. He was very unwilling to leave but he had to be back at the pub by closing time.

When he arrived back at the pub he looked at his classmates and saw that they had been enjoying themselves too. He decided that the only way to get them back on board was to march them. He told them to 'get fell in' outside the pub. They managed it rather more literally than usual. The march back through Portsmouth looked rather more like the conga than a group of marching men but it did the trick and they all slept well.

The following morning after breakfast a PO took charge of them and they were taken in the back of a lorry to HMS *Victory*. It was the first time any of them realised that the court martial would take place on board Nelson's old flagship. Roger felt honoured somehow. It was the first time since he had joined the Navy that he really felt a part of it. As they marched aboard pride in Britain's naval past took hold of him.

He had studied the Napoleonic wars with Mr Emerson at school and the study had been typically thorough. As an old soldier, it was the Peninsular War which had been Mr Emerson's favourite subject, but Roger's interest had been in the battles at sea – the battle of the Nile that had cut Napoleon off from his supplies and the battle of Trafalgar which had given Britain lasting supremacy on the sea.

He was fascinated by the ship, though they saw all too little of it. They were ushered into a small area enclosed in canvas. They sat on benches looking at a fire bucket full of sand in the middle of the square. It wasn't long before the fire bucket began to fill with the dog ends of anxious ratings. Roger was the only one who didn't smoke.

After a longish period of waiting they were marched in their turn, one by one, to the Ward Room to give their evidence. Roger was the last to go.

He wasn't free to look around the Ward Room but it left clear impressions. It was right at the stern of the *Victory* so the timbers curved around giving a low, gently rounded room with portholes shaped like windows, small squares of opaque glass.

He was marched in and halted in front of a highly polished wooden table with three officers behind it, sharing plenty of gold rings between them. Everything about the room was highly polished or scrubbed, the deck was scrubbed; the timbers oiled; tables and brasses polished; everything was immaculate and spotless.

He stood to attention, cap beneath his left arm and eyes facing front. He knew that was where they must stay. He must look at no one, just face front. He had expected to be a bag of nerves but found that he was utterly calm. He gave his name and number and took the oath on the Bible. That niggled him. His word should be good enough. If he were a Quaker or an atheist, it would be good enough. But then, if he were a Quaker he wouldn't be in the Navy. They were pacifists weren't they? A lieutenant began to question him.

"You are a friend of Able Seaman Hemingway?"

"Yes sir."

"I believe that you were the first person to be told about the alleged incident with Petty Officer Ross."

"Yes sir."

"Would you tell us what happened?"

"I was in our Nissen hut sir, standing by my bunk, when James – Able Seaman Hemingway – burst into the hut in a terrible state. He was as white as a sheet sir and only half dressed."

"Had you ever seen him in this kind of state before?"

"No sir. He is normally a quiet, almost timid man sir, and very proud of his uniform. He tries hard always to be smart sir."

"He burst into the hut you said. What happened then?"

"He sat on his bunk and I asked him what was the matter."

"Did he tell you?"

"Yes sir. He said that PO Ross had ordered him to accompany him to his cabin and had ordered him to strip."

"He ordered him to strip."

"Yes sir, so Able Seaman Hemingway began to strip and then the PO said that they were going to have sex together.

"And what did Able Seaman Hemingway do?"

"Objection!" It was another lieutenant. "This witness didn't

45

actually see what Able Seaman Hemingway did."

The prosecuting lieutenant apologised and asked, "What did Able Seaman Hemingway *say* that he did?"

"He fled sir."

"And you believed all this."

"Yes sir. I would always believe Able Seaman Hemingway sir. He is completely truthful and honest."

"Thank you Able Seaman Wallace." He turned to the officers sitting behind the table. "I have no further questions sir."

The defending lieutenant stood.

"You said that Able Seaman Hemingway is honest?"

"Yes sir."

"And he told you that PO Ross ordered him to strip?"

"Yes sir."

"Don't you think that that is a very strange order Able Seaman?"

"Yes sir, I do."

"If somebody gave you that order, would you obey?"

"I don't know sir. It depends on the circumstances. But we are conditioned to obey orders without question sir."

"I didn't ask you to be clever Able Seaman. I asked if you would obey?"

"I don't know sir."

"I put it to you Able Seaman that there is not a lot that you do know. Do you know Petty Officer Ross?"

"I know who he is sir."

"But you do not know him?"

"No sir."

"And you do not know of his outstanding record of naval service which you are now attempting to destroy?"

"I do not know his record sir, no."

"Did you know him even by face at the time of the alleged incident?"

"No sir."

"And were you present in his cabin when the alleged incident took place?"

"No sir."

"So you are prepared to take the word of a trainee rating against the word of an officer with a fine naval record?"

"I saw Able Seaman Hemingway in distress sir, and I believed and still believe his account of the cause of that distress."

"Has it occurred to you that Able Seaman Hemingway may be a highly imaginative youth in need of psychiatric treatment?"

He and I have been friends throughout part one training sir. We have spent a good deal of time on shore leave together. If there had been any sign that he needed psychiatric treatment, I think I would have noticed. I do not believe that he needs psychiatric treatment sir.

"No more questions."

The captain behind the table said, "Thank you Able Seaman Wallace. You have expressed yourself with considerable clarity for which we are grateful."

He nodded almost imperceptibly at the PO who had marched Roger into the ward room.

"Able seaman, Seaman . . . On cap. Salute. Hay-bout turn. By the lift, qui-ick march."

For Roger it was all over. He took command of the other ratings again and they travelled back to HMS *Royal Arthur*. It was only via the grape-vine and later from James himself, that they learned the verdict.

The officers had recorded a verdict of 'Not Proven' but had made it perfectly clear that they believed the charge. They had reduced Petty Officer Ross to the rank of Able Seaman and transferred him to the Persian Gulf, always the destination of men who were in trouble, whether it was trouble in the Navy or trouble at home.

7

A Minor Disappointment

The day after they returned from Portsmouth, Roger was back in his garden shed. A runner came. "The education officer wants to see you in the classroom right away."

Roger locked up the shed and set off. They hadn't used the classroom much. There had been lectures on ship safety; elementary first aid and avoiding VD but not much else. He wondered what else the education officer did.

"DMX 884398 Able Seaman Wallace sir. You wanted to see me?"

"Ah yes, Able Seaman Wallace. Sit down. I've got a disappointment for you I'm afraid. You joined the Navy to serve in education, that's right isn't it?"

"Yes sir."

"And you've been held up here because of a court martial?"

"Yes sir."

"During the waiting period the Navy has stopped taking National Service ratings into education so you are going to have to make a change. What would you like to do?"

Roger was disappointed. There was nothing else he wanted to do in the Navy. "Could I transfer to the RAF or the Army sir?"

The education officer looked at him sharply. No, the lad wasn't trying to be funny. He was deadly serious.

"I'm sorry," he said, "that won't be possible. How would you like to become an electrician?"

"An electrician sir! Oh no sir, I'd be no use at that. I've no practical abilities at all."

"Maybe you could acquire some. You've certainly got to transfer to some other area of work and if you don't make a choice the decision will be made for you."

"Yes sir. It's good of you to give me a choice sir." He paused for a moment or two. "If I become a writer sir, it will save changing uniforms. Perhaps that's what I had better do."

"Well done Able Seaman writer Wallace. A good choice. You can dismiss now."

Roger stood, put on his cap, saluted, turned about and marched out of the classroom. He went back to the garden shed in a flaming temper, swearing under his breath every step of the way. Bloody Navy. He didn't want to be a bloody writer. He wanted to be in education to prepare himself for becoming a teacher after he left the Navy.

But as he began to cool down he also began to question for the first time how much he wanted to be a teacher. His school had only seemed to have three ideas about jobs for school leavers. One was farming because so many boys had been the sons of farmers, and the school wasn't all that keen on that. One was the church because it was a church school, but more than anything else, the Head seemed to want his boys to become teachers like himself.

Roger had admired Mr Emerson, his English and History master, so much that he had gone along with the Head's ambitions. Besides, one of his brothers was going to be a teacher and he admired him too. But did he really want to teach? Did he really want to go to University? For the first time he began to ask the questions. He certainly wanted to go on studying but he wasn't sure about University. It often seemed a bit juvenile to him, a lot of kids postponing doing a day's work and earning a living. At this stage he got no further than the questions. The fact that they had emerged was far more significant than he realised.

Within days he had his transfer to part two training. It was combined with a week-end pass. He and James were going their separate ways, James to some ship in Devonport while he went to HMS *Ceres* in the middle of bloody Yorkshire for goodness sake! He was still feeling very sour.

He picked up his leave pass, his week-end ration card and his railway warrant, and struggled home with all his kit. Once again

c

he cursed that hammock. The kit-bag on its own was heavy enough. He had never used his hammock and couldn't see that he ever would.

Friday night and Saturday at home and then he made the long journey to HMS *Ceres* near Wetherby, between York and Leeds. With all that kit it was a rotten journey: up to London by train, then down onto the Underground, up again and another train and finally the bus from Leeds.

Winter had arrived and the Nissen hut with its single boiler was freezing cold. The men were all strangers and Roger was in a foul temper. Here he was somewhere he didn't want to be, doing something he didn't want to do, wasting his time and his life and all because the stupid government hadn't abolished conscription. What was the point of it all?

On that first Monday they were up at 0600 as usual and introduced to the Chief Petty Officer who was to be their teacher. Roger disliked him on sight. He looked a slimy toad, not someone you could trust. At least their PO during part one training had been straightforward. Roger felt instinctively that this man wasn't.

After breakfast and their normal morning duties they reported to their classroom. They sat at desks. Roger was still in a bad mood. Just like being back at school, he thought.

The Chief came in, they stood to attention, he sat at his desk and they sat. "During this part of your course we shall study service documents. You will learn how to fill them in; how to store them; how to keep them up to date. You will learn their vital importance both for the Navy and for the men themselves."

Roger was grumbling away to himself. He wasn't interested in service documents. He didn't want to learn about service documents. He didn't want to fill in service documents or file them. He had better things to do with his life. He looked out of the windows of the class-room: Nothing to see worth seeing. And so the morning drifted by.

Just before they broke for lunch a physical training instructor appeared. "All right if I have a word Chief?"

"Of course. Go ahead."

"Anyone here any good at cross country running?"

Roger knew as they all did that you never volunteer for anything in the armed services. You never knew what it might

50

lead to. In spite of that his hand shot up.

"Name and number?"

He stood: "DMX 884398 Wallace sir."

"Right Wallace. Report to the gym at 1400. Thanks Chief."

Roger was the only one from his class. The Chief looked at him. "Because you are excused classes does not mean that you are excused work. I shall expect you to keep up with the rest of the class. Is that understood?"

"Yes sir."

That afternoon he reported to the gym.

"Hello Roger. Where have you sprung from?"

He swung around. It was Dave, tall gangling Dave from part one training's cross country runs. "Dave! I didn't realise you were here. Am I glad to see you."

"We'll run together, same as we used to. It's a seven mile run but quite easy going. We do it every Monday. Better than classes eh?"

"You bet." Roger's spirits rocketed skywards. His gloom and misery dispersed like morning mist. He had found someone he knew, someone he liked, and every Monday afternoon he would be enjoying himself.

He soon found that was not all. On the Tuesday morning the PTI came into the classroom and asked, "Anybody here play hockey?"

Roger had never played in his life but hockey couldn't be all that different from football could it? His hand went up.

On Wednesday it was soccer and on Thursday it was rugby. On Friday he found himself stuck in the classroom. There was no escape but from the very first Saturday he also found himself playing rugby for the ship.

That was a real bonus. They travelled widely throughout Yorkshire. The cold of the winter meant that pitches were hard and dry, not sticky mud as they had so often been when he was a boy in Devon and Cornwall. The team played fast open rugby of the kind that Roger loved, and with *Lewis Jones in the centre they were unbeaten. But even after Lewis Jones moved on the team continued to win and kept its unbeaten record to the end of the season.

*Lewis Jones was an exceptionally fine centre three-quarter who played for Wales until he turned professional and played rugby league with distinction.

51

Changing rooms varied from the palatial to the primitive. They changed in a barn high on the Yorkshire moors one Saturday, played their match and came back to the barn to find thirty metal baths laid out, all of them with a few inches of steaming hot water. Thankfully, they stripped and jumped in.

With all of them safely in their baths a procession began. Mothers, wives, girl friends of the Yorkshire team all appeared with more kettles of hot water to top up the baths. The Navy might have won the match on the pitch but off the pitch it was a different story.

Another Saturday they played at Harrogate. Roger noticed a bill-board advertising Eileen Joyce playing the piano that night. He asked the Lieutenant-Commander who captained the team if he could stay behind to hear her play.

"Good is she?"

"I don't really know how good she is sir. She's an Australian pianist and I read somewhere that she is a specialist with Grieg. She's playing his piano concerto tonight."

"You know that you're due back at *Ceres* by midnight?"

"Yes sir."

"Think you'll make it?"

Should he be honest? He was pretty sure he wouldn't.

"If I don't sir, I shall have to face the consequences won't I?"

The lieutenant-commander laughed. "I'll have your pass extended to 0700. If you don't make it by then, I'll give you hell. Understood?"

"Yes sir."

So Roger listened to Eileen Joyce play, caught a late train to Leeds and thumbed it back to Wetherby. He was back on board by 0200 and beginning to think that life in the Navy wasn't so bad after all. He could cope with working half time in the classroom now that his afternoons were organised so well. All that remained was to organise his off duty time as well and as fully as he could.

8

Off Duty

It was Dave who determined the way Roger would spend a good deal of his off duty hours. It began with a seemingly casual question when they were on one of their Monday runs.

"Do you like music Roger?"

"Yes, most kinds. I got to hear Eileen Joyce playing Grieg's piano concerto the other week."

"Lucky beggar. Where was she playing?"

"Harrogate. We played rugger there and I was allowed to stay on for her concert."

"Do you like Gilbert and Sullivan?"

"Yes I do."

"D'Oyly Carte are coming to Leeds for a couple of weeks. I wondered if you'd like to come sometimes. If you are prepared to stand it only costs a *tanner in the gods."

"Yes, I'll come. I'd love to."

"I'm on duty alternate nights so I thought I'd go every night I'm free."

"Brilliant. I'll come with you every time you go if that's all right."

Those two weeks whizzed by. They both knew quite a lot of the songs already and sang merrily to one another walking to and from the bus. *'Behold the Lord High Executioner'*. *'A policeman's lot is not a nappy one'*. *'The flowers that bloom in the spring tra la'*. *'A wandering minstrel I'*. *'Tit willow'*. Roger felt daft when *'Tit willow'* brought tears to his eyes and was

*A tanner was six old pence.

relieved to find Dave blowing his nose pretty firmly after the song was over.

"Why don't you join the choir?" asked Dave one night as they were on the bus back to *Ceres*.

"What choir?"

"The ship's choir. We're doing *Hiawatha's Wedding Feast*, though at the rate we're managing to get the hang of it, we shall never manage a concert performance."

Roger knew *Hiawatha*. They had sung it at school. He didn't mention it. He just said, "How do you join?"

"Come with me on Friday. Of course, it's mostly officers and their wives but that doesn't matter. It's the singing that counts isn't it?"

So Roger went and joined the basses. Because he knew the music, he sang confidently from the first evening and soon the other basses picked up the line from him. The choir-master had begun to despair of ever getting his choir to master the work. Most of the singers couldn't read music and he lacked the ability to enable them to grasp their parts. He was only doing the job because no one else would.

"Oh well done basses. You've got it. That should help the rest of us. Let's try the tenor line on their own please."

Roger sang the line along with the tenors and once again they picked it up from him, though there were notes he had to strain to reach.

"Wonderful. You are getting it at last. Let's try that again."

When he was satisfied he turned to the contraltos and Roger sang away behind them in a falsetto that would have had them all in hysterics if they hadn't been so serious in their efforts to get their line right. And once again, Roger's support proved crucial.

They tried it all together with the sopranos. Without help, the tenors and altos struggled for a while but after a few more shots on their own with Roger's backing, they mastered their lines.

It was not only the choir-master who was excited. The whole choir felt lifted. They had been struggling with no hope of success and now, suddenly, it was all coming right. They sang Roger's praises. His 'sight reading' was magnificent. They didn't know what they would have done without him.

He ought to have admitted that he knew the piece and he blushed to receive praise beyond his deserts. But he enjoyed his moment or two of glory too much and never let on.

The choir gave two performances. The first was a voluntary one which the whole ship's company had to attend. The second was in Wetherby for the local population. It was well attended and the concert was well received, even earning a short write-up in the local paper.

Soon afterwards a Christmas revue style concert was lined up for the ship's company. Both Dave and Roger were roped in. They sang with the whole company and Dave did a couple of dramatic monologues. In terms of sheer talent they were the highlights of the evening.

In part one of the concert Roger sang a George Formby song accompanied by a Chief PO on the piano. Roger sang in uniform. His uniform had never been a decent fit. Standing there bulging out between the buttons of his jacket with his trouser bottoms barely reaching his boots, and a gormless expression on his face, the song was almost irrelevant. It brought the house down.

In part two of the concert he had to sing again, this time a love duet with a petty officer Wren who had been in the choir. In her uniform she looked neat, smart and attractive, and Roger had never seen her in anything else. In their single rehearsal together, they were both in uniform so he was completely unprepared for the sight of her as she came onto the stage from the wings on the opposite side of the stage to himself.

He stood and gaped at her in astonishment. She was dressed in a pink bridesmaid's dress, low cut in front and with a great, billowing full length skirt. It had bows at each breast and on her skirt and she had bows in her hair. Roger couldn't help himself. He just gaped.

There was an uncertain tittering in the hall. The memory of his first song was too fresh, and there he stood looking a bit like Norman Wisdom without a cap. And there she stood looking absolutely gorgeous if you liked that kind of outfit. As he gaped at her she looked at him in horror. 'What on earth had she asked him to sing with her for? She ought to have asked one of the officers who would either have looked smart in uniform or have dressed up for the occasion.' Her heart sank.

The Chief PO began to play. She pulled herself together and began to sing. After a faltering start she sang well.

"Why do they think up stories that link my name with yours?"

Everyone knew the song from Oklahoma. But as they looked at her in all her loveliness and then looked at him it was obvious that this was a take-off, a spoof. They tittered again. It was meant to be funny wasn't it? Surely it was. But she managed to look so serious. Well of course she had to didn't she. It wouldn't be half as funny if she didn't manage to keep a straight face.

Roger pulled himself together. He swung to face the audience and began his line, "Why do the matelots gossip all day behind their doors?"

She sang again with her list of don'ts ending with, "People will say we're in love." She sang it well and the audience began to think that perhaps this was a serious song after all. The tittering had subsided and people listened. Roger had turned towards her and was also listening but then it was his turn again.

He turned towards the audience, "Some people say . . .' Oh crikey. What the hell did they say? He had lost it. The Chief PO played on. Roger struggled in vain to find the words. Now the audience was in no doubt. They loved it. They roared with laughter. A line came back to him, He sang:

"Don't praise my charm too much."

The audience hooted and he lost it again until he came to "People will say we're in love." He sang thankfully but those who looked at his companion's face saw no sign of love at all. She was furious.

Snippets kept coming to him but the more he tried the more the audience howled with laughter and his final "People will say we're in love" brought the house down.

He bowed. She curtseyed. The curtain fell. He crossed the stage to apologise. The curtain rose. She caught him a terrific swipe across the face. The audience roared. He bowed. She curtseyed. The curtain fell and stayed down. She fled in tears and Roger felt that he had never failed anyone so completely in his life. He felt utterly rotten. He went and sat in the men's changing room and the rest of the concert passed him by. At the end of it he heard the Ship's Captain speaking.

But he knew nothing of the captain's words. At the end of his speech congratulating those who had given such a good concert and congratulating the Chief PO who had organised it all he said, "We are going to finish as usual, since it's Christmas, with some Christmas carols. Let's have that Able Seaman Writer back on stage to lead us all."

He stepped off the stage and returned to his place on the front row. Dave ran and fetched Roger.

"You're wanted back on the stage."

"To hell with that."

Dave almost dragged him to his feet. "The skipper has just announced that you will lead the carol singing."

"You're joking."

"For goodness sake, just come."

The two of them ran to the stage. Fortunately the applause had been such when the captain finished speaking that the time-lag wasn't noticeable. The Chief struck up, 'Silent night, Holy night', and Roger began to sing supported by all but one of the concert party. His fellow duettist had left the concert hall long before. A few more carols led to *Good King Wenceslas* and then it was all over. Even the prospect of a week's Christmas leave failed to raise Roger's spirits. He felt so ashamed. That Wren would never speak to him again.

But then, she was a petty officer. She probably wouldn't have done anyway.

9
Jealousy

Roger sent off a small Christmas parcel to Gladys containing a brooch he had bought, a small Royal Navy anchor in dark blue and gold. On his Christmas card to her, he promised to write while he was at home. They were writing more regularly than they had at first.

Both of them were reasonably happy and pretty busy. Each of them had found a friend whose company they enjoyed: Roger and Dave, Gladys and a girl called Sally who was her immediate boss at the hotel. Sally had her own flat in Beddingford and Gladys often stayed the night there when she was off duty instead of being alone in her attic room. But she always checked with Sally to make sure she had none of the 'gentlemen' from the hotel there.

"It helps to pay the rent," Sally explained.

But though they were happy enough on the whole, both Roger and Gladys had an inner core of loneliness which nothing in their lives could satisfy. Their letters to one another gave them the feeling that, if they could only find it, there was a companionship that could take that loneliness away.

Roger didn't find it at home. He looked forward to going home and visiting the new home his parents had bought in the Surrey countryside. The journey that Christmas was so much easier without his full kit. It was ten o'clock at night when he finally left the bus a mile from their house.

It was a cold, crisp night with a good, strong moon. He walked briskly down the hill from the bus through a lane of trees and then out into more open country. He swung away left, revelling in the beauty of the night, and came to the end of the long road where his parents lived. He still had a fair way to go. They were almost at the other end. He came to the first houses, standing well back from the road in large gardens. His dad had done well at work to be able to buy one of these.

At last he was home. It was strange how his parents seemed to have shrunk even since his last leave. He took his mother in his arms, shook his dad by the hand and said an informal hello to his sister Margaret and his brother Gerry. Gerry showed him their bedroom and he changed out of his uniform straight away. What a relief that was.

Christmas brought other family visitors and plenty of food and drink in spite of rationing. But in two days it was over and that inner core of loneliness took hold of Roger with a vengeance. It was strange: here in the heart of his family he was more lonely than ever. He went for long walks in the country, thankful that his parents had moved away from the town. And then he settled down to write to Gladys.

He felt a strange sense of ease and contentment as he wrote, blissfully unaware of the effect his letter would have when Gladys read it.

She read his account of his new home and felt that it only increased the distance between them. Roger's parents were obviously pretty well off. Her parents were not. Why should that matter? What was Roger to her anyway? She hardly knew the boy. She only wrote to him because he was lonely.

And then she read Roger's account of the Christmas concert at HMS *Ceres* and of the mess he had made of the duet. She read between the lines. Roger had been sweet on that Wren. She read much more between the lines than was actually there and she felt angry and jealous. But why should she feel jealous? He had no business making her feel jealous. It was stupid to feel jealous. Hadn't she always told him that he must spread himself about a bit? And anyway, what did it matter to her?

But it did matter. So when Sally suggested that they both go to the cinema with a couple of the commercial travellers who were staying at the hotel, she jumped at the chance. It was time she spread herself about a bit, never mind that Roger boy.

"This is Tom," said Sally. "He's looking after you and Cyril is

59

looking after me." She had already told Gladys that if she wanted, they could all four go back to the flat after the pictures.

But Gladys wasn't her usual self. She was usually so bright and such fun. Tonight she was moody. She left it to Sally to make silly conversation and when any of them spoke directly to her, she answered as briefly as she could.

But she began to relax once she was inside watching the film. She wasn't really a fan of Clark Gable. She thought he was a bit of a smoothie and she didn't like his moustache, but the film was nice and easy.

And then Tom put his arm around her. She didn't really want him to but she didn't make any comment. His free hand fell onto her leg and he began to come on strong, trying to kiss her neck and her cheek.

"Get off," she hissed. "I want to watch the film."

He drew back for a little while and then began to try again. She was angry. She wasn't having any of that nonsense. She got up in a huff, pushed her way past legs and feet out into the aisle and stormed out of the cinema. Tom followed her.

"Clear off," she said. "Leave me alone."

"But I thought that's what we had come for, and to go back to Sally's place after."

"Well you can have another think. What would my boyfriend think?"

"Who cares what your boyfriend thinks. I didn't know you had a boyfriend anyway."

"And I suppose your wife is quite happy for you to behave like this when you are away from home?"

"You leave my wife out of this."

"Yes, that's what you would like me to do isn't it? Never mind your wife just so long as you have your bit of fun. Well you idn' gwain to have it with me, so there. Now piss off and give a girl a bit of peace." Her accent had grown stronger as her temper rose. She turned and left him standing.

She walked down to the riverside with tears blinding her eyes. It was all that bally Roger's fault. Why should she care about him? How could she call him her boyfriend? They had never even been out together. But they had been to bed together. In spite of herself she giggled. 'Oh Roger Wallace,' she thought, 'why can't you come and spend your leave down here. Then we can get each other out of our systems.'

She went back to her room and answered Roger's letter. She told him that she and Sally had been to the cinema with two young men. And then she sat sucking her pen. No, she wouldn't tell him anything more. Just let him think what he liked. She wondered if he would feel jealous the way she had over that Wren. Serve him right if he did.

The letter arrived soon after he had returned to his ship. He hurried away to be on his own to read it. A good thing he did. Jealous? He was sick with jealousy. He tried to reason with himself. Of course Gladys would go out with other men. He meant nothing to her. He was just a boy from school. All right, so they had been to bed together. But that didn't mean anything to her. He wasn't the first and he probably wasn't the last. (He was wrong there.) And she was so much older than he was, so much more up in the ways of the world. He couldn't expect her not to go out with other men. One day she would want to find a husband.

Later, when he had calmed down a bit, he wondered why he was so upset. What did Gladys mean to him? He knew he treasured the memory of her, but was that really her, or was it some dream-Gladys he had built up in his own mind? And he treasured her letters. When he read them, not this last one, of course, but most of them, he could almost see her cheeky face and her pretty little nose. He could hear her laugh and see those sparkling eyes. Oh how he wished he could see her.

When he wrote again he said so: *I wish I could see you Gladys. When I've got a long enough bit of leave, can I come to Beddingford and spend a bit of time with you? I think about you so much. Tell me if I can come.*

Whenever he thought about her during those next few days he was on tenterhooks and when her letter came he opened it in a fever of anticipation.

Of course you can come if you really want to. But you would probably be bored stiff. I don't know how much time off I could get. What would you do when I'm working? She had nearly left it at that, but then she added:

Even if you would be bored, I'd really like you to come. I want to know what you are really like. For instance, do you like the things I like? You're a townie and I'm a proper country girl. I don't even like it here all that much. I like to get out in the country and see the sheep and the cattle and in spring and summer, all the wild flowers. That probably sounds silly to you.

How little she knew the happiness those additional sentences gave him. Yes, he was a townie but it was the countryside he loved, the very things she had written about. She was his kind of girl, he was sure of it. And he repeated one sentence of her letter over and over again:

I'd really like you to come.

That was all he needed to know.

10

Guard Duty

Their letters began to be full of their plans for Roger's visit to Beddingford. But it was to be some time before any of those dreams could be realised. Roger still had the little matter of his naval training to complete.

After their Christmas leave they returned to the study of naval book-keeping. Roger looked at it without interest. The system was unique to the Navy. It would be of no use to him in civvy street. He decided that one of the things he would learn when he had the opportunity was proper book-keeping, cash book, ledger and all that stuff. Now that really could be useful.

He continued to be saved from utter boredom by sport. Bottom of the class in Service documents, he was now bottom of the class with book-keeping, but he did just well enough to progress to the next stage – typing.

Immediately he sat up and took notice. They had a different instructor for typing. He showed them how to dismantle their Imperial typewriters, how to clean them and keep them in good nick.

"You look after them and they'll keep going for ever."

And then he began to teach them to use all their fingers and not just to two-finger type. He put records on a gramophone which thumped out such beautiful melodies as 'a s d f g, a.s.d.f.g.' Roger decided that 'qwertyuiop' was such a superb word that it ought to be added to the dictionary. "The Navy has provided me with a qwertyuiop and I'm learning asd f," sounded so much more interesting than, "The Navy has provided me with a typewriter and I'm learning to type."

After two or three days the instructor said, "I expect you are fed up with these typing records by now. You can imagine what I think of them after all the classes I've taught. So I thought we'd type to proper music from now on."

For the next three weeks until the end of the course, he played his collection of dance records over and over again. Roger enjoyed himself so much that he was almost (not quite) sorry to be escaping in the afternoons. In spite of his absences he leapt up the class test results and did himself proud.

And then training was over. After another passing out parade they were put to 'work ship' while they waited for transfer to their first real posting. Dave had already gone so Roger's sense of loneliness and isolation returned in full force. He wrote to Gladys with a hint of bitterness behind his humour:

You go on about being just a kitchen maid. Well that's what I am. After all my naval training I'm now working in the Petty Officers' Mess. My boss is a drunken killick (a leading seaman). I hoover, dust and polish. I serve meals and wash up afterwards.

Our kitchens back onto the main kitchens. The meals are passed from the main kitchen through a hatch. They are already on their plates, a pile of four separated by metal rings. At lunchtime the first meals come through between 1130 and 1200 and the last between 1300 and 1330. We put them in warming ovens to keep hot until the POs are ready for them.

You can imagine the state they are in when the last POs arrive. The gravy is all stuck to the metal rings and the plates. By the time we come to wash up it is a hell of a job to get the plates clean. The killick sometimes throws them on the floor and smashes them to save us the trouble, but of course that's worse because who has to get down and clear up the mess?

In another letter he wrote to tell her about the cockroaches they collected in bucketfuls and how they ran cockroach races on the draining boards. But there was one night when he wrote to her with real glee.

After our day's work we are sometimes on duty at night as well. We do guard duty marching up and down at the main gates with a rifle (unloaded of course). It's utterly boring and only interrupted when we have to challenge an officer and then salute him as he comes on board.

64

But sometimes guard duty means looking after the prisoners in the cells – usually a crowd of drunks. As long as they are quiet we have a good time, playing cards or reading or writing letters like this one and drinking endless cups of cocoa. Because I work in the PO's mess it usually seems to be my job to go and get the cocoa.

Tonight we've got a special guest in the cells and I've never been so pleased to be on duty all the time I've been in the Andrew. (Have I told you that we call the Navy 'the Andrew'? Don't ask me why.)

Anyway, let me tell you about our guest.

This afternoon our killick came back from his own lunch break as drunk as a lord. We were sitting quietly reading so he got stroppy.

"Nothing to do?" he slurred. "What about . . . what about a bit of cleaning up then? How about that passageway roof then? When was that last done? Put that table yous sitting by against the wall."

There were three of us. We did as he said.

"Now get up on the table, all of you, and take a mop and bucket of water with you."

Who were we to argue? We did as he said.

"You." He pointed at me. "Get hold of the mop and wet it and hold it out of that window."

So I did.

"You . . . and you . . . two of you . . ." he pointed at the other two, pleased that he had managed to count them, "Pick him up and hold him out of the window."

They humoured him, so there I was hanging out of the window with my legs still inside, and my mop dangling down towards the roof of the glass passageway.

The killick looked long and hard. "He can't reach," he said.

"Shall we pull him back in then?"

"NO. Take him hold by the ankles and hold him out properly."

"We can't do that."

"YOU DO THAT. AT ONCETA. THA'S AN ORDER."

"But . . ."

"DO UT OR YOU'LL GO ON A CHARGE FOR DISOBEYING ORDERS."

"Watch out for yourself scribes. Get ready to drop."

They held me by my ankles and I began to try to clean the passageway roof. As I swished the mop to and fro the duty officer passed by underneath. He marched into the POs mess and quietly ordered my two bearers to pull me back in. Then he turned to the killick.

"Who's in charge here?"

The killick did his best to come to attention and salute and then remembered that he didn't have his cap on so he shouldn't salute.

"I am sir. Just super . . . supervising some cleaning sir."

"Report to the guard-room immediately and wait for me there."

So here I am at 0200 guarding the men in the cells and one of them is our killick. Every so often I go and wake him up and ask him if he is all right. It would be a pity to neglect him wouldn't it?

Roger worked for seven weeks in the POs mess and swore that whatever else he did with his life, he would never work in kitchens again. And then at last his transfer came through. He was to go to HMS *Drake* (Devonport barracks). From there he would be posted to the ship where he would probably spend the rest of his naval service.

Once again his transfer was linked in with a spot of leave. It was the ideal time to go to Beddingford, but how was he to tell his parents that he wouldn't be coming home?

Right out of the blue, John Cob, his old friend from schooldays, came to the rescue. He did something almost unheard of in his lifetime. He wrote a letter.

Dear Roger, How's it going in the Navy?

It will soon be time for the annual match between the old boys and the school. I don't suppose you'll be able to come, but I've kept a place in the team for you if you can.

Roger was thrilled. The timing couldn't be better. He wrote to John and arranged to be picked up from Beddingford station. He wrote home and said that he had got a spot of leave before going to Devonport and that he was going to play rugby for the old boys. He gave the impression that he had only got a week-end off though he actually had two weeks. And he wrote to Gladys. He was so excited. He was actually going to see her at last.

11
Not in Uniform

Large numbers of them set out from *Ceres*. Naval trucks took them to Leeds where most of them caught the train to London. They were all encumbered by full kit, kit-bags and those ruddy hammocks. Inside Roger's kit-bag there were a few extras, civilian clothes he had brought back from home after his Christmas leave. At last he was going to be able to make use of them.

Once again he struggled across London on the Underground. He caught the train to Exeter. Once there, he changed out of uniform. Off came his boots, his jacket and trousers and his naval tie. On went a pair of grey slacks, brown shoes and a jumper. The relief of it! The sheer, unadulterated pleasure!

He took his kit to the left-luggage office and arranged to leave it for two weeks. Now all he had was a small grip containing a bit of underwear and a few shirts, a towel and toilet bag and his rugby kit. Light-handed and truth to tell somewhat light-headed too, he caught the train for Beddingford. It was early evening when he arrived. He sat outside the station and waited, too excited to read. It was a pity about the rugby match. He would have liked to cross the river straight away to Gladys's hotel.

Eventually John Cob arrived in a small Ford truck. They shook hands with an old world formality that Roger found mildly amusing. He didn't feel it was necessary to shake hands with old friends or family. As a result he was often caught by surprise when people offered their hand.

"Not in uniform then Roger?"

67

"No. I changed at Exeter and it's a relief to be in civvies."

"Mother will be disappointed. 'Er was lookin' forward to having a sailor in the house." He chuckled.

"I'm no sailor," answered Roger. "They don't even call us sailors. We're 'seamen'."

"Sorry I'm sure," said John and roared with laughter.

It was good to be back enjoying the old, easy friendship they had always enjoyed. They arrived at the farm and John's parents came out to greet them.

"Not in uniform boy? Mother will be disappointed," said John's father with a twinkle in his eye.

John's mother blushed. "Come on in boy. Don't take no notice of they. 'Tis good to zee ee."

A huge meal awaited them and then their chatter took them swiftly to a late night for the family and a comparatively early night for Roger. He slept like a top.

They made an early start. Roger joined John driving in the cattle for milking. He watched as John hitched up the milking machines, attaching the suckers to the udders. Things were changing fast in the countryside. Roger thought back to his own efforts at hand milking on Joe's farm. After milking they drove the cattle back out into the fields.

"Aren't these in the fields rather early?" asked Roger. "I thought this time of year, you'd still have them under cover."

"Yes mostly," said John. "But not this breed. Thoose stay out in the fields all year round. They'm hardy but not such good milkers. If us 'ad more barns us would scrap thoose and 'ave something better for milkin'."

A massive breakfast followed and then the two young men wandered slowly round the 350 acres of the farm. To Roger's inexperienced eye it all looked in beautiful condition. John talked of his dreams of owning a farm of his own and of all he would do with it.

After a light lunch, Roger said his farewells and John took him in the pick-up across country to Perspins College.

"Us 'ad better report to the Head," said John, so the two of them made their way to the familiar study with its heavy smell of old leather and polish.

They shook hands and then the Head looked at Roger with distaste.

"Not wearing your uniform Wallace?"

"No sir. It was a relief to get out of it."

"Shame. It would have set a good example to the boys to see one of their old boys serving the king in uniform." He paused; looking Roger up and down. "We certainly can't have you looking like that," he said.

He fished in a drawer and pulled out an old boys' tie. "Put this on and wait here." He zoomed out of the study.

John was watching in amusement. "He hasn't changed has he?"

"No," answered Roger. "More's the pity."

A couple of minutes later the Head was back with a jacket. "Put this on. You can return it before you go. Oh, and the old boys' tie costs five shillings."

Roger was furious but he curbed his anger. "Right sir. I'll return the tie when I return the jacket. Thank you." They left the study and went off to meet the other old boys as they arrived. They soon found themselves at the centre of a group of boys they had known, boys who were now themselves at the top of the school ladder.

A good match led, unusually, to an old boys' victory followed by a typical school tea and a couple of speeches. Roger returned both jacket and tie to an empty study and walked down the road to Mr Emerson's house. As usual, Mr Emerson had watched the match wearing his old brown overcoat and trilby hat and leaning on his walking stick. He welcomed Roger easily and the two of them sat chatting about Roger's life in the Navy.

"You've finished your training," said Mr Emerson. "You'll probably find time hanging heavy on your hands now. What will you do with it?"

"I don't know sir. If I had the remotest idea about my life after the Navy, I'd know what to do, but I haven't."

"I thought you were planning on University and then teaching?"

"I was sir, but I don't think I am any more. I'm not sure. My dad's a businessman. I think I might follow his example, but I want to go on studying sir."

"You mean to go into the family business?"

"No sir. One of my brothers is already there. No, I thought I'd try to start a business of my own."

"Plucky thing to do. An awful lot of people fail, not that I think you would. You won't have much time for study if you do. Pity. You've got a decent brain. Well, we shall see. If you find you are making the wrong choices or going the wrong way in life, don't be afraid to change direction. Changing is never easy but life isn't easy either. All the best to you Roger."

Roger went back to school and found John. When John finally escaped from a crowd of admiring schoolboys he drove Roger back to Beddingford and dropped him by the bridge. He assumed that Roger was going to visit the people who had looked after him when he was an evacuee and Roger didn't attempt to put him right.

He waved John off and then made his way to the Riverside Hotel. He walked to the small reception desk and rang the bell.

It was Gladys herself who answered the bell. She looked neat and smart in a two-piece suit. There was an unaccountable shyness between them, an awkwardness which Gladys broke with:

"Yes? Can I help you sir?"

They both chuckled and he replied, "Is it possible to have a word with Miss Gladys Hill."

"The chambermaid? Oh I don't know about that sir. We don't usually allow members of our staff to talk to visitors in working hours. I'll go and enquire. Who shall I say has called?"

"Roger Wallace. I'm . . ." he hesitated. "I'm an old friend on leave from the Navy."

"You're not in uniform sir."

"If anybody else says that, I'll crown them," he replied and their formalities collapsed in merriment.

"I'm not off duty until ten," she said. "But here's the key to Sally's flat. It's over the hardware shop in the High Street. You get to it from the back. That's the address. Think you can find it?"

"Yes, of course."

"I'll see you at about ten minutes past ten. Don't do anything silly like coming to meet me."

"Don't I need to get myself fixed up somewhere for the night?"

"No, stupid. That's why you've got Sally's key. Most of the time you are here, she's staying in my room and we are staying in her flat. Now get along with ee and you can take this too." She gave him a small suitcase.

Roger couldn't believe his ears. He looked at Gladys wide-eyed with astonishment. She laughed.

"Go on. Push off. I've got work to do. See ee later."

So off he went. He walked along the riverbank trying to calm himself down and collect his thoughts and then he set off to find the flat. It didn't take him long.

He felt almost like a crook letting himself into someone else's flat. He hung his Burberry over a hook inside the door and took the suitcase and his grip through to the bedroom. It wasn't much of a room. There was a double bed, a wardrobe and dressing table and lino on the floor. The walls had been papered a long time ago with a dull sort of brownish paper.

Then he thought he ought not to put his grip in there. Perhaps Gladys would want him to sleep on the sofa. He went back into the living-room and looked at it. He hoped she wouldn't. He took his rugby kit out of the grip. It was wrapped in brown paper to keep it away from his clean stuff. Then he took his shirts out and hung them over the back of the sofa to take the creases out of them.

The living-room was no bigger than the bedroom. There was a small table with two chairs and there was the sofa and a small cupboard that served as a sideboard. A photo of a middle-aged couple stood on it. Probably Sally's parents, he thought. There was more lino on the floor and the same dull brown wallpaper. There was also a small hand-made rug, made from old bits of cloth. It sat on the floor in front of a small gas fire.

The tiny kitchen served as the washroom as well. It looked as though the bathroom and toilet were communal, serving a number of flats. He went to explore.

Time was hanging heavy on his hands. He was in a fever of anticipation. He took his book out of his grip. He had hardly read any of it on the trains. Now he found he couldn't concentrate to read at all. *Pride and Prejudice* hardly had the power to captivate a man in such a lather. And then at last Gladys was there.

12

A Spring Idyll

She came in carrying a tray covered with a tea towel. Roger got in the way, got out of the way, tried to take the tray from her, thought better of it, and finally allowed her to get to the table and put it down. Then he tried to help her with her coat and made a mess of that too. By the time she had given it to him to hang up, she was in hysterics. He wanted so much to be the gentleman but he was so awkward and clumsy.

He hung her coat next to his Burberry, hugging it to himself before doing so. And then he turned back to the living-room and found himself hugging the contents of the overcoat. That was much better. They clung to one another for a long time before they kissed and then they kissed one another for a long time before they finally released each other. The awkward clumsiness was all gone. How did she make everything so easy, as if they had been kissing one another all their lives?

"Come on boy," she said. "If us idn' careful our food will spoil. Sit up to the table."

She turned and lifted the tea towel from the tray. Two plates with metal covers awaited them. "There boy, just like your petty officers' mess." She lifted the covers and revealed lamb cutlets and a full quota of vegetables.

Roger hadn't realised how hungry he was. "Not quite like the PO's mess," he said. He went to start but Gladys still hadn't sat down. She came in with a glass of water for each of them. She looked at him with a smile. Graciously she said:

"You may begin." And added, "You don't have to wait for me."

But he waited all the same. After the meal he helped her wash up and she made a cup of cocoa. They sat on the sofa and she snuggled up to him.

"We've got the flat until Friday and then Sally wants it for the week-end. Then we can have it again from the Monday."

"That's marvellous. When do you have to go to work?"

"I idn' gwain at all. I've taken my holidays."

"So we're going to be together the whole time." He was thrilled and his voice showed it.

"Mostly," she said. "I shall go to see my parents at the week-end so you'll have to fend for yourself somehow. I'm not taking you with me to see them."

"No . . . I'll probably go and see Miss Holly. She looked after me when I was an evacuee here."

"And now I suppose 'tis bed-time? There was a hint of amusement in her voice and a hint of challenge too.

For the first time Roger felt uncomfortable. "Where do you want me to sleep?" he asked.

"There's only two places you can sleep unless you want to sleep on the floor. One's the bed and the other's this sofa."

"Yes," he said. There was nothing else to say.

"Have you come *prepared* to sleep with me? That's what I want to know."

"You mean?"

"I mean, have you been to the chemist's?"

He was embarrassed. "Well no, I went to the NAAFI."

She roared with laughter. "Doesn't matter where you went silly, just so long as you did your shopping."

"Yes I did. It was awful. So embarrassing. I'm sure the girl knew I'd never bought any before. She kept saying things like, 'My, you ARE going to have a busy leave. Do you think you are up to it?' And she dropped my money. I'm sure she did it deliberately just to make me wait longer. There were other men waiting to be served and they were all laughing. Then she said, 'Shall I wrap them in brown paper sir?' I just grabbed them and ran."

Gladys loved every moment of his account. "Why shouldn't it be you who has to be embarrassed?" she asked. " 'Tis just as embarrassing for me if I have to buy them."

"Yes. I suppose so."

73

d

"So you *are* expecting to sleep with me?" she teased.

He hesitated, embarrassed all over again. "Perhaps not quite expecting," he answered, "but yes, I have been hoping we might."

She got up from the sofa. "You're a good boy Roger Wallace. You don't take nothing for granted. I like that. Well just give me time to get ready for bed and then you can come and join me."

Getting ready for bed involved going down the passageway to the communal WC and then washing in the kitchen. Roger followed her example and joined her in the double bed.

"This is a bit more comfortable than our last time," she giggled.

"You mean out in the school cricket pavilion?"

"You do remember then?"

"Of course I remember. I remember every time."

"And how many ladies have you had since then?"

"You know I haven't been with anyone."

She sighed contentedly. "Yes," she said. "I know. And how many gentlemen do you think I've had?"

He almost whispered, "I don't think you've had any at all, but it wouldn't make any difference if you had. You're here with me now and for this holiday you're mine."

Conversation came to a standstill. She took him happily. Yes, she was his and he was hers. For the time being nothing else mattered.

They slept very little that night, but when they slept they slept well and they loved yet again before they got up in the morning. Instead of feeling exhausted, they felt exhilarated, bubbling over with health and vitality.

Gladys cooked them breakfast and made some sandwiches. They set off through the town up past the grammar school and into the country. They had walked briskly until now but once in the country their pace slowed. Roger's mind went back to childhood walks with his parents. His Dad was always charging on ahead, proving to himself how healthy he was and proudly boasting about the mileage they had covered at the end of the day.

Walking with Gladys was totally different. Once they were free of the town and out on the footpath that led to the sea, she stopped to look at the primroses that still blossomed in the hedges. Brighter celandines were taking over but the primroses had a while to go yet.

She pointed to some ramsons beginning to flower on the edge of a patch of woodland and to a small patch of wood sorrel in the hedge. The wood anemones were almost over but here and there in the hedge the white of greater stitchwort was making its presence felt. She knew the names of all of these but Roger felt that there was much more to it than that. She actually loved the sight of these flowers. He was seeing a side to her that he had never seen before.

They leaned over gates and looked at sheep and cattle. "Ooh look," she said, "down there amongst the sheep."

Roger looked but saw nothing. "What am I looking for?"

"There's a fox sunning himself."

At last Roger saw it. "The sheep don't seem to be bothered. Aren't they worried for their lambs?"

" 'Tidn' very often a fox will have a lamb, and then 'tis the sick ones they go for. But he wouldn't be sunbathing like that if he was hungry. He's probably had a rabbit for his breakfast."

"Or a chicken," replied Roger, remembering how his farming friends hated foxes.

"Oh he'll have chickens all right if he's gived the chance. They're nice and easy to kill. The trick is not to give him the chance. Do you know, my mum and dad keeps a few chickens and they 'ant niver lost one seps once when they left it to me to shut the chickens up for the night and I forgot. Then they lost the whole lot, all in one night."

They left farm land behind and walked through the infant bracken down to the cliff path. The gorse was golden in the spring sunshine and the sea a whole range of different colours. They sat where rabbits had cropped the grass, drank coffee from the flask and ate their sandwiches.

They spent the afternoon on the cliffs and down by the sea, leaping over the rocks, studying the rock pools, watching prawns and crabs and small fish and admiring the colours of the seaweed and the anemones. They caught water in the flask as it fell from the cliffs and so kept their thirst at bay. Evening saw them walking hand in hand into a sea-side village. They were starving. A small café soon put that right and then they caught the bus back to Beddingford.

In the days that followed they took the bus further and further afield. They spent a day at Clovelly and Bucks Mills. A walk through the Hobby Drive and then the clamber down the steps of Clovelly's only street took them to the New Inn for lunch with a half pint of strong cider each. They turned down the chance of riding up the hill on the donkeys.

"My grandparents rode on them once but I don't think it's right," said Roger. "I suppose it might be OK with small children, but it's still a hell of a climb back to the top."

Another day they went to Hartland point and wondered at the ferocity of the sea around the rocks and cliffs. And all the time they talked, getting to know more and more about each other.

"I didn't know you worked in reception at the hotel."

"I do everything. That's what we agreed when I took the job. I want to know everything there is to know so that I can become a manageress. I've worked in the rooms as a chambermaid and in the kitchens helping the chef and slaving away washing dishes and that. I've done waitressing and now I'm on reception for a while."

"Would you like to have a hotel of your own one day?"

"No. No it will be good enough for me if I become manageress."

"Is that what you want in life? Is that your dream?"

"It's not my dream, no. But if I don't marry it's what I shall do for the rest of my life I suppose."

"Do you want to marry?"

"Only if I find the right man."

Roger was tempted to pursue that but then chose to keep his questions more general.

"And if you found the right man, what then?"

"He would buy me a house in the country and I would have a cottage garden all higgledy-piggledy and colourful. And I would grow my own vegetables and have a few chickens."

"And forget to shut them in away from the fox."

They laughed. "Not my own chickens I wouldn't forget."

"Is that all your dream, what you would really like?"

"Pretty much. Of course, if my husband was really well off we could have a few acres as well. Not a farm, nothing like that. I'd have a small wood that was all my own and one or two wild flower meadows. There Roger Wallace, will you buy me all that and give me a family as well – not a big one, just a couple of children would be nice."

76

"Not while I'm in the Navy," answered Roger. "That's for sure. Anyway, how much do you think your dream house in the country and all that land would cost."

"We're not talking about a lot of land," she said. "I don't know. You can buy a little terraced cottage in Beddingford for between fifty and a hundred-and-fifty pounds. But I've never dared look at a proper house in the country. Oh well, I suppose I have too. Just the house and garden would cost anything between five hundred and seven-hundred-and-fifty pounds I reckon, and then there'd be land on top of that."

"So all we've got to do is save about a thousand pounds. I wonder how long that would take us."

"Until we're old and grey I expect," she answered, but Roger was not so sure.

When she had talked about a little terraced house he realised that he could go out and buy a house straight away if he wanted. He had a hundred and forty pounds in the bank which he had saved up ever since he was a child. From a savings point of view it had been a good time to be a child. All through the war there had been nothing to spend money on. Even now, five years on, there still wasn't much. So perhaps one day he would be able to buy Gladys a house to come near to her dreams.

Now who's doing the dreaming? he thought.

13

Separation and Reunion

When Friday came they cleaned the flat thoroughly before having their lunch there.

"We'll have to buy Sally something decent for letting us have her flat."

"It doesn't need to be that extravagant," replied Gladys. "I've paid her two weeks rent."

"Oh my goodness. I never thought. Can I pay you then?"

"No there's no need for you to do that."

"I think I should – and I'd like to. After all, I'm the one who would have had to get a room for myself."

Gladys hesitated. She didn't want to be mean. "No, really. There's no need."

"Maybe not but you can put it towards your savings for a house if I pay. Please let me. All week you've been insisting on paying your share so it's only fair."

In the end she let him pay half and said that he could buy Sally's present.

"But what can I buy?"

"There's a bracelet she wants. It's a bit expensive. Whenever she's got a new gentleman friend she always takes him past the jeweller's and points it out, but none of them has taken the hint so far." She laughed.

"You haven't taken me past the jeweller's shop yet," he said.

"We've been past it lots of times but you don't even see the shop. It would be no use pointing something out to you."

So in the afternoon they bought the bracelet and then they

strolled along the waterfront and on into the park.

"What will you do next week-end Roger? Will you go back down to Devonport early?"

"Not unless you want me to. I thought perhaps we could go to Lynton and Lynmouth. We could stay somewhere bed and breakfast on Friday and Saturday nights and then come back here on Sunday in time for me to get to my ship."

"And would we be Mr and Mrs Smith or Mr and Mrs Jones or would we have separate rooms?"

"Not separate rooms I hope. Could you put up with Mr and Mrs Wallace just for a week-end?"

"Just for a week-end I suppose but I shall have to change my name."

"Why?"

"Well just listen: Gladiss Walliss. It's all hiss. No that will never do. You'd better start calling me Gloria."

"Gloria! No I don't like that. It reminds me of that film star, what's she called, Gloria Swan Song?"

"You know very well that isn't her name," she giggled. "What are you going to call me then? Something nice and romantic. After all, who ever heard of a lover called Gladys?"

He thought for a while. "What's your second name?" he asked.

"How do you know I've got a second name?"

"Your initials on the suitcase: 'G.L.H.' What does the 'L' stand for?"

"Laura."

"Laura, woman of mystery."

She snorted. "Woman of mystery! Poof. There idn' nothin' mysterious about me."

"No not you. Back in the thirteen or fourteen hundreds, in Renaissance times, I don't know exactly when, there was a famous Italian poet called Petrarch. He wrote a whole lot of love poems to a lady called Laura but no one knows anything about her. Was she single or married? Did she love him or was his love unrequited? No one knows. That's why I called her a woman of mystery."

"You haven't written any love poems to me."

"No," he said, "not yet. But I'm not a poet am I?"

"You don't know until you try."

"But will Laura do? Shall I call you Laura because I'd better practise?"

"Yes you can call me Laura. That goes with Wallace all right."

He saw her off on the bus, did a little bit of very personal present shopping, and then retraced their walk. 'Laura.' 'Gladys.' He grinned to himself. What did it matter? He had come to Beddingford because he wanted to see her again. That was all. But it was more than that now wasn't it? Much more. How much more he wondered?

Whatever happened to them in the future, he would always think of her as someone special. That last week had been the happiest week of his life – and there was another to come. But what about the future? How could he think about the future when he still had so long to go in the Navy? And what on earth was he going to do when he came out? She was such a wonderful girl and such a straightforward girl. They would have to have a real heart to heart before he left. They were so happy together. He mustn't damage that.

He walked up the High Street to the tiny cottage he remembered so well. He knocked on the door and Miss Holly answered. She looked at him wondering who could be disturbing her at such a time on a Friday evening, and then she looked again.

"ROGER! 'Tis my boy. Oh my dear soul. Oh my. What be you doing yer? Oh my goodness. Come on in."

He went inside the tiny front room, hugged her and kissed her bristly cheek.

"Sit down boy. Do'ee want some herb beer or shall I make us some coo-coo?"

"Cocoa please."

She bustled about, full of questions. "What are you doing here? How long be ee staying? Where be ee to?"

At last he was able to answer. "I'm being transferred to Devonport and I've got a free week-end." He had prepared his speech very carefully – the truth, but not the whole truth. "I'm not staying anywhere."

"So you can stay here? In your old room?"

"If that's all right?"

"Oh the dear of him. Course 'tis. Oh my." She wiped her eyes on her apron. "And you'm in the Navy now. Just think, my boy in the Navy. Who'd of thought it. Your mother tells me all about it when she writes."

They chattered until bed-time. Before he went to sleep, Roger sat and tried to write a poem *To Laura from her Petrarch*. It was to be the first of many.

"I've got to go to the shop in the morning dear."

"I'll come with you. It'll be like old times."

So the two of them went to her nephew's shop and worked until lunch. They had their lunch at the shop and then he sensed that she wanted him out of the way.

"I thought I'd go and visit Mr and Mrs Guthrie this afternoon if that's all right?"

She almost sighed with relief. He never did learn why, but he remembered that she always got rid of him on Saturday afternoons when he was a kid.

"Yes dear," she said. "You do that. They was very good to you I remember."

Saturday passed and then it was Sunday morning and chapel. "I hopes you still go to chapel boy. I wouldn't like to think of you back-sliding."

No she wouldn't. She would be upset to know how little he went to chapel, so he didn't tell her. Instead he told her about church parades at HMS *Ceres*.

"On Sundays we all parade on the huge parade ground, except for a small number of people who are on duty. We are all there, seamen and Wrens. They divide the Wrens into three groups and the seamen into three groups and we all have to be inspected by the Ship's Captain before we march off to church."

She could picture it all in her imagination. In fact she pictured rather more than there had ever been. In her mind she saw them all with the band of the Royal Marines. How splendid it all was in her mind's eye.

Roger continued his story. "The men and women going to the Church of England march off first, and they go to a chapel in the grounds of the ship. Then the Roman Catholics march off, also to a chapel in the ship. Last of all, the rest of us march off.

"We are a mixed bunch of all the men and women who belong to the Free Churches and the Salvation Army and so on – everybody except atheists. But we don't have a chapel in the ship. We march straight out of the gates and all the way to the Methodist chapel in Wetherby. That's where we go to chapel."

He wondered whether to tell her that they marched behind the

Wrens part of the way and then lengthened their stride and marched straight *through* the ranks of the Wrens just for the fun of it. Somehow he didn't think Miss Holly would be amused.

That Sunday was the first for a long time when he went to chapel twice. He stayed one more night and gave Miss Holly a small anchor to pin to her hat before he kissed her good-bye.

The day dragged by but at last it was time for him to meet the bus. He and Gladys – no – Laura were together again. They hadn't been back in the flat long before he noticed that she kept flicking her fingers. What was she doing that for? There was something different.

"What is it?" he asked. "What are you waving your hands about for?"

She stopped and held them out. On the fourth finger of her left hand there were two rings. "Mrs Laura Wallace at your service," she said with a giggle.

"Where did you get those?" he asked.

"They were my Nan's. She left them to me. I thought they might be useful in Lynmouth."

"You think of everything," he said in wonder.

"Somebody has to."

So began a second idyllic week. Even the weather stayed fine.

14

Serious Matters

It hardly seemed possible that their second week could be as happy as their first but it was. Yet each of them in different ways felt that a small cloud was hanging over them. Sometime before they were parted they were going to have to do some serious talking.

But it never seemed to be the right time.

On the Friday morning they cleaned the flat again, had their lunch, left Sally's bracelet with a thank you note, and then set out on the bus arriving in Lynton early in the evening. They found a bed and breakfast with vacancies and booked in for two nights. Perhaps it was because they had had nearly two weeks together. Perhaps they just seemed right together. There were no raised eyebrows, no hesitations. They carried off their married status as if they had been married for a while.

And that night they finally got round to talking seriously to one another. They had made love and were in that comfortable half and half state when people go on talking until after one of them has fallen asleep.

"Gla . . . I mean, Laura."

"Yes?"

"I know I can't ask you yet but just suppose – well suppose one day I was to ask you to marry me. Do you think you might?"

"Dear Roger," she said, "we've been so happy together haven't we? I can't imagine being happier with anybody. But it's no good you and me thinking about getting married." As she said it, a deep sadness almost overwhelmed her.

"Why ever not?"

"All sorts of reasons. First of all, you and me are from different classes Roger."

"Oh come on. We're not."

"Your Dad's well off. Mine's poor. He doesn't even own his own home. You went to a posh school. I went to the village school."

"You can hardly call Perspins posh."

"Posh compared to mine. You've passed exams. I haven't. You can go on to University and be a teacher. What use would I be as a teacher's wife?"

He was going to speak again but she stopped him.

"No, don't interrupt me. I don't want to say these things but they've got to be said. Just think how long it will be before you can offer marriage to anybody. First you've got to finish with the Navy. Then four years at University getting your qualifications. And then you can't get married right away. You've got to have been earning for a while before you can think about marriage. No boy. Even if we was right for one another, which we idn', 't'wouldn't be no good us talking about getting married."

She felt sick with misery. Why had she ever let things go so far?

"Have you finished?" he said.

"Yes. That's all I've got to say."

If she could have seen him she would have seen that he was as white as a sheet.

"Some of the things you say are true," he said. "I can't ask you to marry me until I'm in a position to look after you as a husband should. But that may not be as far ahead as you think. I don't think I shall be going to University for a start."

She began to interrupt this time and it was his turn to say, "No, let me finish. This decision is not because of you. I've been thinking for some time that I didn't want to be a teacher and I didn't want to go to University. I don't know what I DO want to do yet but my Dad's a businessman and I think I might go in for business myself. So I might be ready for marriage sooner than you imagine. Of course that might not be soon enough. I know someone else could come along and snap you up. But if no one has – well don't rule me out.

"And don't rule me out for your other reasons either. All that talk about class is rubbish. My grandmother was a skivvy who never learned to read and write and she was one of the best people I ever knew. And as for school! You never had the chance to go to what you call a 'posh' school but you're just as clever as me and you've got a darned sight more common sense. You are one of the wisest people I know as well as being the loveliest and the most beautiful and – oh for goodness sake, what do you mean by saying we're not right for one another? We may not get one another but we are absolutely right for one another . . . at least YOU are absolutely right for me."

"Oh Roger, Roger, Roger, how did we ever get to this? We never made any commitment to each other when you left school did we. Well we mustn't make any commitment to each other now. The future is too uncertain. We must both keep our freedom to go with who we want to and to be with who we want to and in the end to marry who we want to."

"But I'm not going to be so far away now. We can go on seeing one another can't we?"

"Yes of course we can. Look Roger. We must always be straight and honest with one another, even if we hurt each other. A little hurt or even a big hurt is better if it is open and honest so that we can respect one another afterwards. For now, we'll just leave the future wide open and wait and see."

"Yes," he said. "You're right. But at this moment I can't imagine that I could ever come to love anyone as much as I love you."

"Come on then," she said wearily, "you'd better prove it, hadn't you?"

Quietly and gently they loved once more that night and then slept and slept until their wake-up call in the morning.

They had said all they wanted or needed to say. The little cloud that had hovered over them through the week was gone. They walked out to the valley of rocks in the morning, took the funicular railway down to Lynmouth and walked up to Watersmeet in the afternoon.

"Gladys," said Roger.

"Laura you mean."

"Gladys Laura Hill," he said, "if ever the day comes when we do marry I shall want to come here to Watersmeet with you. As the two rivers are joined and flow together, the two rivers of our lives will be joined."

She was embarrassed by his seriousness. "I thought you said you wasn't a poet," she said. "You'll be spouting poetry if you'm not careful."

For a little while they were silent and then she said, "But you're right for all that. This is a lovely valley and if two lives together could be half as lovely they'd be pretty good wouldn't they?"

They said very little as they walked back down to Lynmouth, blissfully ignorant of the tragedy that was to strike Lynmouth two years later. They had no need for words and couldn't have found any that were good enough if they had tried. A last meal, a last walk, and a last night that Roger felt was the nearest thing to perfect bliss he had ever known, and then their time together was over.

They took the bus back to Beddingford and Gladys came with him to the station.

"I was going to buy you a ring," he said, "but I wanted to try to find something you could keep no matter what the future brings, so I got you this."

She unpacked her parcel and found inside a small statuette.

"Look underneath," he said.

The statuette was called 'Laura'.

"You were right," he said. "I couldn't find one called 'Gladys'."

They laughed through their tears. She kissed him one last time and the train took him on his way.

15
Guzz

At Exeter Roger collected his kit and changed back into uniform. It was like undergoing the kind of metamorphosis some of the creatures of the natural world undergo. They were not just different clothes. They represented a different life. Did they make him a different person he wondered?

As the train drew into the station in Plymouth Roger heard the first and last clear station announcement of his life, one he was to hear many times:

"This is Plymouth North ROAD, Plymouth North ROAD, Plymouth North ROAD."

Whatever followed was the usual garbled incomprehensible mess but those words were engraved on his mind as if carved in marble. He struggled off the train with his kit-bag and hammock. Outside the station a naval truck was waiting and he joined a crowd of other men clambering on the back. The truck took them to HMS *Drake*, Devonport Naval Barracks. Devonport was known as 'Guzz', though why he never knew.

So Roger's third ship was another dry land establishment. Turfed off the truck, they stood in line and waited for the guard-room PO to tell them where to go and what was expected of them. In Roger's case very little was expected. He was in transit. He was to report to the guard-room twice daily and apart from that, keep his head down.

For a week he did just that. He had learned the value of chits of paper for unemployed seamen. He wrote to Gladys and then carried the letter in his hand while he wandered around the barracks getting his bearings and looking busy. Then he wrote to his parents and did the same. In the NAAFI he bought himself an exercise book and then he found the ship's library. He settled down and copied his poem *To Laura from her Petrarch* into it. Then he tried to write another poem to her. It took him lots of attempts before he had written what he wanted to. He bought another exercise book and wrote both poems into it. One day perhaps he would dare to give his poems to Gladys. The trouble was, she would probably just laugh. But what would she think in private? That was what mattered.

> *I wish I could paint a picture with my words*
> *that would begin to catch the beauty of your eyes.*
>
> *There are times when I catch*
> *a glimpse of gaiety,*
> *or see a smile of sheer delight*
> *that puckers out in little lines of laughter.*
>
> *At other times*
> *there's loveliness*
> *surpassing all I've ever seen,*
> *so quiet, gentle and serene.*
>
> *I wish I could paint a picture with my words*
> *that would begin to catch the beauty of your eyes.*

And then he tried another on the same lines. He called it *Loveliness*:

> *How can I describe*
> *the loveliness I see?*
> *A light that plays about the eyes;*
> *a gay and sparkling merriment;*
> *the warmth of friendship smiling through – and gentle too.*
>
> *And sometimes exquisite and pure,*
> *a moment deep and inward – soft*
> *and rare as any precious stone*
> *and one who sees, adores alone.*

Roger spent most of the rest of the week either in the library or watching the field gun crew in training from the discreet security of his barrack dormitory.

And then he was told of his transfer to HMS *Defiance*, a training ship for torpedo-men, divers and other specialists including those in mini-subs. He was to embark at 0700 on the boat that would take him to his ship.

For the first time since he had joined up he felt a tremor of excitement. He was going to sea – at last. Little did he know what was in store.

Seven o'clock the following morning saw him struggling aboard the MFV with his kit-bag and hammock. He was the only rating in transit. He looked around the boat. It was similar to the small fishing boats that sailed from harbours all around the south west. As they chugged steadily out into the Tamar and headed for the Hamaoze he looked at the lines of great ships, mothballed by a peace-time Navy that didn't need them.

The sun shone across the water, gold and shining in its light. It picked out a host of colours in the wake stretched out astern. It was magical and Roger was entranced. He was at sea!

In far too short a time he found the MFV heading for a group of three old ships moored together – ships with roofs. Noah's Ark came to mind.

"That's 'er boy," said one of the civilian crew of the MFV. "That's where you'm gwain: HMS *Defiance*."

He saw Roger's face drop. What did the boy expect he wondered?

" 'Tis three old 19th century cruisers all moored together. I don't rightly know the name of one of them but that one," he pointed, "she's HMS *Vulcan*, or was. And that one to the stern, she once held the speed record from Cape Town to this country. She was the *Andromeda* and a real beauty."

In spite of his disappointment, Roger's heart stirred. The old civilian had read him rightly. As Roger looked at Andromeda he could see that she had been a beauty – still held a beauty of line and shape that her new function failed to hide. He felt a touch of pride.

The MFV drew alongside with a minimum of fuss and he thanked the seaman before struggling up the gangway with his kit-bag and hammock. He was directed to his mess, told to settle in and then report to the Central Regulating Office at O900.

He went below and found the mess. A dozen men were eating their breakfast. "Just in time scribes. Come on in."

They introduced one another. The killick in charge of the mess said, "I expect you had some breakfast over in Guzz, but you might as well have some more if you feel like it."

Roger did feel like it. He hadn't felt like food before he set sail but he did now. Those few minutes on the water had given him an appetite. Egg, fried bread, bacon, toast, marmalade, coffee. Life was looking up.

They cleared away. "Mick, you're duty rating. You'd better show Roger around before you get the mess ready for rounds."

Mick's showing around was cursory in the extreme. He was anxious to get on with cleaning and scrubbing the mess ready for inspection. So he contented himself with showing Roger where the CRO (the Central Regulating Office) was. Promptly at O900 Roger reported to the office. He was greeted by three Chief Petty Officers.

"So you're the new scribe? There's your desk in the corner. I'm your immediate boss and these two chiefs are my colleagues." He didn't bother to name them. "Our commanding officer is Lieutenant Trelawney. He's Cornish, risen from the ranks and a bloody good officer. He'll be in later this morning. All clear?"

"Yes sir."

"You're fresh from training aren't you?"

"Yes sir."

"Your first lesson is that you don't call Petty Officers 'sir'. After training, only officers are called 'sir'. Understood?"

"Yes . . ." he hesitated, "chief."

"That's better. Now get your cap off and get down to work. There are three railway warrants to write, and make bloody sure you don't make any mistakes. Lieutenant Trelawney has to counter-sign every mistake and he doesn't take kindly to it. Understood?"

"Yes chief."

He settled down in his corner, looked over his sheets of instructions and pulled out the book of railway warrants with the special ink and special pen used for filling them in. Nothing in his training had prepared him for this but it wasn't difficult. As long as he avoided being as careless as he usually was with forms he would be OK.

At ten o'clock on the dot Lieutenant Trelawney appeared. They stood to attention, he told them to relax and called Roger into an inner office.

"Sit down scribes. You haven't got a very good record as a Writer have you?"

"No sir."

"Bottom in Service Documents. Bottom in Ledger."

"Yes sir."

"Well there idn' no service documents in this office and no ledgers either. But you kin type I see. There's plenty of typing to be done."

"Yes sir."

"You seem to be a bit of a sportsman. Us'll have to make use of that. Us have got a cross country on Wednesday so you'd better be prepared to have a go. I shall want you to play a bit of cricket for the ship in summer and rugby and soccer in winter – you do play cricket I suppose?"

"Yes sir, not very well I'm afraid."

"Well enough I expect. Now boy, the chief will tell you about coffee and how we all likes it. Oh, and bring in they railway warrants when you've finished them."

"They're all done sir."

"Well done boy. Coffee first, railway warrants after."

Roger soon discovered that coffee was often the signal for the end of the day's work. The rest of the morning was spent wrestling with the chiefs' three newspaper crosswords, the *Mirror*, the *Sketch* and the *Express*. Roger was only allowed to contribute when the three chiefs were stuck. He soon found that he was no good at crossword puzzles.

Late that evening he asked Mick where they bunked down. He had seen no sign of bunks anywhere.

"Bunk down?" Mick laughed. "We don't bunk down on THIS ship. It's hammocks here."

He showed Roger the hooks in the ship's timbers and pointed out Roger's own allocated space. Later as they all slung their hammocks Roger found that there wasn't a lot of space between hammocks, just enough for each man to swing himself up and in, but he was astonished at how comfortable hammocks were. He slept well. All that hammock carrying had its purpose after all.

16

Filling in the Time

When Friday came Roger found that he had rather more work than usual. He had week-end ration cards to prepare for all those who were off on week-end leave. It was a tedious job but very easy. He was well into it when Lieutenant Trelawney strolled into the office. They all stood to attention.

"Mornin' boys."

"Morning sir."

"Easy."

They relaxed and sat down. The boss wandered over to Roger's desk.

"Ah. Week-end ration cards is it? Make sure those who needs 'em gets their visas."

"Visas sir?"

" 'Ess. And their list of do's and don'ts."

"I'm sorry sir. I don't know anything about any visas or any lists."

With a straight face the Lieutenant said, " 'Tis for all those going into Cornwall."

Roger was pretty naïve but not quite that naïve. "Oh, I see, sir." He grinned. "Don't they have to give us their passports so that we can stick the visas in and stamp them sir?"

"Cheeky bugger," replied the boss with a laugh. "Us caught out your predecessor when he was fresh to the job. But us do have a list of do's and don'ts." He wandered off into his own office and came back with a dog-eared piece of paper which he plonked down in front of Roger.

Roger began to read. *When you cross the Tamar into Cornwall treat the natives with respect even if you don't understand their language.*

Eat at least one proper Cornish pasty and you'll never touch another Devonport 'oggie'.

Cornish cream is more runny than Devonshire cream but 'tis taken the same – in lavish helpings.

Don't try to bargain with Cornish shop-keepers. The more you try to push the price down, the more they push it up.

Don't have sex with Cornish women. They are all called Delilah and will leave you weak as kittens. Then their menfolk will give you the hiding of your lives.

Unless you are fourteen stone and tough with it, avoid rugby like the plague. And do not support visiting teams.

The list ran on.

"Would you like me to type this out again for you sir? It's looking a bit tired."

"Yes boy. I'd appreciate that, but finish off they ration cards first. And before that let's have a cup of coffee."

Roger fetched the coffee and settled back into his work.

"Earwaker," he exclaimed. "What a funny name!"

The next thing he knew he was stretched out on the deck with the chief PO who sat behind him standing over him.

"That's my name," he said, "and it's pronounced Ear Wacker."

Roger felt that he knew why. He apologised, got up and dusted himself down. He risked no further comments during the course of his work.

Even with the additional work he was still finished by lunch-time. By the end of the day he was bored stiff. That evening he wrote to Gladys.

I've got an address that looks fairly permanent, he wrote. *I've got a pretty boring, easy job but it looks as though I shall still get a fair bit of sport. My boss is a decent chap with a host of stories. He's risen from the ranks to become a Lieutenant. He wants me to play rugby and football and cricket and I've already been for one cross country run so life shouldn't be too bad.*

He seems to understand that for most of us conscription is just a blooming nuisance, a waste of time, stopping us from doing what we want to do in life. I think if I wanted to do any training or study or anything he would help me so that I could prepare for civvy street again. The trouble is, I don't really know what I want to do. I'll have to give it some serious thought.

The one thing that I DO know that I want to do is to see you again as soon as possible. Write and let me know when you've got a free week-end and if I can get the same week-end off I'll come up, or you can come down if you prefer it.

But it wasn't to prove as easy as all that. Gladys had very little time off and it rarely seemed to coincide with Roger's. Besides which, their only means of contact was by letter. Neither of them was on the telephone and Roger wasn't allowed to telephone her at the hotel. It became even more frustrating than it had been when he couldn't see her at all. But it took time for all that to dawn.

That Saturday he went ashore and wandered around Devonport. As he did, he wondered about his own future. More and more he felt that he wanted to run some kind of business. He hadn't a clue what but he realised that if he was going into business he would need to learn book-keeping. And that became his first goal.

Devonport didn't seem to have much to offer. He caught the bus to Plymouth and found the city library. He managed to find a few addresses of correspondence colleges, took the liberty boat back to his ship and wrote off for information. That short journey on the liberty boat was obviously going to be all that he was going to see of the sea. He loved it and determined to make the most of it.

So the following morning he went to line up with the liberty men again. He thought he'd spend a bit of time walking in Plymouth and then come back again.

"Roger, what are you doing here?"

It was James. He hadn't seen him since part one training.

"I'm working in the CRO. How about you?"

"They kept me here after training. I'm ship's company too. Where are you going?"

"Just thought I'd go into Plymouth and start getting to know the place."

"No. You must come with me."

They lined up, were inspected and allowed to leave. They boarded the liberty boat and James continued.

"I go to the Methodist Central Hall. There's a crowd of us. Then we all go back with Uncle Stan for lunch."

"Who's Uncle Stan?"

"He belongs to the Central Hall choir. He's a bachelor and takes us all home with him. We have lunch. Then we all go out in a crowd until it's time for evening service. Then we go to the canteen fellowship before returning to our ships."

Roger allowed himself to be led. He was surprised by the congregation. It was the largest he'd ever seen, perhaps three or four hundred and the singing was real west country hymn singing. He didn't think even Welsh singing came up to the west country.

At the end of the service he noticed a man hurry down from the choir seats behind the pulpit. He was small, thin and walked with quick, jerky steps. He caught them in the entrance lobby.

"James, who's this? Introduce us."

"This is Roger, Uncle Stan. He's on board *Defiance* with me."

"Nice to meet you boy. James will bring you home to my place for lunch."

Before Roger could respond, he was gone.

There were about sixteen of them to lunch that Sunday, all of them naval ratings except for one Nigerian student. John Bilson was the first African Roger had ever met. Friendship blossomed immediately. John was so open and so naturally friendly.

Lunch was presided over by Miss Crawford, an elderly housekeeper, a cockney who belonged to the Salvation Army and was rather deaf. The old hands teased her mercilessly but she gave as good as she got.

"Need yer be rude as well as ugly?"

Roger found the house itself fascinating. It was approached through a corridor from the garden gate with statues at each end, usually made up and dressed in articles of naval uniform. The house itself struck him as being grey – grey inside and out.

Uncle Stan was a bachelor living in the old family home. He had probably done nothing to it since his parents had died. It looked that way.

"Come upstairs," said James. He led the way up to a narrow corridor between bedrooms. "Be careful where you walk along here. This is bomb alley." He showed Roger a hole in the floor and a patched up roof overhead. "A bomb fell through here in the blitz and failed to go off. Uncle Stan either can't have anything done by way of repairs or else he just doesn't bother. I sometimes stay here for the night when it is more convenient than going back on the late night liberty boat. He'll let you do the same.

"He's an amazing man. He looks after the canteen at the Central Hall. After he's locked up for the night, if he finds any matelots the worse for wear, he brings them back with him, puts them to bed and then gets them up in the morning in time for them to catch the 0700 boat. And if there isn't enough room, he puts them in his own bed and on the sofas and sleeps in an armchair himself. He's an amazing man, the most practical Christian I've ever met. And he never asks for anything in return."

Roger was impressed and was to remain impressed, both by Uncle Stan and by his housekeeper who Roger came to know simply as Auntie. They were a formidable pair.

After lunch some of the men went off on their own but a group of them including James, Roger and John Bilson, went back to the Central Hall. There they met a similar number of girls. Roger's heart sank. He didn't want to waste his time with a lot of silly girls but he was trapped. They walked down towards the Hoe. It soon became clear that John Bilson wasn't interested in the girls either so Roger paired off with him and began to ask him about his reason for being here and about his home and family.

What amazed him was that friendship with this black man was easier and more natural than with any of the others in the group. It was obvious that the colour of your skin didn't matter. He thought about Epicurus from ancient Greek times and his teachings about friendship. Epicurus was right. There was nothing more important than friendship, ordinary good old common or garden friendship. He laughed. 'Common or garden' that was good. Epicurus met with his friends in his garden.

As they meandered about the Hoe and the sea-front one of the girls attached herself to them. John treated them as he treated everyone else, with open friendship. Roger couldn't. He had no experience of girls, had never been out with them like this, and anyway there was Gladys to think about.

He thought about Epicurus again. HE treated everyone the same, men, women, children even, Greeks, foreigners, citizens, slaves, he made no distinction between them. It struck Roger that he was streets ahead of the Christian Church. Parts of the church still didn't allow women to be priests. He thought about it. Even his own church didn't have women ministers.

"But the real point," said Roger to himself, "is that *I* don't treat women the same as men. I don't feel free to be friends with them on the same terms."

Most of the women soon got the message and left him well

alone. That pleased him on the whole. That afternoon and many more like it kept them going until it was time to get back to the Hall for the evening service.

This time Roger really was astonished. He went with the group up into the balcony and found that he was part of a congregation of about a thousand. And yet, apart from the hymn singing, the service didn't seem to mean much. The prayers seemed to have nothing to do with anything that mattered. He listened carefully to the Bible readings.

If he was going to start going to chapel again, he'd better give it a real go. The Old Testament reading was just a bit of old history. Why bother with it? The New Testament lesson came from Paul's letter to the Romans. The minister didn't seem to read very well and whatever meaning there was, failed to come across.

By the time they got to the sermon, Roger was already losing interest but he did his best to give the Minister his attention. It didn't last. The sermon was dull. Roger got to wondering why this minister was here with this large congregation when his own minister at home was so much better and only preached to about a hundred.

After the service a crowd of them went into the canteen for the after-service fellowship. There was a lot more singing and the minister led a discussion. He was a pacifist and with so many servicemen there it was a wonderful opportunity to air his views and then have a knockabout discussion. At last Roger found himself interested.

He wasn't a pacifist. That was obvious. He wouldn't have joined the Navy if he had been. Yet he had a great deal of sympathy with the pacifist position. He almost wished he could be a pacifist. At least it made life simple, just as being a jingoistic patriot did. The pacifist would never go to war. The jingoist would follow his country's call without question. Roger felt that both positions were too simple.

He was quite sure in his own mind that it had been right to fight Hitler. But his knowledge of history made him feel that there had been times when countries went to war for no good reason. Leaders didn't give a damn for the fact that many of their men would die. They were only interested in things like power, making a name for themselves, getting rich, receiving a peerage.

A lot of wars could have been avoided. If he had been alive at the time would he have made a stand he wondered? He wouldn't

e

have had to in England, not before the First World War, because England had never had conscription – apart from the press gangs of course. Perhaps he would just have kept his head down. The question fascinated him.

After that Sunday he began to see quite a bit of James but he also made sure that he kept his independence. He often stayed on board when he could have gone ashore with James. He chose his correspondence course and worked at it. And he bought a cash book and ledger and began to keep a day to day account of his own money, just as his grandfather had done when he was a child. He remembered totting up his grandfather's figures. The record had been kept to the last farthing, which is perhaps how his grandfather managed so well on a small income. He began to do the same.

At first he kept forgetting things but then he started making a note. There wasn't much to enter. On pay day he received twenty-seven shillings and sixpence plus one shilling and ninepence in lieu of rum. As a teetotaller Roger never took his daily tot of rum.

Every week Roger put a pound into savings and lived on the rest, but he was usually able to save some of that too. He bought very little when he was on board: a pint of milk a day and a piece of shortbread. And he rarely spent anything ashore except for coffees in the canteen. Occasionally the group from the hall went to the cinema and he went too, but if there was a queue he pushed off. No film was worth queueing for. And then he decided to learn to drive.

He booked a course of nine lessons. That would cut his saving down badly. He went out in a little Morris 8. Once his nerves began to settle he found that he loved every minute of it. He wrote excitedly to his parents.

Dear Mother and Dad, I'm having driving lessons with the British School of Motoring.

When I get out of the Navy I'm going to set myself up in business and I shall make sure that I have a car too.

His letter rambled on about his life on HMS *Defiance*. He was surprised to have a letter by return from his father.

Dear Roger, It was good to hear from you. I was pleased to read that you are having proper driving lessons. If you pass your driving test write and tell us and I'll reimburse you for your lessons.

But don't be in too much of a hurry to get a car. They are expensive things to run. Alfie is thirty years old now and he's got a good job with the family firm but he hasn't got his first car yet.

If you want to run your own business, first you've got to decide what kind of a business it's going to he. Then you've got to make a success of it. And only then, when you know the business can afford it, can you start to think about a car.

And this idea of running a business: you haven't got any qualifications. I still think you should go to university first and perhaps you should think again and go for something safer than business.

But Roger was not inclined to take much notice. He was enjoying driving too much.

In fact, what with driving and sport and time spent with James and his widening circle of new friends, Roger was beginning to enjoy his life too much to think too seriously about anything. So although he wrote back to his dad in fairly conciliatory terms, he preferred to shrug it off.

"He made a success of his business, so I don't see why I shouldn't."

The fact that he hadn't a clue what sort of business he would have seemed pretty irrelevant. What was much more important was the fact that he managed to get up to Beddingford a couple of times to see Gladys.

But each time they only had a day together. It was worth it, of course, but it wasn't enough. He wrote another poem for his exercise book and called it *Frustration*.

He left her as late as he dared and that got him back to Plymouth too late for the midnight liberty boat. He made his way from Plymouth North Road station to Devonport Park and dossed down on one of the park benches. At half past five in the morning a policeman came around and moved them all on. Roger made his way to *Aggie Weston's for a wash and tidy up and then caught the 0700 liberty boat back to his ship.

That early morning boat with the sunlight on the water was special. It was a strange thing. Wet though Plymouth's climate was, it hardly ever rained for that 0700 boat. Life wasn't so bad after all.

But then the Korean War broke out.

*Aggie Weston's famous hostel for seamen, providing basic accommodation etc., finally closed in the year 2000.

17

The Korean War

The Korean War put Roger into a real tizzy. It began by making him angry. Conscription was extended from eighteen months to two years. Six more months had been stolen from his life. He felt as if the government had been guilty of bad faith. They had demanded eighteen months and now had conned him out of another six. It seemed dishonest and dishonourable somehow.

No one in the mess knew where Korea was but the chiefs in the CRO knew. All of them at one time or another had served in the Far East. So had Lieutenant Trelawney. The outbreak of war led to morning after morning of hilarious reminiscences.

But Roger was depressed and his depression wouldn't go away. He had a sneaking suspicion that this was a war we ought not to be fighting but he didn't know enough about it to be sure. He read the chiefs' papers after they had finished with them but they were hardly the right papers to give him a real insight. They were all jingoistic, full of rubbish about our brave boys going out to fight alongside our American allies. Had they forgotten the lessons of the First and Second World Wars so soon?

Roger studied maps and began to understand the anxiety of people in Australia and New Zealand. They had given us magnificent support in the World Wars – and, of course, they had been threatened by Japan's initial success.

Was it not right that we should return the compliment and give them support now? But they weren't the ones who had gone into the war were they? It was the Americans with their paranoia about communism.

100

Was communism such a threat? Certainly communism in a country like Korea posed no threat to western Europe. Roger wished he knew a bit about South Korea. Would communism there be a disaster or would it be an improvement on what they already had? And what did the people of Korea want? Nobody seemed to ask that question.

One day, when he was in the inner office, he plucked up the courage to ask Lieutenant Trelawney. "What do you think of this Korean War sir?"

The Lieutenant looked at him. "What do you mean scribes?"

"Do you think it's right sir? Do you think we ought to be involved?"

"Sit down boy. Now, what makes you think we shouldn't be involved?"

"Well sir, as far as I can make out, if it wasn't for the Americans there wouldn't be a war at all."

"Don't forget that it was the North Koreans who invaded the south. And yet you're probably right. Go on then boy."

"The Americans are only fighting because they've got this obsession with communism, but is communism all that bad sir? Is it any worse than what the Koreans have already?"

"I don't know boy. Do you think communism has been good for Russia or East Europe or China?"

Roger paused. "Not for East Europe, no I don't. But I think life is probably better in Russia and China than it was before the communists took over."

"You may be right. I don't know. But I think life could be a lot better still, don't you?"

"Yes sir I do. But that still doesn't make it right for us to fight in Korea."

"No it doesn't. And I don't understand these things any better than you do. We just don't know enough about it do we? But the government thinks it's right and the United Nations has given its backing to the Yanks too."

"It's a pretty half-hearted backing sir. There are less than twenty countries prepared to give real support to the Americans and most of those are like us – we're so anxious for American friendship that we dare not stand up to them or oppose them."

The Lieutenant laughed. "Ah. Now that's an argument I'm not prepared to go into. But tell me boy, why do you think the

101

Russians haven't opposed this war?"

"They haven't supported it either sir. I think they are sitting on the fence watching to see which way the wind will blow. They don't want the Chinese to increase their influence there, but they wouldn't mind it if the Americans were given a good hiding."

"And the Americans do seem to be getting a good hiding at the moment," the Lieutenant said. "But let's come back to you boy. Suppose you come to the conclusion that we shouldn't be fighting in this war, what will you do about it?"

"That's really what I've come to see you about sir. Isn't there some kind of tribunal I could go before?"

"Yes there is. Do you know what a tribunal would do with you boy?"

"I've got a rough idea sir. They'd either stick me in the cells or send me off to work as a Bevin boy in the coal mines."

"So you know that you wouldn't be going for a soft option. It might be worse than you've suggested. Take this business of being sent to the cells. They can keep you there indefinitely until you change your mind. And then you would come back into the Navy to serve your time, only your time in the cells wouldn't count, so you would go on beyond your two years. You don't want that do you?"

"No sir, but it would be a matter of principle wouldn't it?"

"A matter of principle eh? Beware of 'matters of principle' scribes. They and their holders are too rigid by half. Life demands flexibility, not rigidity."

"But it's possible to be too flexible, isn't it sir?"

"Yes that's true too. Look scribes. this matter has become important to you. For the time being, until you know your own mind, just go on doing your work and fulfilling your service."

"Yes sir."

"You go to the Central Hall on a Sunday don't you?"

How did he know that, Roger wondered. "Yes sir, I do."

"Then how would it be if I arranged for you to go and have a chat with your chaplain in HMS *Drake*?"

"If you think it would help, yes sir, I'd like that."

Lieutenant Trelawney picked up the phone and made an appointment for 1030 the following day. Shortly before 1000 he called Roger and led him out of the office, down and astern to the old *Andromeda*. He led him to the spot where the captain's barge

102

was moored. It was a superb launch, all polish and shining brass.

"Cox'n," called the Lieutenant.

"Sir."

"Just off to Guzz to collect the skipper aren't you?"

"Yes sir."

"Drop my scribes over there will you – somewhere discreet? He's got an appointment with the padre."

"Yes sir," the cox'n grinned.

"Get on board boy and stay out of the cabin."

"Yes sir." Roger saluted and boarded the launch.

She drew gently away out into clear water and the cox'n called for increased power. She surged ahead, her bow rising in the water. Roger's excitement was obvious.

"Never been in one of these scribes?"

"No chief. She's a beauty isn't she?"

"Not so bad lad, though I've known better. But she's smart enough."

He dropped Roger off at one mooring and then moved on to his appointed collection point. Roger made his way to the chaplain's office feeling on top of the world. He didn't really want to discuss the Korean War much.

"Lieutenant Trelawney tells me that you are bothered about the Korean War and whether our country should be involved in it."

"Yes sir."

"And he tells me that you go to the Central Hall."

"Yes sir."

"So I suppose that pacifist has been getting at you has he?"

"No sir. We discuss pacifism of course. But I'm not a pacifist, though I admire their principles."

"Oh you do, do you? Well you won't expect me to will you. After all I wouldn't be a naval chaplain if I did."

"It's possible to admire them without agreeing with them isn't it sir?"

"You think so? Well I don't know how you expect me to help you. You've heard of the doctrine of 'the Just War' I suppose?" It was a useful doctrine. He often quoted it though he had never really understood it and couldn't even remember what it was now.

"No, I haven't sir."

"Every Christian seaman should study the doctrine Wallace. You can take my word for it, this Korean business comes under

103

the definition or our headquarters staff would be screaming blue murder by now." Would the boy realise he was talking about the Church's headquarters staff? "I'm talking about the Church lad, you realise that?" He didn't add what he thought of them, 'a crowd of reds and pacifists, every last one of them'.

"So you feel that we were right to go to the help of the Americans sir?"

Blast the boy. No he didn't. He didn't like the Americans. It was no good asking him why. He didn't know. And here was this lad raising questions he hadn't thought about for years.

That doctrine of the just war for instance. He had always thought it was typical of the churches' teaching – casuistical justification for things that couldn't be justified, the work of theologians in their ivory towers, all of them too clever by half. There was no moral or intellectual justification for war. Nobody who had been through the blitz as he had, or who had seen death on the battle-field or in prisoner of war camps could believe in a just war.

War was simply the result of one set of humans attacking another and the second set of humans and their friends fighting back. You might be able to justify the fighting back, and that was what the United Nations was doing in Korea, but you couldn't justify the first aggression or the horrors that war always brought.

Roger was standing patiently waiting. The chaplain looked up at him. What was it that he had asked? Were we right to be involved in this Korean business? How on earth did the boy imagine he would know? He hadn't the faintest idea. He hadn't joined the Navy to think about questions like that.

Why had he joined the Navy? Simply because he had grown up in Plymouth and always wanted to join the Navy. Joining as a chaplain had been brilliant. He had no rank but was treated as an officer and was a member of the officer's mess. He had an officer's uniform and officer's pay and because he was a chaplain, any parade ground incompetence was glossed over – expected almost. And of course, if anyone important came he was always there and introduced to them. He was rambling. He must deal with this boy and then get off to the mess. He had an unfinished snooker match with the MO to complete.

"Listen lad: the force in Korea is a United Nations force, not an American one." He could see that Roger was not convinced and he finished lamely, "Even if most of the troops are American. When is your next week-end leave?"

Roger was surprised at the sudden switch. "I don't plan to take it sir, but it is this coming week-end."

"Then you should take it. Go home and discuss these things with your parents. See what they have to say."

"Yes sir. Thank you sir."

"Very well. On your way." He waved Roger out. "Dismiss or whatever it is."

Roger put his cap on, saluted, turned about and left the chaplain's office. The beggar never even told him to 'stand easy', let alone sit down, he thought. But then, he didn't seem to know how to dismiss him either so perhaps he just didn't know what he was doing. He didn't like the way he spoke about the minister at Central Hall. He might be a bit dull but he was thoughtful and thought provoking. Roger must ask him about this doctrine of 'the Just War', not what he thought about it but what it was. He couldn't see himself going to see the chaplain again.

He returned to the *Defiance* on an ordinary MFV. As he looked out over the water he realised that he preferred sailing on this to being in the captain's barge. He had longer on the water and more time to look around. The smell of diesel, tar, timber and rope seemed to be becoming part of him.

He reported to Lieutenant Trelawney. "I don't think I'll go to see my parents sir. They wouldn't understand. I think I'll go back to my old school sir. My history master was a soldier in the First World War but he will examine my thoughts and ideas fairly and push me further. What I mean is sir, he won't try to tell me what I should do, but he will try to help me to think the subject through properly so that I can make up my own mind."

"Then he sounds to be just the man scribes. Yes, you do that."

Which meant, thought Roger, that he'd have to see the Head and if he asked him what he thought he knew how he'd answer. He'd give him a treat. He's go in uniform, then the Head could show him off to the school."

18

Back to School

Roger wondered what to do about Gladys. He knew she wasn't free that week-end so there wasn't really much point in going to Beddingford. But would she be upset if she knew he had been so close and never visited? It would be best not to mention this trip at all. After all, these thoughts of his about the Korean War wouldn't mean anything to her. She would just tell him not to be so serious.

He caught the train to Exeter and then found that he really was tempted to take the connection to Beddingford. But he stuck to his plans and travelled on the other line to the small halt that was as near as he could get to the school. Because he wasn't going to see Gladys he had decided to just make a day trip of it.

The station was six miles from school. He began to walk. It was hot in uniform so he took his jacket off and slung it over his shoulder. He wasn't likely to meet any naval police here. A farmer was driving past, stopped and gave him a lift most of the way.

When he arrived he put his jacket back on and made his way straight to the Head's study.

"Wallace! What are you doing here? In uniform I see." He looked at the uniform and was not impressed.

"I was up this way, sir, so I thought I'd call in."

"Good. Old boys are always welcome. The cricket teams are all playing away today so the school's pretty empty."

"Are they doing well sir?"

"Not as well as the team in your day – but then you never got

106

into that team did you?"

"No sir. I do play a bit now for my ship sir."

"Good. Of course we are at war now so you've got a real opportunity to serve your country."

"Do you think we *should* be at war sir?"

"What an odd question! Of course. This is United Nations business and our government has given its full support."

"Yes sir." There was no point in pursuing this any further, "Thank you, sir."

"Good of you to pop in." Pity the boy was so shabby. It would have been useful to have paraded him around the school but . . . whatever was the Navy doing letting him out looking like that? And to think that he had once thought of making the lad head boy!

Roger left with relief and walked out onto the road. Mrs Petherick was looking out of the kitchens as he passed. When she saw Gladys a week later she said, "Do you remember that boy as borrowed your kilt that time? He was out to school last week. In his uniform too. Looked ever so smart."

"When was he there?"

"Saturday. I seed him coming out of the school. He'd been to see the Head I reckon and was just gwain up the road to see Mr Emerson."

"Did he stay all week-end?"

"I don't know do I?"

So why, thought Gladys, hadn't he said anything to her about it? Why hadn't he come to see her when he was so close? Was he beginning to cool off?

But when Roger had walked out of the school he had known nothing of the storms ahead. He had arrived at Mr Emerson's house and been welcomed in.

"Hello Roger. Come in. In uniform I see. Was the Head pleased?"

"I don't think so sir. It's not exactly smart is it?"

Mr Emerson's eyes twinkled. "Not exactly. Come and sit down. Would you like a cup of coffee? Joan, look who's here."

Mrs Emerson shook Roger's hand, echoed her husband's welcome and went to make the coffee. She was pleased for her husband. He liked it when old boys turned up. She would not intrude.

107

"Is this just a social visit Roger or does it have a purpose?"

"It has a purpose I'm afraid sir. I'm bothered about this Korean War sir."

"Ah yes. You wonder whether it is a war too far?"

"Yes sir. Do you think we are justified in fighting sir?"

"Justified? That's a difficult one isn't it? We, the general public that is, haven't been told very much have we? Do you know anything about the history of Korea Roger?"

"No sir."

"Nor did I." He handed Roger a book. "I've just been doing a spot of home-work. Perhaps you'd like to take that with you. Korea is one of those countries that has suffered from other countries being too interested in it, notably China and Japan but more recently Russia and America."

"A bit like Ireland and us sir? Thank you for the book. I'll make sure you get it back."

"As to whether we are justified, I'm not sure. On balance I think that we probably are, but it's a border-line case. In our ignorance perhaps we should give the government the benefit of the doubt."

"Can we do that sir? Don't we have to work these things out for ourselves?"

"Hm. Perhaps. We can't all be experts in every field though Roger. Some things we have to take on trust. However, since we don't know the answer to your question let's approach it in a different way."

This was more like it. Roger wriggled in his chair. He had been right to come to old Emerson.

"The North Koreans invaded the south and have driven far into South Korea already."

"Yes sir."

"Suppose the United Nations succeeds in driving them back into North Korea and in securing South Korea's future. Will that be good for South Korea and will it be good for the peace of the world?"

Roger pondered. "As far as the world goes, I suppose the government would say that we need to halt the spread of communism."

"Would you agree with that?"

"I'm not sure sir. I mean, I'm not a communist – well, you

108

know that. But perhaps communism is an advance on what they have already – a step forwards rather than backwards."

"So you think that United Nations' success might not be for the good of the South Koreans?"

"It might not. How do we know? Suppose it happens. Will they have elections like ours? Will they really be allowed to work out their own future, or will the Americans dictate it? If communists stood for election and won, would the Americans allow them to govern? And even if they do have free elections, will they stay a democracy or will they slip back into some kind of corrupt dictatorship?"

"What a lot of questions Roger. We don't know the answer to most of them, though we could perhaps hazard a few guesses and I don't think you would find our guesses comforting. However, since we have no actual answers to your questions, we have to live in hope.

"What both you and I hope is that the United Nations is fighting to give the South Koreans the opportunity to work out their own destiny."

"I suppose we have to assume that that's why we are there sir, but I think it is much more to do with the American obsession with communism."

"You think that Roger, and you could be right, but you don't know. If you are right, then you should be glad that this thing is no longer entirely in American hands. The involvement of other nations may well calm the Americans down a bit. Meanwhile, in the absence of real knowledge and understanding, we have to give our government the benefit of the doubt – or do you think otherwise?"

"So you feel that on balance we've got to go ahead sir?"

"We can't do any other now can we?"

"And you think that, as an individual, I should give the government my support?"

"Only you can answer that Roger. You mustn't ask me to try to make your decision for you."

"No sir. I am leaning a little bit in that direction. The issues are not clear-cut enough to make me feel that I've got to make a stand. I only wish I knew what was best for the poor South Koreans."

"Yes." Mr Emerson was pretty sure that 'the poor South

Koreans' were in for a rotten time whichever side won. "Suppose that you did make a stand Roger, what would happen to you?" He knew perfectly well what would happen but it was important to be sure the boy knew what he could let himself in for.

"Either the cells or the coal mines sir, I expect."

Mr Emerson smiled. "You have just given yourself two excellent reasons for not rocking the boat unless it is absolutely necessary."

As if on cue Mrs Emerson came in with a tea trolley, sandwiches and cakes. This time she stayed, they discovered Roger's intention to walk back to the station and Mr Emerson took him by car. He was still driving the little Standard with its Union Flag symbol at the head of the bonnet. Roger wondered how long he had had that car.

They shook hands affectionately and Roger returned to his ship.

19

The Beginning of the Troubles

It had taken Roger a little while to sort himself out. Now he suddenly found his existence in the CRO justified. For two weeks he worked flat out. Each evening when he finished work he was exhausted. At the end of the two weeks he was so flat out that he felt he couldn't bear to be with anybody, couldn't even face ordinary conversation. He just needed peace and quiet and the silence of his own company.

The cause of all this toil and turmoil was the annual summer leave. It was his job to type list after list with a host of complex detail. It was his job to provide passes, travel documents, ration cards for fifteen hundred men.

The relief when they actually went off on leave was enormous. His own leave had already been taken of course. But even if it hadn't, he was never allowed to go with the main body. While they were away a skeleton ship's company remained and Roger found that he was always a part of that skeleton crew. For two weeks he had virtually nothing to do and no opportunity of escape.

It was as he was recovering from his exhaustion that it dawned on him that he hadn't heard from Gladys for a while. So he wrote to her to tell her about the work he had been doing. He knew nothing of her conversation with Mrs Petherick so he was totally unprepared for the coolness of her response.

She never wrote long letters but this was short almost to the point of being curt. And the last paragraph shook him to the core. *We always said that we would be straight and open with each other. Well I intend to keep that promise whether you do or not. Two young men have started coming courting.* He was so shaken that the formal language failed to amuse him. *One of them is a policeman in Beddingford and the other is a farmer from home – a man with his own farm and farmhouse.*

When Roger read that last sentence his heart sank. How could he hope to compete with a man who had *his own farm and farmhouse?* Weren't those the very things on which Gladys had set her heart? He sat right down and wrote a desperate letter pleading with her not to forget him and not to write him off. *Please let me know your free week-ends and let me come to see you again.*

Gladys read his letter with pleasure. So she had managed to stir him up had she? And he sounded as if he hadn't cooled off after all. But she decided to let him sweat for a while. She left it for a week before replying. *Yes, you can come to see me if you really want to, but I can see my two young men whenever I'm free. I've always told you not to get too serious.* She wondered if she was going over the top. After all, she did feel for him in a way she didn't feel for either of these two. And there was no real point in putting pressure on him was there? He couldn't do anything about his situation.

That was the trouble, of course. He was stuck. It would be a long time before he was free to carry their courtship forward and she wasn't at all sure that she wanted to wait. She wasn't getting any younger. She was nearly twenty-four after all. And anyway, however much she liked him she kept coming back to the simple fact that they would be a mix-match. But she gave him her free week-end dates and they arranged a week-end when he could come. Both of them felt that it was too long to wait but it was the best they could do.

In the interim the Evangelist Billy Graham came to England. James was full of excitement and he was not alone. In Christian circles his visit created quite a buzz. There was also a good deal of controversy. Roger hadn't realised that a fair number of Christians disliked the kind of emotional excitement Billy Graham stirred up. Attitudes became polarised but at Central Hall most people were in favour of Graham's mission and were eager to hear him when he came.

Roger was very unsure about his own attitude to Billy Graham.

The man had a tremendous reputation: but wasn't an evangelist someone who went out to non-Christians and tried to convert them? And then there was the question of his reported salary. Jesus was poor. Francis of Assisi was another one who had embraced poverty. Ministers and clergy weren't poor like that, but they didn't have large salaries. Graham was said to earn £5,000 a year. That was twenty times the stipend of one of the young ministers he knew and sixty-five times his own earnings.

Roger knew that Americans earned a lot more money than English people did – an American private soldier in the war had earned as much as an English major – but wasn't it a bit obscene for an evangelist to have that kind of money?

So it was with mixed feelings that he went to hear Billy Graham. Choir singing, hymn singing in that great congregation all built up a powerful atmosphere. Roger could see that James was completely carried away by it all.

Billy Graham himself made an immediate impression. He emphasised point after point of his address with the recurring refrain, "The Bible says . . . ." There was no doubt about it, he was good and very impressive. He ended his address with an appeal to people to come forward to the communion rail and give their hearts to the Lord while the congregation sang.

Roger was astonished to see Uncle Stan make his way down from the back of the choir and go to stand at the front of the congregation by the rail. Other people were moving out of their seats all over the hall and making their way forward. But what was Uncle Stan doing there? He was already a Christian. Had he gone forward to encourage other people? Or was this some kind of rededication? Roger was baffled. And then James tugged at his sleeve. "Come on. We must go down."

Why? They were Christians. Christians didn't need to be converted to Christianity. It didn't make sense. He stayed put.

"Please come with me." James was pleading with him. He was so much in earnest that Roger felt obliged to go. So the two of them made their way down from the balcony of the hall and right down the side aisle to join about thirty others at the front.

Billy Graham prayed, thanking the Lord for these new converts. The meeting ended and they were led through to a room where counsellors divided them into small groups. They were all very excited, as though the people who had come forward had

113

done something wonderful. They gave them booklets of Bible studies to read every day and information about the Billy Graham Organisation.

James came away in a state of euphoria. Roger badly wanted to ask Uncle Stan what his presence there meant, but he felt that he couldn't do it. These were surely matters that were too private to be enquired into. Nor was he at all sure about his own feelings. He was pretty confused by it all, but he would give the Bible readings a go.

He wondered what Gladys would make of it all. He was due to see her the following week-end and he was growing increasingly excited, though his excitement was mingled with anxiety.

And then his Burberry was stolen.

The loss of his Burberry was bad enough but his wallet and pay book had been in the pockets, not that there was much in the wallet. He reported the loss and promptly found himself on a charge. He was astonished.

"You've no business leaving your pay book in your Burberry scribes. You are supposed to carry it at all times and even to keep it with you at night."

So he appeared before the captain. The hearing was exceedingly brief. The charge was read. There was no defence.

"Seven days stoppage of leave."

Roger's heart sank. His visit to Gladys was off. He felt sick as he wrote to her. He told her exactly what had happened.

"What do you make of this?" Gladys asked Sally. "Roger says his pay book was stolen. It was in his mackintosh. And now they have stopped Roger's leave for letting his pay book get stolen. Can you believe that?"

"Doesn't make sense does it? Do you think he's got another girlfriend he doesn't want to tell you about?"

"I don't know. He's always seemed very straightforward. But he visited Perspins recently and never told me anything about it. I wonder what's going on?"

"I should tell him to get lost," said Sally.

"I don't know. I like him better than either Bob or Jack but I'm not going to stand for being messed about. He wants to make a new week-end date. What do you think?"

"I should tell him no. If he cares enough about you he'll come anyway."

114

"Yes. that's right. He will won't he?" So she wrote to Roger and told him not to bother to come. She was too busy with Bob and Jack.

Her letter filled Roger with despair. It was made worse by the fact that his Burberry and pay book, though not his wallet, had been found stuffed down behind some cupboards. He wrote straight back to Gladys but he felt absolutely helpless. And then he poured out his anguish in another poem, never for one moment considering that it was a complete waste of time and effort because she would never know the anguish he felt.

What else could he do? There was no point going to Beddingford if she didn't want to see him. He couldn't force himself on her could he?

When he received no reply he decided that the only thing he could do was to go on writing to her in the hope that she would give up her two suitors and come back to him. The more he couldn't have her, the more sure he was that she was the girl for him.

Meanwhile, every night he read one of Billy Graham's Bible Readings. There was one about the story of Jesus walking on the sea of Galilee. 'I don't believe that,' Roger thought. Strange. Why had it never struck him like that before? He had never really thought about it but now he did.

What about the other miracles? Did he believe them? He didn't really think that he believed in miracles at all yet he had listened week by week in church and his lack of belief had never entered his head. The next time he went to the canteen fellowship he asked the minister whether he believed the miracle of Jesus walking on the water. The minister didn't give him a straight 'yes' or 'no'. Instead he said, "A lot of time passed between the life of Jesus and the writing of the New Testament. As a result we can't always be quite sure just what happened. People read the miracle stories and interpret them in different ways. You'll find that the miracles can always be interpreted in a way that strengthens our faith."

"I see," said Roger but it was clear that he didn't see very much.

"Come to the office," said the minister. "I think I've got a book there that you might find helpful."

So they went to the office and the minister produced a book by

115

C.S. Lewis called *Miracles*. "I'd like this back when you've finished it," he said.

Roger found it fascinating. By the time he had read it right through he felt that the whole of Christian theology hung on two miracles. If they were true, the edifice that had been built upon them was also true. Or, if not true, at least it could be justified. But if those two miracles hadn't happened, then the whole of Christian theology came tumbling to the ground. Christianity was just a Jewish sect.

Roger was incredibly excited by this discovery. He would never have thought that ideas could excite you so much. He was at the very heart of things. So now he had to ask himself, "Do I believe in the miracle of the Incarnation or not? And do I believe in the miracle of the Resurrection or not?"

Billy Graham had made a lot of the Bible. Roger's church did too. He thought that he would read the whole of the New Testament and see what it actually said about those two miracles. Perhaps that would help him to decide what he actually did and did not believe.

Meanwhile he continued to go to the Central Hall with James and continued to go around with the group from the hall. It was then that the group was joined by two new girls from the London area, Susan and Philippa.

20

Fatal Fascination

Holidays in the south west with their families had convinced Susan and Philippa that they would like to live there. They had found a flat in Plymouth and then found secretarial jobs. When they joined the group at Central Hall, there was an immediate, almost electric attraction between Susan and James.

As a result, at the end of their Sunday evenings with the group, James and Roger began walking Susan and Philippa home. Philippa was tall and slim with shoulder-length fair hair. She had long, athletic legs and a shortish body but far more important than these things was her personality. It was vibrant, full of life and energy. Susan was altogether different, as often happens in pairs, quiet, composed, private. Yet she was the one who had captivated James at once, which left Roger with Philippa.

At first they walked home as a foursome but it was not long before James and Susan were finding ways to break apart, leaving Roger and Philippa on their own. As a result, Roger found himself watching her when they were part of the larger group. It wasn't difficult. She was always at the centre of things, bubbling, laughing, teasing. Life was fun and she was going to drain the cup of life to the dregs. Roger was fascinated. He had never come across a woman like this before. And yet, although she often attracted him, there were times when she irritated and repelled him too.

Sometimes her fun was at the expense of others and when it was just the two of them walking together, she would talk of some of the others in disparaging terms. Roger felt that she was one of

117

those suburban Londoners who feel that they are superior to any other human being on earth.

He was drawn by her colour, her vitality and her vivacity, but there were also moments when he was quite clear in his mind that he didn't like her very much. And always when he walked her home, he found himself thinking about Gladys. If only she were here and he could walk her home. Should he tell her about Philippa? They were supposed to be open and honest with each other but this didn't seem to be a good time. And anyway Philippa was nothing to him. Or was she?

Meanwhile he got on with his book-keeping course and received a certificate when he had completed it. He wasn't sure what value the certificate had but he had completed the course with honours. He also completed his course of driving lessons and went for his test.

He was a bag of nerves but he managed to draw away from the kerb without problems, having completed the drill including looking in his mirror and signalling his intention to draw out. He moved through the gears easily and began to lose his nerves and gain confidence. He was driving OK. It was going to be all right. And so it was as they drove around Plymouth, completed an awkward reverse around a corner, did a three point turn. Roger was actually beginning to enjoy himself when he was called on to do an emergency stop. Then they drove on into a narrow street. A bus was coming towards them. There was certainly no room on the road for both of them.

Roger slowed and dropped down to second. Gently, he pulled the car up onto the pavement and drove past the bus. Now he really was on a high. That had been beautifully done. But when they arrived back at the office he found that it was that manoeuvre which had led to his failure. He was bitterly disappointed.

He arranged for three more lessons and a second test. How he would have loved to have driven away from that second test in his own car instead of still being in the driving school car with its L plates and advertising board. But at least he now had his licence. He wrote to Gladys to tell her and he wrote home with great excitement.

The letter that came back from his father was a bit of a dampener. It began with warmest congratulations. But then his father went on to point out that if buying a car was expensive,

118

running one was prohibitive. Once again he reminded Roger that Alfie, his eldest brother, was thirty years old, had a good job with the family firm, but still didn't have a car.

Roger felt flattened after he had read the letter. It gave him one more reason for feeling that he didn't want to work in the family firm. He wanted to branch out on his own, but he still hadn't the faintest idea what he wanted to do. It must be something with a car, he thought. He had come to love driving even in those few lessons.

Throughout all of this time he was still in the Navy, though there were times when you wouldn't really have thought so. He spent almost as much time ashore as he did on board. A good deal of that time ashore was organised for him by the Navy. His anxieties about the Korean War had convinced Lieutenant Trelawney that he needed to keep his scribe occupied. The less time he had for thinking the better.

So on Wednesdays Roger was sent ashore to play soccer and on Saturdays he played rugby for the ship. He was given more time off for training sessions and then he was sent over to Devonport Services for trials. That led to rugby of a different style and calibre to anything he had played before.

At his first training session the coach said, "What position do you play scribes?"

"Either wing forward, fly half or centre three sir."

"How heavy are you?"

"Ten stone eight sir."

"Then you can forget wing forward unless you want to go away and put on two stone. We'll try you on the wing."

Over the weeks Roger found himself playing in all sorts of different positions, mostly on the wing though and even occasionally at full back. After the matches teams stopped off at pubs on the way home. Roger was teetotal. When the coach arrived back in Plymouth it circulated from one officer's home to the next. Roger assisted the officers to their front doors and often assisted them inside as well.

At last the coach arrived back at the dockyard gates with about eight to ten ratings, all the worse for wear. Roger lined them all up, linked their arms, took his place in the middle of the line and led them through. It was often quite fun but Roger began to suspect that he was only in the team because of his usefulness afterwards. This was not rugby as he had known it and enjoyed it. He found that he was beginning to look forward to the end of the season – but it was still a long way off.

When the Chinese came into the Korean War in November in support of the North Koreans Lieutenant Trelawney kept a close eye on his writer, but he had no need to worry. Roger's only reaction was an immense outpouring of fellow feeling towards those who had to face the terrifying onslaught of Chinese troops who attacked in huge numbers, screaming aggression as they came.

Roger had dealt with his problems about the war and put them behind him. His mind was now fully occupied with his New Testament studies and with the question of his religious beliefs. But if his mind was fully occupied, what was the state of his emotions?

He was more and more uncertain. He wrote every week to Gladys but she never replied. More poems found their way into his exercise book, less personal, more about the nature and meaning of love:

> *Love, the tender plant of all our hopes and dreams;*
> *the inspired author of all our wildest schemes;*
> *the mother of fears and doubts and questionings.*

That was all that his love was but there must be more to it than that. When it all worked out properly surely true love did bring its 'happy ever after'? He wrote a fourth line and dreamed that one day it might become true for him. 'Oh Gladys,' he thought, 'if only you knew.' He crossed out the full stop after 'questionings' and added his fourth line:

> *and then, the firm sure knowledge of eternal things.*

Writing his letters to Gladys and his private book of poems helped him but he so longed for a response. And he was more and more confused by Philippa.

They had now been walking home together for almost two months and he hadn't laid a finger on her. He had learned a good deal about her though. Her father was a wealthy doctor, practising in Harley Street and living in Reigate. They even had a tennis court in their garden.

Philippa had been to private school, done reasonably well,

enjoyed a lot of sport, been a prefect. It all sounded very familiar.

Gladys had always told him how unsuitable she was for him because she had never had any of these advantages. But were they advantages? Hadn't they made Philippa too sophisticated for him and a bit of a snob? And what would her expectations in life be? Could he possibly give her the kind of life she would want?

In spite of her many attractions he kept his distance. And that irritated her. She began to torment him, to tease and tempt him, to seem to offer herself to him and then to pull away. He hadn't a clue how to handle her. Eventually, well into November, when they had arrived back at the gate to her flat, instead of just going indoors as she usually did, she turned and put her arms around his neck and kissed him full on the lips.

Instinctively his arms went round her. She moved her arms to give herself a better grip on him and then she kissed him again. His whole body responded and she knew it and revelled in her power over him. She began to toy with him, pressing herself against him, kissing him, tormenting him, bringing him into a state of intense lustful desire.

And then she let him go, brushed her hand quite deliberately against the hardness of him in his trousers, and ran with peals of triumphant laughter to her front door.

Roger was hot, flustered and furious. He was tormented by his hunger for her and repelled by her treatment of him. He walked away, found a quiet, dark alley and wanked himself off furiously. The release of it left him empty and depressed. He felt guilty and ashamed. He wasn't conscious that anyone had ever spoken to him of masturbation but he knew that if anyone had, they would have done so with strong disapproval. His mother would be horrified, his church disgusted and condemning.

He was fiercely angry. He'd had it with that bloody woman. He wouldn't actually want to hurt her but he would never take her home again. That was for sure. He was wild with himself for wasting so much time on her. And he felt guilty as his mind switched to Gladys. Maybe there were no formal ties between them. Maybe he had already lost her. But he felt as if he had been unfaithful all the same. It was ridiculous. He knew it was ridiculous but that was how he felt. Fortunately he was about to begin two more hard weeks slog preparing for annual Christmas leave and thus clearing his mind.

f

21
An Ending and a Beginning

Two more desperately hectic weeks of work left Roger utterly exhausted and very depressed. While almost everyone else went home on Christmas leave, he remained on board.

He wrote to Gladys and wrapped up her Christmas present. He had found two Victorian prints, one of a cottage garden and one of an adult and a child walking through a wild flower meadow. They were a touch sentimental and pretty-pretty but he liked them for all that and he thought she would. He wrapped them carefully, hoping like mad that the glass would be OK, and sent them off with his letter and Christmas card. In his letter he told her how much he missed her, how much he wanted to see her or at the very least to hear from her and he signed off *with all my love*.

Her Christmas card and letter crossed with his in the post. He opened it with sweaty fingers, excited beyond words. It was not long before his excitement was dashed:

Dear Roger, I hope you have a happy Christmas and that this letter doesn't hurt you too much. I have agreed to marry my farmer friend Jack. We are going to get married next August. Please don't write to me any more. I shall always remember you with love.

The letter filled him with despair. He paced the decks up and down, up and down. Eventually he sat down and wrote one last letter.

Dear Gladys, Thank you for your letter. I shall honour your wishes and not write to you any more but there are one or two things I feel I must write.

First of all, I must thank you. You have done so much for me and given me so much. I shall never forget you and whenever I think of you it will be with love. So far you are both my first love and my only love.

But the other thing I must say is that I wish you every happiness with Jack. With all my heart I hope he will make you happy and enable you to fulfil your dreams.

There is so much more I could write but it is best if I stop now. Good-bye Gladys. Your loving Roger.

The tears poured down his face as he wrote. It would perhaps have comforted him to have seen Gladys, both when she received his Christmas present and when she received his letter. She wept over both of them. She knew she ought to be happy over her engagement to Jack. After all, he was everything that was right for her, and yet she had never felt so miserable in her life.

Nor had Roger. For two weeks he was more or less a prisoner on board with nothing to do. He took his Bible into the office and finished his study of the New Testament accounts of the birth and resurrection of Jesus. Well it was Christmas after all. What better time to study the birth stories. But that's all they were to him.

He was surprised that there wasn't all that much and most of it was just stories full of miracles and wonders and signs. Oh the stories were nice enough, most of them, but he didn't believe them. They were not a description of things that had actually happened. They were not historical facts.

The first chapter of John's gospel was different. It was beautifully written and a fascinating piece of, what would you call it, philosophy? He was sure that people who believed it would find it very valuable and meaningful, but it was all ideas wasn't it. Again, there were no solid facts, just extreme claims. He decided to try to write down his own beliefs about Christmas. Gosh! If the birth of Jesus wasn't a virgin birth, then Mary was just another naughty girl and Joseph a naughty but honourable boy.

If only he had made Gladys pregnant, he thought. She might have married him instead of Jack. It was no use thinking along those lines. He had lost her and that was that. When he finally brought his mind back to the New Testament he began to write.

He wrote what he thought would be the final poem in his exercise book and called it *Lost Love*. Then he dragged his mind back to the New Testament and wrote another poem, not about Gladys this time and not for her exercise book. He must buy another book for the poems that were nothing to do with her. This poem expressed his new view of Christmas:

> *Would not a god*
> *who identifies*
> *with 'publicans and sinners'*
> *go the whole way?*
>
> *It's Christmas*
> *and a child is born*
> *conceived out of wedlock*
> *by a woman in love.*
>
> *She married the man,*
> *the man whom she trusted.*
> *He gave her a home*
> *and fathered his child.*
>
> *No shepherds or wise men*
> *and certainly no angels,*
> *just ordinary people*
> *and the birth of a child.*

So that dealt with the birth of Jesus. What about the resurrection? Was that 'just stories' too? He had noticed a few stories which claimed that Jesus raised other people from death to life. But with one exception, Jesus always claimed less than other people claimed for him. People said that Jairus' daughter was dead but Jesus said that she was only sleeping.

The only exception was the story of Lazarus. What on earth was he to make of that? He had always taken it at face value, but should he? Now he was allowing himself to doubt, didn't the whole story seem contrived? And what was the point of it, except to give Mary and Martha joy? If Lazarus, why not other people? Roger was genuinely baffled.

Nor did he find the resurrection stories about Jesus convincing any more. They seemed to try too hard. It was as if the New Testament writers felt that people wouldn't believe what they were writing so they put details in to make their stories more believable. But the details only made the stories less believable: that business about Jesus eating fish for example, or making Thomas stick his hand into his wound from the spear when he was upon the cross.

No he didn't believe any of that. Besides people were so gullible weren't they? They still were after all these centuries. Some churches still claimed to have bits of bones from the apostles or bits of the wood of the cross, and there was that Turin shroud. And then you had all these weeping statues of Mary and that sort of rubbish, but people believed it all.

The minister had lent him a book called *Who Moved the Stone?* It examined all the people who might have moved the stone from the entrance to the tomb of Jesus, all the people who might have moved the body of Jesus. It came to the conclusion that no one had moved the stone or the body and that therefore Jesus must have risen. It was very convincing. Could it be right? Was Jesus something more than just a very fine teacher and faith healer?

Roger rephrased that in his mind. Some of the teaching of Jesus was marvellous, but some of it was awful if the New Testament record was accurate. All that stuff about judgement for instance. But was the book right? Had Jesus risen from the dead? He started to read the passages about the resurrection in the New Testament again.

Wallop! It caught him smack between the eyes. Why hadn't he seen it before? There it was, plain as plain in Matthew's gospel. Matthew talked about earthquakes at the time of the death of Jesus. That's what happened! That's what moved both the body and the stone. Of course!

It was like a moment of great illumination and of release too. He was free from all the beliefs he had been loaded with throughout his childhood and youth. He was free to work out his own beliefs and his own path in life. He was free!

For a little while his joy at his new-found freedom was so great that it overlay his depression and despair at his loss of Gladys. But it was not long before he sank back into feelings of doom and gloom. Wryly he pointed out to himself that he now had nothing: thanks to his spat with Philippa he no longer wanted to have anything to do with the Central Hall lot; thanks to the destruction of his faith he no longer wanted to have anything to do with

125

Central Hall or any other church come to that; and thanks to the ending of his friendship with Gladys he now had nothing in the world that he valued except his family. Well at least he would be seeing them soon.

It was with such gloomy thoughts as these that he went ashore and wandered around Devonport. He found himself looking at all the bomb damage from the war. He had never really paid attention to it before. After all, there had been plenty all around his home and plenty more in London. After a while you stopped noticing.

But today he did notice. Devonport had been hit pretty hard. And as he looked at the damage in Devonport he thought about the damage in Plymouth. Golly! The whole centre of Plymouth had gone. It had been tidied up now, of course, and they were even beginning to rebuild, but it must have been awful.

His troubles were nothing were they? Not when you thought about what people must have been through. It was no use just moping around feeling sorry for himself. He must start looking ahead. After all, the new year was just about to begin and he would be demobbed before next Christmas came.

What the hell was he going to do with himself when he was demobbed? He strolled down towards a bus stop to catch a bus to Plymouth. He passed a small taxi office. There was a board outside with notices pinned up on it. He read about a lost cat; about a jobbing builder willing to tackle anything – 'no job too small'. He read about the taxi firm inside needing part-time drivers and help in the office. He walked on to the bus stop.

'Part-time drivers and help in the office?'

He stood while a bus came and went. How flexible could they be? he wondered. There was only one way to find out. He went back to the taxi office and walked inside. A man was sitting doodling by a telephone.

"I've come about the notice on the board outside."

"What about it?"

"Well. As you can see, I'm in the Andrew. But I get a fair bit of time ashore. I wondered whether I could do some part-time work for you?"

"Not for me you couldn't. You'll have to see the boss – in there." He pointed to a door leading to an inner office.

Roger knocked and when he heard "Come in," he went inside.

126

The office was tiny, with a desk, a couple of filing cabinets, and room for a chair either side of the desk.

"I've come about the notice on the board outside."

"Sit down. What's your name?"

"Roger Wallace."

"Mine's Michael, Mike to everyone here. What about the notice?"

"I get a fair bit of time ashore and I've no commitments. I wondered if I could do a bit of part-time work for you?"

"I doubt it," answered Mike. "Our drivers work shifts: 6 to 2; 2 to 10 and 10 through the night to 6."

"I couldn't do the first two, but I could do the night shift pretty often. I'd finish in time to catch the 0700 boat."

"Hm. Have you got a clean licence?"

"Yes," said Roger and produced it.

It was perhaps a little too clean. "How much driving have you actually done?" Mike asked.

"Not a lot."

"Just passed your test I expect," said Mike and roared with laughter. Luckily he didn't imagine that anyone would be so stupid as to ask for a driving job when he had only just passed his test. He looked at Roger's arm-badges. "You're a scribe aren't you."

"Yes."

"Navy book-keeping isn't much use to us. More's the pity. I hate these bloody books."

"I *am* a qualified book-keeper," said Roger stretching the truth a little. "Not just for the Navy," he added. "I've a civvy street qualification back at home. I could get hold of it when I go home on leave next week and bring it to show you if you like."

"How long are you going home for?"

"Two weeks – but if you want me to work for you, I'll stay at Aggie Weston's for a week and cut my visit home short."

"You couldn't do it the other way round could you? Work for me for a week and then go home?"

"Yes I could, why?"

"I don't actually keep my books up to date very well. And it's time for me to bring them up to date so that I can complete my annual accounts. You see all this lot." He pointed to piles of papers. "That's all the bills and receipts for last year. I've never got round to entering them up. If you can get them written up and transferred to the ledger by the end of next week, I'll give you a fiver."

"Right," said Roger. "When can I start?"

"Now if you like."

So he showed Roger what he normally did, moved out of his chair and installed Roger in his place. "I'll go out and take the telephone off Jack so that he can go driving. If you need me you know where to find me."

Roger began work. There was nothing difficult. Only rarely did he have to ask Michael for help. The piles of paper began to shrink and to disappear into box files, each one carefully labelled and put away in a filing cabinet.

Back on board ship, he wrote home to say that his leave had been curtailed because he was needed to do some urgent book-keeping work. He didn't tell them what the work was.

Every moment he had ashore he spent in the tiny inner office of the taxi firm. By the Wednesday he had finished writing everything up. It gave him an immense feeling of satisfaction, almost of power. He was doing something only the boss could do, something the boss found a pain in the neck.

"I've finished," he said. "If you want me to I can type the accounts up ready for the tax man. And I can give you a break-down on the accounts showing up the things you are spending most money on and that sort of thing." He felt quite cocky. He could show where money was being wasted and help Michael with advice on how to run his business better. But luckily he had the sense not to say so.

Michael was delighted. He gave Roger the portable typewriter and told him to get on with it. When Roger finished, Mike paid him £7-10-0 and told him to come back after his leave. "I don't want you coming here in uniform any more in case I have to send you out driving. But mostly you'll work in the office, if that's OK."

"Yes, that's fine." With seven pounds and ten shillings in his pocket Roger was game for anything.

"We'll talk about pay when you come back, but I'll pay you by the hour – cash so you won't need to tell the tax man."

Roger was over the moon. All his depression was gone – almost all of it. He tried not to think about Gladys, just to concentrate on the wonderful luck he had had.

22

Parents in the Picture

The following week Roger went home. Gerry was still on holiday from university. Margaret was back at work at the insurance company but she was at home in the evenings. Lilian was happy to have most of her family around her. She took out her card table and made the most of the company while George read his newspaper or listened to the radio.

One evening, as they were putting the cards away, George stood in front of the fire, tapped his pipe against the chimney, and drew out his tobacco pouch.

"Oh dear," thought Lilian. She knew the signs.

So did Jerry. He caught Margaret's eye and the two of them slipped out of the room. Roger knew the signs too but it was time to have a chat with his dad. Besides, it could end up by being quite useful.

"How much longer have you got in the Navy son?"

"I finish in September."

George had filled his pipe to his satisfaction. He lit it, drawing deeply and filling the lounge with the smell of his St. Bruno. For Roger it was one of the familiar smells of home.

"Which University do you hope to go to when you come out?"

Had he forgotten or was he deliberately ignoring all that Roger had said about going into business?

"I was planning to go to London but I've changed my mind."

"Bit late for that isn't it?"

"No. I mean, I've changed my mind about going to University. I'm not going to go."

"What do you mean, you're not going to go?" George was angry. What had been the point of all that education if the boy didn't go to university?

Lilian was uncomfortable. She murmured to herself, "Oh dear. Oh dearie me."

"I've decided that I don't want to go into teaching," Roger replied, "and there's no point in going to university if I'm not going to teach."

George agreed with that. Neither he nor Roger saw university as the gateway to anything else. "So what are you going to do then?"

"I've decided to go into business like you."

"And what do you know about business my son?" He paused and Roger decided to let him carry on without an answer. "I suppose I could take you into the family firm but I'm not having anyone saying that my children have it easy. You would have to train in the evenings, go to evening school and that sort of thing. And Alfie is already in the business. He will be the one to go into senior management. He will always be over you. I suppose you realise that?"

"Thanks Dad. I really appreciate your offer, but I'm not intending to add to your burdens in the business. I want to go into business on my own."

"Which brings us back to my first question. What do you know about business? Don't you think you are a bit young to be thinking along those lines? And what sort of business are you going into? Have you thought about that eh? These are serious matters we are talking about."

"Dad," Roger hesitated. "How old were you when you went into business? And how much did you know about business?"

He knew the answers. His dad knew a good deal about selling because he had been a commercial traveller since he was sixteen, but he knew virtually nothing about manufacturing. He had bought his business during the First World War and had a fortnight in which to learn the ropes. He had been nineteen or twenty at the time.

"Things were different then," George grunted.

"Yes," said Roger, "I'm sure they were, but look what you've achieved, not just for yourself but for all of us and for all the people who work for you."

Lilian smiled to herself. It was going to be all right. The boy understood his father. George was intensely proud of his achievements – and why not? He'd done it all with none of the education her children had been given. She was proud of her husband too.

Roger pressed home his advantage, knowing that he had pleased his father. "I've been thinking about this for some time Dad. Since I joined the Navy I've done a book-keeping course and came out of it with an honours certificate." That would impress the old man. "And I've been working part-time doing the books for a local taxi firm which has begun to give me a bit of experience. I did the whole job for them, preparing their accounts for the tax man."

"There's more to accounts than just getting them ready for the tax man," answered George, impressed in spite of himself. He still didn't understand accounts.

"Yes I know," replied Roger. "They help you to see where you are and what's going right and what's going wrong. I've studied all that. And I've been reading books about how to run your own business."

"Books are all very well. But they are no substitute for actual experience. It is only by doing the job and finding out what works and what doesn't that you learn. And it's no use learning that sort of thing when it is your own business. You can easily learn too late to prevent disaster. Do you know how many new businesses fold every year?"

"It's about ninety-eight per cent isn't it? I know. That's about as discouraging a statistic as you can find. But that's why I'm learning all I can now, working for this taxi firm." He deliberately gave the impression that he had been working for the firm for a while.

"I'm surprised they let you drive. You've only just passed your test."

"I mostly work in the office," said Roger, "doing the books, answering the telephone and sending the other drivers out. I'm more or less a part-time manager," Roger said humbly. The more he could build this thing up the more his dad would accept his plans.

"What does the Navy think of all this?"

Roger hadn't attempted to find out but he assumed that the

Navy wouldn't care as long as it didn't know. "My boss understands that as a conscript I've got to prepare for civvy street. He's with me all the way. He even gave me time off to go and have my driving lessons." That was true anyway.

"And is it taxi work you want to do? It's a very cut-throat business. And there'd be no scope for it around here."

"I know that Dad. I haven't made any definite plans yet. Perhaps I could set up a small office in Croydon. There must be plenty of work there, and I could live at home."

"I'd have thought Croydon was pretty saturated with taxi firms, but it might work. I expect I could find you a small office on my premises. That would cut down on your expenses." George knocked out his pipe. "You're sure this is the sort of thing you want to do? Business isn't easy you know."

As they had talked Roger had become more and more sure. Their whole conversation had confirmed his thinking, and yes, why not a taxi firm. That particular idea had never entered his head before but that was the obvious thing to go for. By the time he left the Andrew he ought to have enough experience to help him avoid the worst pitfalls.

George cleaned out his pipe, blew the dottle into the fire and took out his tobacco pouch again. "Well son," he said, "if you do decide to have a go, keep me in the picture and I'll do what I can to help. I can probably come up with a loan if you need it."

"I'm trying very hard not to need much help Dad. I've been saving hard ever since I joined up and now I'm putting my taxi wages away too. I should have about three hundred pounds by the time I leave the Navy."

Now George really was impressed. He turned to his wife. He didn't often discuss money matters with her. You couldn't expect women to understand finance. Come to that, he didn't understand it himself. But Lilian sensed his excitement and his pride in a son who, in a way, was going to follow in his footsteps. She knew what he was going to offer. He couldn't resist it. She was glad. It was the sort of man he was – generous to a fault. She nodded in answer to his unspoken question.

"Look son," George said. "Let's forget about loans. If you manage to save three hundred pounds, your mother and I will give you another hundred. How's that?"

Roger was overwhelmed. His eyes shone. "That's marvellous

Dad. I've already saved over two hundred. Oh gosh. With all that money I could almost buy a house as well as start my own business."

They laughed together and Lilian felt that she had heard enough about business. Without realising it she brought Roger crashing down from the heights of his excitement to the depths of a personal misery.

"Have you met any nice young ladies while you have been in Devonport? You keep writing to us about this group you go out with from Central Hall. There must be some nice girls there. Are you interested in any of them?"

Roger had known that the question would be asked, but her timing couldn't have been worse. "No mother," he said. "The only girl I was ever really interested in was a girl I met while I was still at school. We wrote to each other quite a lot after I joined the Navy, but that's over now. She's going to marry a farmer."

He managed to say it easily enough, but it tore at him.

"There's no point me getting interested in girls," he added, "not until I'm doing well enough to support a wife and a family."

Lilian sighed. He was just like his dad. Women had no significance except as prospective wives. Perhaps it was just as well. After all, that's what she wanted for him wasn't it. As least he wouldn't be playing fast and loose. But she did wish her menfolk weren't quite so serious.

"No dear," she answered, "but it will be nice to see you settled with a good wife."

"I'm still a bit young for that Mother. You've got to get Gerry lined up with someone before me."

Roger was glad to get both these conversations out of the way, but talk of girls had brought Gladys right into the forefront of his mind again. He told Gerry that he was going out for a bit, slipped out of the kitchen door and went for a long walk.

Losing Gladys was rather like a bereavement. As long as there had been a shred of hope he had been like a man whose wife is terminally ill. As long as there was even a glimmer of hope he had gone on hoping, hoping against hope. But there was no hope left and he was as grief-stricken as if she had died.

He walked without thinking where he was going and the tears ran down his face. He had loved her so much but she obviously hadn't felt the same about him, even though she really had seemed to love him. But she had always warned him against getting too serious hadn't she? He could almost hear her merry laughter and sense the lightness of touch with which she faced life. She was so real and close and yet she was unreachable – like Orpheus with Eurydice. He sensed her presence but knew that if he turned to grasp her she was lost for ever.

"Well Gladys," he said, speaking out loud as if she could hear, "I wanted to make a success of my life *for you*. But even though I can't have you, I'm going to go full steam ahead and nothing is going to stop me.

"One day I'm going to have my own business and I'm going to earn enough money to end up with a house in the country and a cottage garden. I don't know about the rest of your dream. That may be beyond me, but if I manage part of your dream I shall always be able to think of you. You'll be my inspiration."

At that moment he felt he never wanted to look at another woman. He was nineteen after all!

He returned home, slipped back into the house and went to bed.

"Are you all right?" asked Gerry.

"Yes," he said. "Woman trouble, that's all."

"Oh tough." Gerry didn't want to hear. He knew all about woman trouble. He'd had a girl at university and thought he was going places with her. Then she had left him for someone else. No. He didn't want to hear about Roger's trouble.

Luckily Roger didn't want to talk. 'Woman trouble, that's all,' he thought. If only it was as trivial as that. He could almost picture Gladys beside him in bed, almost feel her. Oh crikey, he was getting a hard on just thinking about her.

He got up, went downstairs and got himself a glass of cold water. He got pen and paper and began to scribble:

> *I love her*
> *for the beauty of her form;*
> *I love her*
> *for the beauty of her face;*
> *I love her*
> *for the beauty of those eyes;*
> *I love her*
> *for the beauty of her self.*

He took each one of these statements and began to try to amplify it but nothing came right. Sheet of paper after sheet went into the waste paper basket. At last, exhausted, he wrote:

> *How long the day,*
> *how dead the night with ne'er a hint of you in sight.*
> *The empty house stands silent, bare,*
> *it is not home with you not there.*
>
> *The place is cold and hard as stone.*
> *Nowhere seems welcoming now you're gone.*
> *From room to room I wander through*
> *and all I'm looking for is – you.*

Dull with misery and exhaustion he made his way to bed, slept like a log and woke refreshed. Life looked better in the morning, a bit dull but better.

23

A Very Long Sunday

Time began to drag as Roger's leave drew to a close.

He packed his suitcase on the Saturday evening. His dad brought him a brown, double breasted suit. "I managed to get this for only ten bob," he said. "I thought it might be useful when you get out of the Navy.

Roger wasn't pleased. He didn't like the suit. But he thanked his dad and gave him ten shillings. Then his dad gave him a cheque for one hundred pounds.

"That'll earn a bit of interest before you are ready to use it, but you are not allowed to use it until you have saved three hundred pounds."

From being displeased, Roger was over the moon. "Gee, thanks Dad. That's terrific. You and Mum are wonderfully generous."

Embarrassed, his father left him to himself. As Roger went to hang the brown suit up in his wardrobe he had a brain-wave. If he had it dyed black and put badges and buttons on it, he could use it as a number one uniform. Brilliant! He folded it carefully and put it in his suitcase.

The following morning he put his case in the car and the family all drove together to their church back on the edge of Croydon where they had always lived. The church of his childhood had been bombed. The new one was pleasant, light and attractively designed but he had no sentimental attachment to it.

And now of course, he had no faith either. There was no point in telling his parents. It would only upset them. He went with

136

them and sang the hymns lustily, but found that he was taking more notice of the words than he had ever done before. He felt uncomfortable. Should he sing words he didn't believe?

They came to the sermon and the minister announced his text: "In the beginning God created the heavens and the earth." He began to talk about evolution and the way Darwin's theories had forced them all to rethink their ideas about creation. "But evolutionary theory need not undermine our faith in God," he said.

Roger's mind began to wander. He hadn't taken his thinking far enough had he? He didn't believe in Jesus as the divine Son of God anymore, but what about God himself? Did he believe in God at all?

He began to hope that he didn't. After all, if there was a God who had created everything and who had created man as the crown of creation with authority over the whole of creation, he'd made a pretty fine mess of it hadn't he? Look at the kind of things humans did to one another, let alone to the world they lived in.

He thought about the war against Hitler and about the horrific things the Nazis had done to the Jews and the Gypsies and other groups too. 'And we never learn,' he thought. 'The First World War taught us nothing. The Second World War has taught us nothing. Now here we are back at war fighting in Korea. All this talk about God as a creator who loves us is barmy.'

After the service the congregation stood around outside chin-wagging. Roger was out of it. He had been away too much and too long to belong any more. His mother turned to him, "You don't want to stand here waiting for us," she said. "Why don't you take Jennifer home?" And then in the kind of stage whisper you could hear a mile off she added significantly, "She's a really nice young lady."

Roger looked at Jennifer. He had known her off and on ever since they were kids. It was true. She was a decent girl. She had heard his mother and was grinning at him.

"Shall I?" he asked.

"If you like," she answered.

So he said his farewells to the family, took his case out of the car and walked her home. They walked slowly with the width of the pavement between them. Conversation was hard work. She asked him about his life in the Navy but his heart wasn't in this at all. At any other time perhaps . . .

137

He tried to turn the conversation back onto her. What was she doing with herself now? What did she do with her spare time?

They arrived awkwardly at her house.

"I must be going I'm afraid," said Roger. "I've got a train to catch."

They both knew that there were plenty of trains. He didn't have to rush. She made nothing of it.

"Thank you for bringing me home. It's been nice seeing you again."

"Yes," he said. "Well good-bye then."

She was amused. He hadn't a clue had he. "Good-bye," she said and opened her garden gate.

He walked away without another word or a backward look. 'Oh Mother,' he thought. 'Why do you have to stir me up all over again. I keep trying to turn my mind away from Gladys and you keep forcing me to think of her again.'

He walked back to the station and caught a train up to London. From London he caught the train to Plymouth and settled down for the long journey. He was pretty miserable one way and another. "I'm a proper lost soul," he said to himself wryly. "I don't belong at home. I don't belong in the Navy. I've lost the only girl I ever cared about. Let's hope Michael can give me the kind of work I need if I'm to learn about the taxi business."

At last the long journey was over. "This is Plymouth North Road, Plymouth North Road, Plymouth North Road."

He made his way straight to Michael's taxis.

"Hello scribes. Didn't expect you until tomorrow. Have you had a good leave?"

"Yes thanks. I thought I'd call in just to make sure you want me tomorrow."

"You can start now if you like. We're short handed this evening. If you take over the phones, Jack can go out on the road."

"Which is where I'd much rather be," said Jack.

"Yes, OK. I'd love to."

"All right until 10 o'clock are you?"

"Yes. I'm in no rush to get back on board."

Jack told him where the other four drivers were, reminded him of the drill: everything went into the diary; drivers took jobs in strict rotation from when they became free; and advanced

138

bookings had to be taken with care. If there were no cars available they said so, but there was a list of regular customers. If they could possibly look after them, they did.

And then Jack took his car keys and was gone. Roger took over and Michael watched him for a while. The boy had learned well before he went on leave. "Look lad," he said, "I'm going to be off home. My home number is there if you have any problems but I'm sure you'll be OK.

"Do you think you could cover the phones for us every night this week from six to ten?"

"I'm sure I can but I'd better ring you when I've checked."

"What I hope you are going to be able to do for us is one week six to ten, which is a half shift; and one week ten at night to six in the morning. I'll pay you two pounds when you do a week's half shift and five pounds when you do a full week of nights. That all right?"

"Yes, that's fine."

"I shall want you to keep the books up to date as well as look after the phones, and perhaps write a few letters for me. And sometimes you may have to do some driving too. Now, is there anything else before I go home?"

"No I don't think so. Oh, yes there is. It's nothing to do with business. I've got a suit I want to have dyed black. Any idea where I can get it done?"

"Give it to me and I'll give it to the missus. She'll see to it for you."

So Roger handed over the suit and Michael left him on his own. He felt very excited and the phones were busy enough all evening to keep him happy. When he was relieved at 10 o'clock he walked the short way to the dockyard, bought himself an oggie and ate it as he walked through the dockyard to the liberty boat. As pasties go, it wasn't very good, mostly crust and potato, but it filled a hole. Roger realised that it was rather a large hole, but at least he had some of his mother's coconut buns in his case. He wouldn't starve.

He stepped aboard the liberty boat and revelled as always in the short journey back across to *Defiance*. He loved that trip. It was the best thing the Navy did for him. The moon shone clear and silver on the water and the old familiar smells made him feel that he had come back home.

24

Trelawney's Armada

Roger lay in his hammock that night surrounded by the creaks and groans of the old ship. It was curious. When he had been a boy he had wanted to join the Navy, thrilled as he had been by the exploits of people like Raleigh and Drake, Howe and Frobisher and of course Nelson.

But once in the Navy he felt very differently. 'The Navy' as such meant nothing to him. It was just a nuisance, a two year stint that had to be endured. And yet here he was lying in his hammock on board ship, cosy and contented. There was nowhere else in the world where he felt so much at home. He slept and slept well.

His contentment continued over breakfast in the mess. He got on well with everyone in the mess yet there wasn't a single man there who had become a personal friend. Even the fact that he was duty rating didn't spoil his contentment. He scrubbed, dusted, and swept the mess clean. He washed the deck, checked it all over carefully and then waited for the duty officer's rounds.

Mess inspection satisfactorily completed, he made his way up to the CRO. Even that failed to intrude on his spirit of contentment. He liked the chief POs in the office and no longer feared them and he recognised that he had a boss in a million in Lt. Trelawney. People said that naval officers were either swine of the first order or the very best of men. Lt. Trelawney was one of the best of the best. He'd risen from the ranks without ever forgetting where he had come from. There was none of the arrogance and bullying that often marked men who wanted to forget their roots but lacked the self-confidence of those whose whole naval career had been as officers.

But when Lt. Trelawney arrived that morning he seemed jumpy somehow. He was in and out of his office like a yo-yo, striding out onto the deck outside, pacing up and down, returning to his office for five minutes and then out again. He called to his staff, and he was never more Cornish than when he did so:

"Yer boys come and have a look at they. Idn they 'andsome then. Gyaw, just look at 'em come."

They stood and watched as an MFV swung around the stern of the *Andromeda*, giving the larger ship a wide berth. She was towing three other boats in line astern. The first was a decked hull and little more, but newly painted, sleek and beautiful. She had been an air/sea rescue launch and her lines were such as to excite the most ignorant land-lubber. Behind her was a whaler and then a small dinghy.

"I'll be over with they if anyone needs me," said Lt. Trelawney and off he went.

They watched as a small boat pulled away from *Defiance* with Lt. Trelawney aboard and four ratings. They rowed over to where the MFV held her place steady against the incoming tide. The seamen moored the air/sea rescue launch about a hundred yards from *Defiance* and secured her fore and aft to separate buoys. The MFV cast off and sailed away. The men with Lt. Trelawney hauled the whaler with its attendant dinghy to the side of the launch. Two of them jumped into the whaler and cast off. They drew in the dinghy and passed its painter across to the launch. Then they rowed across to the *Defiance*.

It was only then that Roger noticed that one of the life-boats from the *Defiance* was missing. Its supporting davits were out over the water with a crew in attendance. The whaler drew alongside and tackle was lowered from the davits and fastened fore and aft. It was all done with a minimum of fuss. The whaler was lifted from the water and drawn up on board. The ratings manning the davits, brought her over and secured her on blocks on the deck outside the CRO. Roger and his companions noticed that she needed a fair bit of attention.

The missing life-boat appeared close to the bow of the *Vulcan*, the old iron cruiser that made another of the three ships moored to create HMS *Defiance*. She drew up alongside, the davits went out again and the tackle was lowered and secured before the life-boat was lifted aboard to her proper position.

Lt. Trelawney took his dinghy and rowed himself back to *Defiance* leaving two men aboard the launch. He returned to the office minutes before the skipper appeared.

"That looked a very efficient life-boat drill Lieutenant," he said with a smile.

"Very satisfactory sir," responded Lt. Trelawney.

"Must keep the men up to scratch eh?"

"Yes sir."

"Nice launch by the look of her but needs some work to bring her back into commission I fancy."

"Yes sir."

"This whaler too."

"Yes sir."

"Carry on Lieutenant."

Roger, standing with the chiefs to attention, could have sworn that the captain winked at Lieutenant Trelawney before proceeding on his lordly way around the ship.

The lieutenant rubbed his hands with delight. He was immensely pleased with himself. "Coffee I reckon scribes." He went to his telephone while Roger made coffee for all of them. Then he came into the outer office.

"Well boys, what do ee think? Bit of all right eh?"

He rubbed his hands in high glee. "The launch will make a vitty motor cruiser when us have done with un. And I'm gwain to put a small motor in the whaler and then 'er ull do fine for a bit of off-shore fishing."

It was only now that Roger realised that these were Lieutenant Trelawney's own boats. The old rogue had bought them from scrap. Now the ship's chippies and engineers could get cracking to provide him with craft fit for a far more wealthy man than a mere Lieutenant.

Nor did they waste any time. The two men left on board the launch were chippies. Lt. Trelawney had provided them with plans and they were busy measuring up and marking out, deciding what materials they would need. Two more chippies came to the office and Lt. Trelawney took them out to his whaler. He didn't need to tell them what to do. There were planks that needed replacement and others that needed repair or patching. The whole boat needed to be waterproofed with tar and then varnished. By the time they had done with it, it would be as good as new.

Work began immediately and in due course, Lt. Trelawney found an engine for the whaler and a pair of diesels for his launch. He rubbed his hands with delight.

"Cost me ten pounds each," he said. "She's gwain to be one of the sturdiest motor cruisers afloat."

All this work added a new dimension of interest to Roger's life. He watched as the superstructure began to appear on the launch, and he watched the work on the whaler closely.

Meanwhile, in his own modest way he took something old and made it new. Towards the end of that first week back at work, Michael brought him his suit. It cost him half a crown to have it dyed black but it looked fine. He took it back on board with him, stripped it of its buttons and replaced them with uniform buttons. Then he added gold badges. He had a number one uniform as smart as any you could buy now and he lined up proudly with the liberty-men, no longer ashamed of his appearance. It was the first uniform he had worn that fitted.

But all this was after his conversation with James. The very first day he was back on board, James had come to his mess at lunch-time and asked him to come up on deck. James was clearly excited about something. Roger finished his meal hurriedly and the two began to pace up and down the deck like two old seamen, heads slightly bowed, hands clasped behind their backs.

"Well, what is it?" asked Roger.

"You know Susan?" said James. "I went home with her for part of my leave over Christmas. I asked her to marry me and she said 'yes'."

"Well done. Congratulations."

"We're going to get married in June."

"JUNE! That's a bit quick isn't it?"

"Yes. It's not what you think." Roger hadn't actually thought anything but he knew what James meant. "No, it's, you see, Susan wants us to get married while I'm still in uniform. She thinks it will add something special to the wedding photos."

"Oh, yes, I see what you mean." James had always been very proud of his appearance in bell-bottoms.

"We wondered if you would be my best man?"

Roger was astonished. "Isn't there someone from home that

143

you would want, someone from before the Navy?"

"No," said James. "I've always been a bit of a loner but you did so much to help me when we first joined up and over that court martial business and so on."

"I'd be delighted," Roger lied. He didn't much fancy the idea of being a best man.

"We don't mind if you don't want to wear YOUR uniform," said James. "We know how you like to get into civvies as soon as you get ashore."

Roger laughed. "What you really mean is that you hope I don't wear my uniform. That's OK. I'll spare your blushes. Fix your wedding date and I'll see the boss and try to make sure he gives me week-end leave. As long as you keep well away from the main leave period there shouldn't be any problem."

At the end of the week, when he saw how smart his new uniform was he wondered whether he ought to say anything to James but he decided not to. He felt so much more relaxed in civvies.

25

All Work and No Play

Early the following week Roger was surprised to have a letter from Jennifer. She thanked him for walking her home from church.

We've known each other for a long time haven't we? she wrote, *but I don't know very much about you. When you write back tell me all about your life in the Navy. Why don't you wear your uniform at home? A sailor looks so romantic in uniform.*

Roger wasn't at all sure that he wanted to write back. Jennifer *was* a nice girl. There was no doubt about that. And it would please his mother, well both his parents, if he courted a girl from their home church. The trouble was, whenever he looked at a girl he thought of Gladys. He had never met anyone who stirred him as Gladys did. There was something about Gladys that had filled him with a sense of gladness and cheerfulness just being with her. He felt comfortable and easy, a feeling of being at home with her. He had never felt that way with any other girl. Perhaps he ought to write back. It was only good manners wasn't it? So he did:

Dear Jennifer, Thank you for your letter. You asked me about my life in the Navy and my uniform. I don't wear my uniform because it doesn't fit and I'm glad to get out of it. Nor is there anything romantic about my life in the Navy. You catch the bus in the morning and go to the office. You work there all day and then catch the bus home. I do the same, except that I don't catch a bus. When I want to go to my ship, I catch a liberty boat. But I work in an office just as you do. I'm at the office from nine to five with a break for lunch and I'd be very surprised if your job is as easy

g

as mine.

So began a correspondence that was more enthusiastic from Jennifer's end than from Roger's. *I want to know ALL about you,* she wrote. *Where do you go to church? What do you do in your spare time?*

He told her that he used to go to Central Hall and that he had got to know a group of people there. *We did all sorts of things together,* he wrote. *We went to the cinema sometimes and on Saturdays we took the bus out of Plymouth and walked on the edges of Dartmoor up the Plym Valley from Plympton and from Yelverton to places like Sheepstor. It's all very beautiful around there. I especially like the river valleys.*

One of my friends is a seaman called James. We have taken a boat from Defiance *to Antony in Cornwall sometimes and walked all around Crafthole and Portwrinkle. You can find these places on the map. Or we've gone in the opposite direction around Rame Head to Penlee Point and back via Cawsand and Mount Edgcumbe to Cremyll where we have taken a boat over to Stonehouse in Plymouth. Everywhere around here is worth visiting.*

As he wrote he thought of a week-end he had spent with James. *That* had been romantic if you like. They had taken the train to Looe via Liskeard and spent the night on the cliffs between Looe and Polperro in a two man tent. All night, above the gentle sound of the sea, there had been the ringing of a bell as its buoy rocked in the swell.

The following day they had walked on to Polruan and taken the ferry to Fowey. There were plenty of places where there was no path but they were determined to stick to the coast. They battled on round Gribbin Head and spent another night under canvas near Par. It was dusk before they set up camp. As they approached the end of their journey, with Roger ploughing on ahead, there was a shout from James. Roger turned round and couldn't see him. Where the hell was he? This was no time for messing about or delays. They must find somewhere to stop.

James shouted again. Roger went back and found him shoulder deep down a hole – probably a badger sett. He helped James out and they continued on their way. The following day was Sunday. They pressed on as far as Mevagissey and then returned to Plymouth by bus and train. Roger spoke enthusiastically of doing a series of week-end walks right around the Cornish coast. But he had the feeling that James was not as keen as he was. They had never gone again.

In her next letter Jennifer picked up on the fact that Roger said he 'used to go' to Central Hall. Where did he go now? She hoped he was keeping up his church going.

Her hopes only made him feel less enthusiastic about this correspondence. He decided that it was time to tell her how he was trying to prepare for civvy street.

When I finish my work on board, he wrote, *I go ashore to a taxi firm. I have been working for them, learning how to run a business, and keep the books and so on. I work in the evenings one week and the next week I work nights. So I don't have either time or energy for church.* He'd better not tell her that he didn't believe in church anymore, he thought.

He sealed up the envelope and then sat back and thought about his evening job. He really had been lucky. On board he had the best boss in the world. Ashore he also had an excellent boss. He had picked up quite a bit of information about taxi firms. Some bosses were slave drivers who seemed to think that their drivers could drive round the clock, nor did they pay very well. Some of them used owner-drivers who worked for them for a few months and then discovered that they weren't actually making any money. They were just wearing out their cars.

Michael owned his own cars, a couple of Austin 10s and two Morris 12s plus a rather tired Vauxhall 14. He paid his drivers by the hour whether they were on the road or not, and he insisted on them taking two twenty minute breaks in their eight hour shifts. "I want my drivers to stay with me," he used to say, "and I want them to last. I don't want them burning out after a few years."

Because of his attitude, drivers from other companies turned up from time to time to see if there were any jobs going. It was Roger who often saw them first and heard all their moans about the firms they worked for. He felt that Michael's was a good firm, one worth imitating when he had his own.

His own pay was geared to a five day week. If he worked extra days he was given extra pay. He didn't work extra nights. Five nights on top of his day job was quite enough. Curiously enough it was Jennifer who rammed home a message he was beginning to be aware of himself.

You seem to be doing nothing but work, she wrote. *Don't forget that 'all work and no play makes a Jack tar a dull boy'.*

She was right. Perhaps after a week of nights he should take up his old dream of walking around the Cornish coast. In mid-March he took a Friday night off, went to Mevagissey and spent the week-end walking and camping. He reached St. Mawes, took a boat across to Falmouth and then returned to Plymouth, well tired and well content. He wrote to Jennifer and told her what he had done. Her reply alarmed him.

If you let me know your future week-end plans perhaps I could come down one week-end and go with you.

No, thought Roger. He didn't want her to come. He enjoyed being on his own.

Her letter continued, *Of course, if I am to spend a week-end with you, there are a few things I must make clear before I come. We shall be sleeping together in a tent. I shall expect you to respect my privacy. And I want to make it quite clear that I don't want you trying anything on. I am saving myself until I marry so that I am pure for my husband.*

Roger gasped. Well, that really was telling him. He grinned. He wondered if that's what his mother meant when she said that Jennifer was 'a nice girl'. He had been very ambivalent about this correspondence but he was feeling less and less like keeping it going. Jennifer was all church and virtue. He wondered if she wasn't a bit of a prude, too good to be true.

He wrote back emphasising that it was tough going around the coast with no footpaths half the time. But if she really wanted to come it would give them a chance to get to know one another at close quarters. Then he wrote: *As to sleeping in the tent, you don't need to worry. I would never try to have sex with anyone who didn't want me to. I respect your point of view. But perhaps I ought to mention that I haven't kept myself for marriage. My wife will not be the first woman I have slept with.*

Weeks passed. Slowly it dawned on him that he was never going to hear from Jennifer again. It was a bit of a relief. Cornwall had never looked so beautiful as it did on his next week-end's hike.

26

Martha's 'Cornish Rhapsody'

Towards the end of April the nearest life-boat to the CRO was lowered into the water. Four seamen rowed her away a short distance and lay on their oars. Others moved Lt. Trelawney's whaler to the life-boat's position. She looked beautiful with her fresh varnish shining in the morning sunshine. They raised her on the davits, and swung her out over the water. Lt. Trelawney and two seamen were aboard.

"Lower away petty officer."

"Yes sir: Lower away. Gently does it."

Down she went into the water. The seamen released her and rowed her quietly to her mooring astern of Lt. Trelawney's launch. The men in the life-boat rowed across and picked up the men from the whaler. They dropped them off at *Defiance*'s permanent forward gangway before returning to the position below the davits and being hoisted aboard.

Back in the office Lt. Trelawney rubbed his hands together. "That's that one vitty. Now then boys, us'll soon have to give the launch a name. Got any bright ideas have ee?"

One of the chiefs said, " 'Admiralty Spares' sir?"

They all had a good chuckle at that and the boss clipped him playfully round the ear.

"Why don't you give her your own name sir? 'The Trelawney'," said the second of the chiefs.

"Or your wife's name, 'the Martha' sir?" added chief Earwaker.

"Hm. You got any ideas scribes?"

" 'The Cornish Rhapsody' sir?"

"Us'll have to see won't us?"

A few days later Lt. Trelawney said to Roger, "I want you to come to the office wearing your number eights tomorrow."

"Yes sir." Why, he wondered? Why had he got to wear the clothes he wore when he was working ship? It sounded ominous. Some cleaning job in store for him he reckoned. Whatever it was, he did as he was told.

He was surprised to find the three chiefs all wearing sweaters instead of their jackets. When the captain came on his rounds, they all lined up outside under the direction of the senior Chief PO. Five more men were there, a Chief Engineer and four chippies. They all lined up together. As Roger looked straight ahead he noticed that Lt. Trelawney's whaler was missing. But he couldn't say anything.

The captain gave them a cursory examination. "Bit of a motley crew this morning Lieutenant."

"Yes sir," grinned Trelawney.

"Sea trials today isn't it?"

"Yes sir."

"I trust everything will go smoothly. I'm sure it will."

"Thank you sir."

"Carry on Lieutenant."

This was normally the signal for dismissal into the office. But the chief quietly gave the order, "Lieutenant's men, men right turn. By the left quick march."

What on earth was going on? The lead man seemed to know where he was going.

"Mark time. In your own time, down to the lower deck and form up again. First, second, third . . ." he directed them all to the lower deck and off they marched again the short distance to the for'ard gangway. Down again and Roger discovered where Lt. Trelawney's whaler was. They all crowded aboard. Everyone seemed to know what was going on except Roger. The chief engineer started the engine, they cast off and made a full circuit of *Defiance* before drawing up astern of the launch and holding their station at one of the buoys. The chief switched off the engine.

"She sounds fine," said the Lieutenant.

"Yes sir."

They hauled the dinghy alongside the whaler and Lieutenant

150

Trelawney transferred to it, sculled out of sight alongside the launch and then came back with a woman in the dinghy. Like half of the rest of them, she was dressed in bell bottoms and a heavy sweater. Roger reckoned that she was a pretty sturdy woman even without her togs. She was in her early forties, he thought, and looked to be full of fun. She had a great mop of fiery red hair and a weather-beaten, freckled face.

The chief roared, "Men, men stand at ease." They stood and faced the dinghy and the whaler rocked a bit. "Men, attention." They managed it. The chief saluted.

"Most of you know my wife," said the Lieutenant. "She's going to do the honours for us." He bent down and came up with a bottle of champagne which he gave to her. Then he took an oar and sculled gently to the stern of the launch, holding the dinghy steady.

Crash!

His wife smashed the bottle against the launch. "I name this . . ." she hesitated: ship? boat? Her husband would never forgive her if she used the wrong term: "vessel, 'Martha's Cornish Rhapsody'. May all who sail in her do so with delight."

The chief raised his cap, "Hip,hip," and all of them joined in three cheers. Roger dared not look but there was more cheering behind them.

"Right lads, line 'em up and let's have you all aboard."

He and his wife went aboard the *Cornish Rhapsody* and the others followed, hoisting the dinghy to her place athwart the stern and securing the whaler astern with a tow rope.

The launch was pretty crowded. There was only room in the bridge for four but the others spread out around the deck rail.

"Start her up chief." One of the two engines burst into throbbing life. "Cast off astern." The nearest passenger cast off. "Cast off for'ard." Again, the nearest man cast off. "Slow ahead chief."

As they drew away from their moorings there were more cheers from *Defiance*. Roger looked across. It looked as though virtually the whole ship's company was there.

"Right boys, relax and have a good time. There'll be a tot or two coming round in a minute." Lt. Trelawney rubbed his hands together in delight. As the men sat on the deck and stretched their legs over the side he came round with drinks for them all, thanking the chippies for all their work and singing their praises.

Roger looked around him. The bridge led down to an inner cabin. He couldn't see very clearly but it looked as though there was a cooking and eating area down there, though he guessed that they would eat up above most of the time. He assumed that sleeping quarters were further ahead near the bows of the launch.

The paintwork, the varnish, the brasses all looked perfect. No effort had been spared. No wonder the boss was proud. He came round with rum for them all but he knew that Roger was not a drinker. He brought him a coffee. "All right scribes?"

All right? This was a darned sight more than all right. "Yes sir. It's marvellous sir."

"There boy. You'm getting a bit of sea time after all."

They sailed gently out into Plymouth Sound and both the boss and his wife plied them with pasties and sandwiches. After an hour or two in the calm waters of the sound they drew in to Stonehouse. The three chiefs from the office thanked the boss and left, free for the rest of the day. The four chippies transferred to the whaler and started her engine.

"Right boys, you know what to do. Come up to the house when you'm safely home."

"Yes sir."

"Away we go chief."

The chief engineer drew away in the launch and began to increase her speed. The whaler waited a little while and bucked in the wake of the launch. Then it set off for its destination – still unknown to Roger. He and the chief engineer were now the only two on board apart from Lieutenant and Mrs Trelawney. He was excited beyond words.

The engineer switched on the second engine and there was a fresh surge of power through the launch. She lifted her bows a little and they sailed steadily out into the open sea.

"You're working tonight boy I suppose?"

Roger blushed. He didn't know that the boss knew about his evening work. "Yes sir."

"What time do ee start?"

"Not until ten sir."

"That's fine. Us 'ave got all the time in the world then." He turned to his wife. "This yer boy doesn't want to stay in the Navy. He's gwain back ashore to a civilian job when his two years is up.

Must be maised."

"Don't you listen to him," said Martha. "The Navy has been very good to him but it isn't the same for everybody. What are you going to do when you've finished your time?"

"I hope to start my own business."

"That's why he's working for a taxi firm ashore," interrupted the Lieutenant. "Thought I didn't know. The beggar must be raking it in."

"Is that the sort of business you want?" asked Martha.

"I think so. Lieutenant Trelawny helped me to get my driving licence and I've always loved cars. Now I find that I love driving them too."

"You don't do much driving though do ee? Mostly in the office isn't it?"

"Mostly, yes sir. I need to know how to run a business, not just how to drive for one."

The lieutenant took over the helm. "Right chief, let's see what her can do?"

For a while there was no conversation at all. The Lieutenant put her through her paces. She had tremendous power. He was concerned to see how she behaved in a variety of ways. He swung her hard to port and starboard; threw her about all over the place until Roger was feeling as sick as a dog. Finally he eased her down to a steady cruising speed and said, "Come on then boy, you take the helm for a bit. D'ee see that headland over there? Just keep her pointing towards that."

His stomach had been beginning to settle down but now it had a new reason for churning – sheer excitement. He took the helm from the Lieutenant. "Yes sir," he said, "but aren't we going the wrong way?"

The Lieutenant was puzzled. "What d'ee main boy?"

"Sir, that's the Devon coast. Shouldn't we be heading towards Cornwall?"

Both the Lieutenant and his wife roared with laughter. "Just because us be Cornish doesn't mean us got to live in Cornwall," the Lieutenant said. "How many Irish or Scots live outside their own countries? The chief here is Scottish idn' you chief."

"Yes sir."

"There's nobody so patriotic boy as those who live away from home, but us don't live far away." He turned back to the chief.

153

"Guide the boy in and take over when you think fit."

He and his wife went for'ard, still chuckling that Roger felt they were bound to be going to Cornwall. They stood hand in hand. They had been married for a long time and were devoted to one another.

Eventually the chief took over the helm and sailed the launch gently inland from Wembury Bay to the safe haven of Newton Ferrers. The Lieutenant had a mooring there. They made the launch fast, lowered the dinghy into the water and Roger rowed them ashore. As they had approached from Gara point he felt that he had never seen anywhere so beautiful in his life and that feeling was underlined as he looked all around from the mooring, and again as they walked from their landing place to the Lieutenant's home. In all his week-end hikes in Cornwall he had never seen anything more beautiful than this.

They came to the Lieutenant's garden gate and Martha said, "Have a wander round the garden and then come inside and don't be afraid to look around."

The garden was an astonishing place. There were ship's figureheads, anchors, benches made from ships' timbers, collections of things picked up on the shore arranged decoratively and everywhere, a mass of flowers. Roger didn't want to leave it. It was a fantastic garden. Yes, he thought, fantastic was exactly the word. Fantastic in all its meanings.

He was called inside for tea and before long the four chippies arrived to join them. Roger's eyes wandered around the room. The Lieutenant watched him with amusement.

"Go on boy, have a look around the house. Don't be shy."

But Roger WAS shy. He didn't feel he could nose around in someone else's house. Martha took him by the shoulder and began to lead him from room to room describing everything he saw. All the furniture had been made from ship's timbers. Sometimes pieces were oddly shaped just because the boss had found something he wanted to use. A rudder marked 'Admiralty drum' formed one end of a dressing table so the other end had to be shaped like a rudder too.

Martha showed him from room to room. He had never seen a house anywhere that was so personal. It seemed as though there was nothing in the house that did not speak of the Lieutenant's life in the Navy or his love for the sea.

The men all stayed to dinner and stayed on over drinks while the Lieutenant regaled them with some of his famous maritime stories. He never seemed to run out and Roger had never heard any of them more than once. At half past nine he turned to Roger.

"If you're caught ashore in number eights you'll be in trouble. There's a chit here as will look after that."

He gave Roger an envelope. "Martha's gwain to run ee to your taxi firm. I'll zee ee in the morning."

Roger began to try to express his thanks but was silenced. Martha took him out to the garage. To Roger's astonishment she wheeled a large khaki wartime 350cc Royal Enfield motor-bike out, kick started it and told him to jump on and hold tight. It wasn't long before he found that it was no good being shy. He needed to hold on tight as she zoomed along the narrow lanes from Newton Ferrers, climbing steeply, throwing her bike around tight corners and generally driving like a maniac. He hung on for dear life and was outside the taxi office on time.

There was one last surprise for him. He dismounted and turned to try to say thank you adequately to her. She lifted the bike onto its stand, took him in her arms, gave him a crushing hug, kissed him full on the lips and said, "My husband thinks the world of you boy. I hope all your best dreams come true."

And then she was back on her bike and away. Roger went into work in a complete daze. When he had finally cooled down a bit and come down to earth in the bleak early hours he wrote a long and careful letter of thanks, not just for what had been one of the most wonderful days of his life, but for all the kindness his boss had shown him throughout his time at the CRO.

On a separate sheet of paper he wrote out John Masefield's poem *Sea Fever*. He hoped his memory was accurate. Then he added a PS to his letter.

I expect you know this poem. It's one of my favourites and sounds just right for you.

He posted the letter and poem off to the Trelawney's home address before catching the morning liberty boat back to *Defiance*. As he stepped aboard from the gangway he was pulled over.

"Number Eights scribes?"

"Yes chief. I've got a chit here."

The chief looked at it. "Right. Carry on."

He went below to the mess, washed and freshened up, changed into his proper uniform, had some breakfast and was ready for his normal day job.

Two days later the boss thanked him for his letter and the poem. "Us didn' know it scribes. 'Tis a vitty poem. I've told Martha to have it read at my funeral." He roared with laughter. But he was clearly pleased that Roger had felt so indebted to him and had taken the trouble to write such a careful letter.

27

Korean Postscript

In May 1951 the Korean War ended in stalemate. The North Koreans and Chinese had been driven back to their own territory just north of the 38th parallel. The United Nations forces were not allowed to advance further. Truce negotiations began and were to drag on for two years.

In spite of his concerns about the war when it began, Roger had paid little attention to it. Only when he had to prepare travel documents for men being sent to Korea had he thought about it, or on those rare occasions when it had found its way onto the front pages of his colleagues' newspapers.

Now that it was over he wondered what had been achieved. For nearly forty years he was to go on wondering. In North Korea a closed society endured a rigid communist dictatorship. Perhaps anything was better than that but the situation in the south was little better. One corrupt and tyrannical government succeeded another until the end of the 1980s when student riots led to national uprisings, genuine democracy and the beginnings of South Korea's emergence as a successful nation in economic terms.

In 1951 these things were all unknown. Of much greater concern to Roger was the excitement James showed every time they met. His wedding day was drawing near. In early June he and Susan set off for her home in Kingston.

28

Going to a Wedding

The Friday before the wedding, Roger dressed in his dyed black suit, his smart number one uniform, as usual. He lined up with the liberty men and the officer of the day began his inspection. He was just passing Roger when the petty officer accompanying him coughed discreetly.

The officer looked at Roger again, looked at the rating next to him and again prepared to move on. Again the PO coughed. The officer turned and the two of them had a quiet conversation. The officer turned back to Roger.

"Where did you get that uniform scribes?"

"It was a suit my father gave me sir. I had it dyed, changed the buttons and sewed on my badges."

There was a bit of tittering around him. "Silence in the ranks!" roared the PO.

"You do realise that ratings' uniforms do not normally have top pockets? Nor are they double-breasted, nor do their pockets have flaps."

Oh hell! "I'm sorry sir. I hadn't noticed."

Again there was muffled laughter and the shout, "Silence in the ranks."

"You hadn't noticed." The officer's voice was heavy with sarcasm. He had already forgotten that he hadn't noticed either. "How long have you been wearing that suit as a uniform scribes?"

"Almost six months sir."

"SIX MONTHS!" God, this would make a good story in the

mess. "Then I suggest that you go and get it off and never wear it again."

"Yes sir."

"Rating," bawled the PO as if Roger were a hundred yards away, "Rating, three paces forward MARCH."

Roger stepped forward three pages.

"Sorry scribes," whispered the PO. "I'll hold the liberty boat for four minutes if you can change that quickly." And then in his usual bellow, "DI . . .UGH . . .S . . .MISS."

Roger fled across the deck, up one gangway, across to another ship, down two gangways, across another deck into the mess. He emptied his pockets, threw off his jacket, then his boots, then his trousers. His old number one uniform came out of his locker and on. He threw his smart, incorrect uniform inside. Boots back on, pockets refilled and off across one deck, up two gangways, across to another ship, down one gangway.

The PO was watching for him from the top of the gangway to the liberty boat. He waved to an increasingly impatient civilian liberty boat skipper.

"Cast off for'ard . . . Cast off aft."

"Go for it scribes."

Roger flew down the gangway and leapt for the boat. Willing hands grasped his arms and hauled him aboard. His cap flew off into the drink. The civilian who had cast off aft grabbed a boat-hook, caught the cap and hoisted it aboard. There were cheers for Roger, cheers for his cap, and Roger turned back to the ship and gave the PO a thank you thumbs up.

"Did you really wear that suit for six months scribes?"

"Yes."

"And nobody noticed?"

"No."

"But you must've known."

"No I never gave it a thought."

"Blimey. Bloody scribes get away with murder."

He slammed his wet cap on to walk through the dockyard and out to the taxi office. There he changed into his civilian suit. He was just about to leave to catch a bus to the station when Michael said, "You've forgotten your button-hole Roger. Can't let the best man go to a wedding without a button-hole. He produced a dandelion." Roger was as amused as the rest of them and carefully inserted the dandelion into his lapel.

"Jim," said Michael, "drop the boy to the station." He turned to Roger. "It's on the firm boy. Have a good time."

So Roger travelled in style to the station. He travelled up to London alone on the train, if you could call it alone. The train was as crowded as usual. He stood in the corridor wishing that he was doing something else that week-end. Almost anything would be better than going to a wedding. Weddings were for women. Men endured them under sufferance. But he was happy for James and Susan all the same. They genuinely seemed right for one another.

He changed trains in London for the short journey out to Kingston. Someone had left a *Surrey Herald* on the train. He picked it up and flicked through the pages idly. He wasn't really very interested in Surrey news. 'Surrey Car Hire Boss to quit', he read. He turned the page and flicked on until he came to the motoring pages and looked at the adverts for new and secondhand cars. The new Ford Consul seemed to be pretty well rated.

Suddenly something clicked. What was that he had read. He began to turn back the pages hastily. Papers were so difficult to control when you were after something. What was it? Yes, there it was. 'Car hire boss to quit.' He read about a man called Hill who was aiming to sell his luxury car hire business and retire. Hill: that was Gladys's surname. Was that an omen?

Where was this business? A place called Hersham. He'd never heard of it. 'Luxury car hire': it sounded as if it would be beyond his means even if he was interested.

Was he interested? Of course he was interested. He stood up and looked at the railway map on the wall of the compartment. Because he didn't know where to look it took him a moment or two to locate Hersham. It couldn't be all that far from Kingston. Perhaps when the wedding was over he could . . .

But his thoughts were interrupted by his train's arrival in Kingston. He went to W.H. Smith's and bought a map of Kingston, got his bearings and then set off for Susan's house. An elderly lady opened the door to him.

"I'm Roger Wallace, James's best man."

"Come in. Come in. I expect you'd like a cup of tea."

Susan's voice called out from the stairs. "Is that Roger? Don't give him tea Gran, give him coffee. He doesn't like tea."

Roger looked up the stairs. Three women leaned over the rail

160

at the top, all wearing white masks. It looked spooky. What on earth were they wearing masks for? Roger was appalled.

"Hello Roger," one of the masks called. It was Susan's voice. "Do you think we look beautiful? We'll be down in a minute but you'll have to excuse our faces."

Roger decided to risk it. He asked Susan's Gran, "What are they wearing those masks for?"

"Masks? What masks? Oh. You mean their mud packs. Haven't you ever seen those before? They are supposed to help them look their best tomorrow."

One of the three masked ladies came downstairs. "Hello Roger. You must excuse us looking like this. I'm Susan's mother."

The front door bell rang and Susan's mother fled back upstairs. It was James at the door. Susan's grandmother let him in. There was a good deal of giggling upstairs but no sign this time of the three masked women. They were carefully keeping out of sight.

James had come to take Roger to meet his parents at the small hotel where they were staying overnight. They left the women to their beautification and walked together.

"What do you want to do for your stag night James?"

"Hide," answered James.

It was precisely what Roger would have expected – and what he would have wanted for himself if it had been his wedding.

"Actually," James went on, "I thought we'd have a quiet meal with my parents. They're looking forward to meeting you ever so much."

It was true. James had told them so much about the way Roger had nursed him through his early days in the Navy and supported him through that awful Court Martial ordeal that they had a rather inflated idea of Roger's virtue and quality.

The introductions were formal and a little on the stiff, awkward side. James's parents were a gentle couple who had married late and had their only son late. It was obvious that he was immensely precious to them and that they both doted on him. Nothing in their lives meant more to them.

Roger found their adoration of their son a bit stifling as if they were in a greenhouse and James was the favourite greenhouse plant. Over dinner he held back and let the three of them talk to one another as if he were not there. Soon after dinner the two of

161

them escaped and went for a long walk beside the Thames.

The following morning James flapped about anxious that he should look his best in his uniform. Roger did his best to make the right noises but he was bored stiff. He didn't feel that he could push off and be on his own, nor did he feel that he could sit down and read a book. He had to be all attentive but James fussed about just as he had when they were getting ready for their first passing out parade. It was a relief when the four of them left the hotel and walked the short distance to the Parish Church.

Roger didn't know much about parish churches but a man in a black cassock met them, some sort of church warden or verger or something. He seemed to be worried but perhaps that went with the job. It was so important for people that a wedding should go well.

"The vicar will be here soon," he said. "He is such a busy man that he often doesn't arrive until the last minute."

James's parents took their place inside the church. They were disappointed that their son was being married in church and not in their home chapel. But they took comfort from the fact that Susan would be going to chapel rather than church after the marriage. They looked around. The church was cool and on the dark side, but very pleasant with nice stained glass windows.

Guests were milling around outside. Some of the Central Hall crowd had come. He saw Philippa arrive with a sub-lieutenant in full dress uniform. They drove up in a small Morris 8 sports car. So Philippa was happy, thought Roger. This was more her style than a naval writer. As James saluted, Roger thanked his lucky stars that he wasn't in uniform. He carefully paid no attention at all to Philippa and her escort.

The verger began to flap around the guests ushering them into the church. Susan's sister arrived in an orange bridesmaid's dress – that's what Roger would have called it anyway. In fact it was peach coloured with a matching bouquet of roses. Susan's mother arrived with her daughter and busied herself straightening the dress and generally making sure that her daughter looked her best.

James fished around inside his bell bottoms and took out the small box containing the ring. He gave it to Roger and the two of them took their places in the church. There was still no sign of the vicar but the church had been nicely prepared and was spotlessly clean. On one side of the altar there was a stand of flowers obviously designed to suit the bridesmaid's colour scheme. On the other side was a throne style chair.

The organist was playing quietly and took them all by surprise when he broke into the wedding march. Susan's mother hurried down the aisle and took her seat with an encouraging smile in the general direction of James and his parents. The vicar came in from the vestry. He was elderly and seemed somewhat unsteady on his feet.

Then at last James and Roger were aware of the bridal procession led by the verger carrying a cross. The verger carried on out of the way, Susan and her father drew level with James and Roger, and they joined the bridal party. James looked at his bride in her long cream dress. His eyes shone with adoration and devotion.

Susan's sister stepped forward and took the bride's bouquet, almost identical to her own. Then she helped Susan lift her veil back from her face and the vicar announced a hymn. After the hymn he began to read the wedding service, swaying a little as he did so. He wiped his brow and leaned back against the altar. And then suddenly he keeled over.

The verger ran forward and Roger jumped over the rail. Strewth, thought Roger as the alcohol fumes hit him, he's drunk. He felt violently angry and was none too gentle as he and the verger helped the vicar to the chair. The verger whispered, "He's an alcoholic. I've been dreading something like this but it's never happened before."

Roger's anger turned to pity. But what were they going to do? He turned to the congregation and said, "We shall now sing the second hymn on your hymn sheet."

The organist struck up, the congregation began fitfully to join in and Roger turned his attention back to the vicar. The verger was standing there wringing his hands helplessly. It was clear that he would be no use. The vicar opened his eyes, looked at Roger and said, "The lesson," then he closed his eyes again.

The lesson? Roger's head was swimming. What to do? The lesson, he thought. Yes of course. So when the hymn ended he went across to the lectern with its huge Bible fronted by the usual eagle.

"Please sit down," he said. "The lesson today is taken from St.

Paul's 1st letter to the Corinthians chapter 13." The Bible was open at the right place. Suddenly he felt wonderfully calm. He began to read. This was the version of the Bible with the word 'charity' in it. Modern versions substituted 'love' for 'charity'. He did the same as he read. He thought back to his schooldays. Mr Emerson had drilled him well for all those speech day readings he'd had to do. That training stood him in good stead now. "Here endeth the lesson."

He looked across at the vicar who had seemed to be asleep. But now he opened his eyes and held out his service book. He pointed at Roger and said, "My curate. Read the service."

Roger took the book and looked at the verger who nodded frantically. He looked at James and Susan. They would have heard the vicar but not many others would have done.

"Do you want me to?" he asked.

James looked at Susan. She didn't hesitate. "Yes please Roger. You heard what he said. You are his curate."

So Roger began to read the service, beginning where the vicar had tailed off. When he came to "if any man can show any just cause why they should not be joined in matrimony let him now speak or for ever hold his peace" he half expected someone to protest that he shouldn't be doing this. From time to time he paused and looked at the vicar. He did no more than open one eye and nod that Roger should continue.

Then in the margin of the service book he saw the words 'sit them down for homily'. Oh golly. "Please would you all sit down," he said. He looked at the vicar.

"Go on," mouthed the vicar.

"At this point," said Roger, "the clergyman would normally offer words of wisdom to James and Susan. I can't do that, I'm afraid. But perhaps I could just say one or two things I was going to say at the reception – no," he added, "not the rude bits, just the serious bits.

"Those of us who saw James and Susan when they first met soon realised that this was one of those rare occasions when two people who are absolutely right for one another have come together. Their rapport was instant and they have never looked back. We feel sure that they never will. We wish them every happiness and," he hesitated. He knew what they would wish him to add and he knew what their parents would wish him to add but it was difficult. He had already been reading things he didn't believe. All these things raced through his mind in a flash and then he added, "and those of us who believe in him wish them God's blessing."

He turned back to the service book and asked the congregation to stand for the vows. Did the vicar really want him to do those? Yes, he did. With intense care he led them through the vows. Next came the ring. The ring! Oh golly, he had the ring somewhere. He fished in his pockets, found it and gave it to James. He looked back at the service book. Thank goodness all the instructions were there. "James, say after me, 'With this ring . . .' "

"With this ring . . ."

" 'A token and pledge . . .' "

"A token and pledge . . ."

At last it was all over. They came to the final blessing. The vicar hauled himself to his feet and gave the blessing before leading the bridal party into the vestry. The marriage book and marriage certificate lay on the table. The vicar turned to Roger.

"Special ink and a special pen. Fill up the register and the certificate please."

That was no problem. It was the same ink that he used in the CRO for official documents. He sat down and got to work. The bride, groom, witnesses and the vicar all signed and then with immense relief took themselves in procession back through the church. Roger had Susan's sister on his arm.

"I don't even know your name," he whispered.

"Jane," she replied and clung on to his arm rather more tightly than was strictly necessary.

Photographs took for ever but at last they were on their way back to Susan's house for a reception in the garden.

29

A Job Well Done
and a Job Begun

At the reception all the early talk was of the vicar and of how wonderful Roger had been. Roger found it all highly embarrassing. And he also found himself defending the vicar.

"No you mustn't confuse him with an ordinary drunk," he said. "The man's an alcoholic."

"Then why doesn't he give up?"

"He probably doesn't realise how bad things are."

"I'd have thought it was pretty obvious this afternoon. I don't know why they don't just sack him."

"They probably can't. Some of these livings become the vicar's own and no one can sack him. He's there more or less for life if he wants to be."

"Well someone ought to do something. It's a disgrace."

"Yes, the church officials ought to try to get him to have treatment but they can't force him. And they may not even have tried. You know how people are with vicars and priests. They seem to think they are untouchable no matter how bad the situation is."

Philippa's sub-lieutenant said to her, "This able-seaman-best-man seems to be a bit of a know-all doesn't he. I wonder how he became such an expert?" he added sarcastically.

Philippa giggled but Jane had overheard the remark and rounded on him. "I didn't notice any officers showing much wisdom or leadership," she snarled. "But that's always the way isn't it? Officers are just educated figureheads who follow the leadership of men who are real men and real leaders." She stalked away.

"Sorry I'm sure," mocked the officer but his face was crimson and he very soon persuaded Philippa to make their excuses and leave.

Conversation settled down to the usual mundane subjects as people who hadn't seen each other in a while caught up with one another. There was plenty of food and drink, buffet style in the garden. Eventually Roger called for silence for the usual run of speeches. When it was his own turn he said:

"You have already heard most of my speech so I'll content myself with commenting on how beautiful the bridesmaid is – *almost* as lovely as her sister. She has done a wonderful job and supported me all the way through. So I'd like to propose a toast to the chief bridesmaid, the one and only and the best." He raised his glass of orange juice wishing that it looked a bit more like champagne in a champagne glass. Why did people never give teetotallers decent glasses to drink from? He loved decent china and glass. Oh well, never mind. There was no point in making a fuss.

After the speeches were over Susan and James disappeared to get changed, came back to farewells and more confetti, and left by taxi for the station. Jane wanted to go to the station and give them a rowdy send-off but, apart from Roger and a few of the Central Hall crowd, she was about the only person there who was young enough to be interested. She didn't know the Central Hall crowd so she tackled Roger.

"I'll go with you if you like," he said, "but James would much rather be left on his own. He's very quiet and shy you know. He doesn't like fuss."

"Oh all right. Only it seems a bit tame. The whole wedding is fizzling out like a damp squib."

"I think a lot of weddings are like that. When the bride and groom have gone people feel like spare parts. They don't know whether to stay or to go. They don't want to be the first to go or to seem rude but there isn't any reason for them to stay any longer is there?"

"So what are you going to do?"

"I've got to go to a place called Hersham. I've got someone I need to go and see. Do you know how to get to Hersham

167

from here?"

Jane was disappointed. She had been hoping that Roger would take her out – perhaps to the flicks. "I could come with you if you like and show you."

"There's no point," he said. "I don't know how long I'll be and as soon as I've finished I'm going back to my ship."

Poor Jane felt absolutely flat. "Well at least let me change and walk with you to the bus station," she said.

As soon as she was ready, Roger said his farewells, received yet another set of effusive thank yous for all he had done, and set off with Jane for the bus station. She took his arm possessively. She so much wanted more than his company to the bus station but his mind was on his destination and she soon gave up. He was a waste of time. She showed him his bus, pecked him on the cheek and waved him away.

Every nice girl might love a sailor, she thought, but there wasn't much point trying to love a sailor like this one. She kicked a stone into the gutter and set off miserably for home.

Roger's bus dropped him off in Queen's Road but he had no idea where to go next. He wanted Woodside Avenue but he hadn't the faintest idea where it was and there didn't seem to be anybody to ask or any shops. He started to walk aimlessly along Queens Road and almost the first turning on the right was Woodside Avenue.

How lucky can you get? he thought. He walked slowly along the road. Nice property, he thought, and his heart sank. This was going to be a complete waste of time. 'Luxury car hire' the article had said. These houses were as nice as the one his dad had brought them up in. The firm must have done pretty well for the owner to have a house like these. He walked right through the avenue and turned left without thinking where he was going. In next to no time he found himself by Walton station. Perhaps he should just jump on a train and go back to *Defiance* or he could even go home for a day . . .

He stood for a while watching trains come and go and then he pulled himself together. "Damn it," he said to himself, "I'm not going to lose anything by finding out and I might learn a lot that's useful."

He strode back to Woodside Avenue. The house he wanted had two Rover saloons in the drive. They were nice cars but a bit elderly. He resisted the temptation to study them carefully, went to the front door and rang the bell. A man in his sixties came to the door.

"Yes?" he said.

"Excuse me for bothering you. I'm in the Navy and I'm on week-end leave. I saw the article about your business in the *Surrey Herald* and wondered if the firm is still for sale?"

Still for sale, thought the man. That's a laugh. There hasn't been so much as a nibble. "Come in," he said. "There are a few people interested but I can tell you about it if you like." He looked at Roger. What on earth was the point? This was just a boy. Oh well, he'd nothing better to do . . . "Like a cup of tea?" he said.

Roger thanked him and said yes. There was no point in telling the man that he didn't like tea much.

"Ethel," called the man, "could you make a couple of cups of tea? I've got a visitor."

"So you're interested in my business?"

"Yes sir."

"My name's Mr Hill. And yours?"

"Roger Wallace sir."

"Know anything about the car hire business do you?"

"I know a bit about taxi work sir. I'm a part-time manager for a firm in Plymouth but I know that car hire is different from taxi work."

"Yes it is different, but it's similar. Do your cars work from the rank or from the office?"

"From the office, but it is right by the dockyard gates."

"Ah, a good spot then. All our work comes in by telephone. We just run the two cars now. I'll introduce you to Roy in a minute. He's my driver and he'll be coming to pick up one of the cars soon."

Mrs Hill arrived with tea and biscuits. She seemed a pleasant woman, fussily busy and anxious to please. They introduced themselves and she left the two men together. They drank their tea and Mr Hill went on talking.

"This was my dad's business before me. He began with horses and carriages and then turned over to cars in the 1920s. He ran a couple of bull-nosed Morrises in those days. Then in the 1930s he turned over to Rovers. Of course the war just about finished us. I was working with Dad by then. He gave up and I got a job as a

169

h

chauffeur for the War Office. We just laid our own cars up."

"So you drove all through the Blitz?" asked Roger.

"Yes lad and I could tell you a tale or two about all that." He paused lost in his memories. "Anyway, when the war was over I got our two cars out again and started the business from scratch. Roy was in the Army and found it difficult getting a job so he joined me. Come and have a look at the cars."

30

'Hill and Son, Luxury Car Hire'

They went out and began to look the cars over. Roger thought about his dad's cars. His dad drove an Austin 16. These Rovers were certainly better than that. But what about his dad's firm's Vauxhall HMG 1? He never understood why his dad drove the Austin when he could have driven the Vauxhall. Were these better than that? He didn't really know.

"Know Rovers do you?"

"No I don't. I think I've only ever been in one once."

"Nice cars. Real quality, not like these tinny new things that are beginning to come out now – all flash and no quality most of them."

"Rovers are still making these aren't they?"

"That's right. Why change when you are making one of the best?"

Roy arrived and Mr Hill introduced him.

"This young man is thinking of buying the business," he said with a wink. He obviously thought this young man hadn't a hope of buying him out.

"Well I hope you'll keep me on if you do," answered Roy. "It isn't easy to get work these days and I'm happy driving."

Roger said, "We've only just begun to chat, Mr Hill and I. But if I did decide to buy, you would be the first person I would need because you know the customers and they know you. They will need to know that they can trust the business to go on looking after them."

"Thank you," said Roy. "Well that's nice to know. I'll be on my

171

way now shall I Guv'nor?"

He took the Rover nearest to the road, leaving his bike against the side of the house.

"I'll take you for a spin," said Mr Hill. He called to tell his wife what he was doing, Roger jumped in and the two of them set off. "Know this area do you?"

"No," said Roger, "I don't. I come from near Croydon so it's that side of Surrey I know."

"Well lad, it's the LUXURY side of the trade we serve so it's business people and people with a bit of money who use us." He drove slowly through Burwood Park. There were not many houses and each of them had extensive gardens. Roger felt that he had never seen a more beautiful housing estate in his life.

They drove out of the park and turned right onto Burwood road. It was pleasant and lined with trees. At the crossroads they went straight over and found themselves in St. Georges Hill.

Mr Hill drove around the hill carefully. It was amazing how large it was. "Believe it or not," Mr Hill said, "the first people to settle on the hill were a crowd of squatters. They were harmless, peaceable people who just wanted somewhere to live a quiet life growing their own food and being no trouble to anybody. The owner drove them off. Now the people who live here are some of the wealthiest people in the country."

Roger looked about him in astonishment. He had never seen such wealth. He noticed the cars too: big American ones, the new Jaguar, Rolls Royce, and some smart sports cars. He couldn't imagine most of these people being interested in old Rovers somehow.

Mr Hill interrupted his thoughts. "A lot of foreigners live here," he said, "diplomats and that. And some of the best known entertainers too. Get a few of these as your customers and you don't need anything else."

"I expect you're right," said Roger. "How much are you asking for your business?"

"Five hundred pounds," answered Mr Hill. "That's for the two cars and the goodwill. It's a darned sight easier starting with a diary full of customers than starting from scratch I can tell you."

Roger kept his thoughts to himself. There was no way this business was worth five hundred pounds. He wondered how much Mr Hill would come down.

172

"Would you be prepared to let me take your books for the last three years? I'll study them overnight and let you have them back in the morning. If I'm interested in the business then, I'll tell you what I'm prepared to offer."

"Know an accountant do you?" asked Mr Hill anxiously.

"No," said Roger. "I understand enough to be able to work things out for myself. If I buy the business I shall look after the books. I don't need anyone else."

Mr Hill was both impressed and relieved. "Yes," he said, "you can take the books. Where will you be staying?"

"I expect there's a hotel near the station isn't there?"

"Right across from the station, yes. You go through the underpass."

"Then I'll stay there."

They arrived back at Mr Hill's house.

"Go back into the lounge and I'll get the books for you."

"Could I use your toilet please?"

"Of course. Upstairs, turn left and its the end door on the right."

As Roger came back downstairs he noticed the telephone in the hall and a diary beside it. There was no one in sight. He flicked through the pages of the diary. There didn't seem to be a great deal of work. He went back into the lounge and as he waited the door bell rang. It was Roy.

"Hello Roy. Everything all right?"

"Yes guv'nor."

"You'd better hang on to the car. You've got an early start in the morning. If you don't mind waiting for a minute you can run Mr Wallace to the station."

So Roy waited until Mr Hill had handed over the books and then off they went. It was only just around the corner, not worth the ride really.

"Do you think you'll buy the business?"

"I shall know better after I've looked at these," said Roger. "I'm certainly not prepared to pay five hundred pounds for it."

"Is that what he's asking?"

"Yes."

"He offered to sell it to me. I talked it over with my Doll but she said 'no'. She was right too. I'm all right with driving but I'd never be able to run a business. I probably shouldn't tell you this

173

but he was going to let me have it for three hundred and fifty pounds."

"Really! Roy, how old are these cars?"

This one's the 1935 12 horse power long wheel base saloon and the other's a 1939 12 horse power 4-light Saloon. Of course they were laid up for five to six years during the war so they aren't really as old as all that."

"But this one ought to have been changed for something newer two or three years ago and the other's ready for changing now isn't it?"

"That's for the guv'nor to say."

"But you have a private opinion."

"Just between you and me?"

"Of course. You see I get the feeling that Mr Hill has had retirement in his sights for some time and has been willing to see the business go downhill a bit."

"We're certainly not as busy as we used to be. I know for a fact we've lost one or two good customers and, well yes, it's because of the cars – this one in particular. It's a lovely car. It's not for nothing that people call these 'the poor man's Rolls'. But I suppose this one is showing its age a bit."

"Have you got a bit of time to spare Roy? Not long – say half an hour or so?"

"Yes."

"Do you know any garage round here that sells cars and that would still be open for business?"

"There's one at the halfway that might still be open."

They drove there and it was. Roger gave a quick look along the cars for sale. Most of them were small Austins and Morrises but there was a Bentley and there was also a nice looking Armstrong Siddeley.

"That'll do," said Roger. "Hang on here."

There was already a salesman hovering.

"I'm afraid I'm only here to make a few enquiries at the moment," said Roger. "I shall be wanting to change this car next September for something similar to your Armstrong Siddeley there. What sort of trade-in price could you let me have on the Rover?"

"What age is the Rover?" The salesman was already giving it a careful looking over. "It's in nice nick, I'll give you that, but it's

174

too old really and a pretty high mileage too. We'd have a lot of trouble selling it on. There are so many new cars coming out now. I don't think we could let you have more than about seventy pounds sir."

"Seventy pounds. Hm. Yes that sounds pretty fair to me. Thank you very much. I'll have to see what cars you have available in September."

"Here's my card sir. If we haven't got what you are looking for, I'm sure we can get it for you. Just come in and have a chat."

"Thank you, I might well do that."

Roger jumped back in the car.

"Where to now guv'nor?"

"Could you just run me slowly round that hill where all the wealthy people live?"

"St. Georges Hill?"

"That's the one. Have you got a few customers from there?"

"We used to, but there's only one left now."

Roger took out his diary and began to scribble in the early pages of the year: Rolls Royce, MG sports, Riley, Jaguar, Humber, Bentley, Austin 16 (that was a surprise), Rover . . . he listed all the cars he saw and how many of each. He was surprised to find that there were quite a few Rovers. Wolseley was another fairly popular car. Perhaps all he would need to do would be to upgrade the Rovers . . .

"OK Roy. I've seen enough. Could you drop me back to the hotel by the station please?"

"Yes guv."

It amused Roger to be called 'guv'nor'. "Do you get paid a regular wage Roy?"

"No I'm paid by what I do."

"So things are not very good at the moment?"

'No."

"Do you ever think of leaving Mr Hill?"

"My Doll says I should go taxying but Mr Hill has been very good to me. I wouldn't want to leave him until he retires."

"I've no business to ask this of you because you don't know anything about me. But if I decide to buy this business I'm going to need help and you are the best person to give me that help. If you can hang on until Christmas to see how things go I'd be very grateful."

"Thank you guv'nor. I'm happy doing what I do so I expect that'll be all right. My Doll will be glad to hear you want me."

"Well I shouldn't tell her just yet. I've got to go through these books yet and then see if Mr Hill is willing to come down to what I want to offer."

"I'll wait and see then."

"Yes, you do that – what's your surname and your address and telephone number. I'll keep you in the picture."

They were at the hotel by now. Roger jotted down Roy's details, thanked him, shook his hand and gave him a ten shilling note. "Treat your Doll for me Roy. If I get this business I'm sure we shall be all right."

As Roy put the money in his pocket he thought so too. This young lad was a real gent.

31
A Happy Conclusion

Roger booked into the Ashley Park Hotel for the night and took the *Surrey Herald* with him to the dining-room. He studied the used car pages and was hardly aware of what he was eating. He should be able to get something pretty decent for about two hundred pounds, he thought. Then he could hang onto the other one for a year. It would be OK as the second car he felt. And he'd stick with Rovers for a while. It would give continuity with the old firm. He wondered what the housing situation was like around here?

He turned to the housing section of the paper. Gosh, some of those prices! That place Mr and Mrs Hill lived in must be worth nearly seven hundred and fifty pounds. Strewth. But there was a fair bit of cheaper property about. There were a few terraced houses for a hundred pounds or so. "Daft when you come to think of it," Roger said to himself. "I shall probably pay more for a car than I shall for a house."

He drank his coffee and made his way to his room. He looked at the accountant's statement of accounts and then he worked his way quietly through the books himself. There was no doubt about it. The firm had gone down badly and it was unlikely that lost customers would come back. If he was going to turn the firm round, they would have to find new customers. But there was just about enough work to keep them going while they did.

So did he want it? And if so, how much was he prepared to spend to get it? After all, he could probably live at home, rent an office from his dad and start from scratch in Croydon. But he knew that his Dad was planning a move to Crawley New Town. That would be a good place to start, but how long would he have to wait and what would he do while he was waiting? No, this opportunity looked too good to miss if he could work out a deal Mr Hill would accept.

But could he? He started to do his sums. In the end he worked out a deal he was pleased with. He thought it was fair, even a bit on the generous side. He also felt that he could afford it, but would Mr Hill go for it. It wasn't as straightforward as the old chap would probably want.

He spent time working out how best to present the deal, trying out various alternatives. He'd just have to be as simple and straightforward as he could, he thought at last. If they went for it, well and good. If they didn't, he hadn't lost anything.

He went to bed. 'Hill and Son'. He wouldn't be able to keep that name, but people knew that name. 'Hill and Son under new management'? 'Hill and Son, new proprietor'? 'Hill and Wallace.'

'Hill and Wallace!' If only it were. "Oh Gladys, Gladys, Gladys, why did you have to go and find that farmer? We'd have made such a team." He started to wallow in self pity, ticked himself off, remembered what it had been like when they had that wonderful holiday together, remembered what it had been like in bed together, got himself all steamed up, tossed and turned, got up and stood at the window until he began to cool down, had a drink of water, went back to bed, tossed and turned some more and finally fell uneasily to sleep.

After breakfast the following morning he went for a walk. He wondered what time the Hills got going on a Sunday. He didn't imagine that they went to church though he didn't know. Eventually at a little before ten he rang their door bell.

"Come in young man, come in." Mr Hill was effusive in his welcome. "Ethel," he called, "could we have a cup of tea? It's Mr Wallace come again."

They went into the lounge and Mr Hill was obviously having difficulty waiting for Roger to break his news, good or bad. His impatience threw Roger a bit and his carefully prepared presentation went out of the window.

"Sit down. Sit down please."

Roger sat. He must obviously put the man out of his misery as

178

quickly as possible. "Mr Hill, I'm prepared to buy your business but not for five hundred pounds and my offer is a little bit complicated. Are you interested in hearing what I'm prepared to do?"

Mr Hill's face was a picture of conflicting emotions. He had hoped for five hundred pounds, dreamed of five hundred pounds but in his heart of hearts he had known that he would never get five hundred pounds. This young man had seemed his best chance. His naïve innocence might just have done the trick.

Ethel brought in their tea.

"Ethel, you'd better stay dear. This young man has come with an offer for the business so let's both hear what he has to say."

"Yes dear," she said. "I'll just fetch my cup of tea then shall I?"

The two men sat in awkward, uncomfortable silence while they waited for her. She came and sat herself down. She had given Roger time to collect his thoughts.

"Let me begin with the negative things," Roger said, "and then tell you what I am willing to do – what I would like to do.

"First of all, I am not demobbed until the middle of September so I would need you to keep things going until then. If we DO agree a deal, I shall need to take a few week-ends off to come up and find somewhere to live, and I might be grateful for the use of a car if one is free – I'd pay for the petrol of course."

"Have you got a young lady in mind to share your new home with?" asked Ethel irrelevantly.

Had he got a young lady in mind? Hadn't he just? And hadn't that young lady given him hell last night thinking about what he had lost? But perhaps she could help him now. The sniff of romance might encourage Ethel to support his bid.

"Well yes," said Roger, "there *is* a young lady in mind. In fact it was her surname that was one of the things that made me feel that this business of yours might be the right one. You see she's called Hill, 'Gladys Hill'."

"Gladys Hill. Nice sensible name too. Does she come from around here?"

"No. She's from Devon. We met when I was still at school."

"Oh lovely, childhood sweethearts."

"Ethel," interrupted her husband, who was just about exploding with frustration, "we want to hear what this man has to say about the business, not about his love life."

179

"I'm sorry dear, but she does sound nice this Gladys. We haven't got any relations down in Devon have we?"

"No we haven't. Please go on Mr Wallace."

"I wish you would call me Roger . . . Anyway, I've looked at the market value of your cars and I've looked at the question of 'goodwill'. It's always difficult to judge the value of goodwill in pounds, shillings and pence. Someone who has been one of your customers for years may take an instant dislike to me, though I hope he wouldn't. Anyway, I reckoned goodwill at a little bit over one third of your profits over the past three years.

"I can't afford to buy you out in one lump sum but what I would like to do is this:

"The moment you agree to a deal with me I'll pay you seventy-five pounds. Then in September when I take over I'll pay you another seventy-five pounds. One year after that, I'll pay you fifty pounds. After the second year I'll pay you seventy-five pounds and after the third year I'll pay you one hundred pounds.

"If you add all that up you'll find it comes to three hundred and seventy-five pounds and if you need someone to stand as guarantor for the sums I shall owe you after September, I'm sure my dad will do so. He's quite a well-known businessman in Croydon. Naturally, I don't expect an answer right away. But I'll put my offer down on paper and send it to you. When you've had time to think about it, let me know. I shall have to know fairly soon of course because of finding a house and all that."

"Thank you young man. You've obviously given it all a great deal of thought and chatted with your dad I shouldn't wonder. You've let your tea go cold. Ethel, let's go and make another one shall we?"

Ethel caught the lift of his head and went with him to make a cup of tea. Roger was left twiddling his thumbs but they weren't long.

"Would you like to just go over those details for me again young man while I jot them down?"

So Roger went through them again.

"And yes," said Mr Hill, "that comes to three hundred and seventy-five pounds in all. Hm. It would be nice to see Dad's company going to help a young man get established in life."

"A young couple dear," Ethel interposed. "You will bring your Gladys to see us when you settle down here won't you Roger?"

Roger felt a complete fraud. "I don't know that I'm going to come here yet Mrs Hill but if I do I'd love to bring Gladys to see you." And then in his mind he added, 'yes I'd love to, but I never will because she's marrying a blasted farmer, lucky sod.'

Mr Hill stood up and coughed. He had an important announcement to make and he wanted everyone's full attention.

"We, Ethel and me, we have given your offer our careful consideration young man, er, Mr Wallace er, Roger." He was finding this embarrassing but it had to be done properly. "We, Ethel and me that is, we both think that you have been very straightforward and very fair and we'd like to take this opportunity" (you'd have thought that he was addressing a public meeting) "of thanking you for the way in which you have conducted these negotiations which we can now bring to a happy conclusion."

"What he means dear is that we'll be happy to accept your offer for the business," added Ethel.

"That's marvellous," said Roger. "Oh that's wonderful news." He jumped up and shook both of them by the hand. Then he said, "Excuse me a moment while I get my suitcase." He brought it into the lounge, opened it up and took out his cheque book. There and then he wrote out a cheque for seventy-five pounds.

"Here's the first instalment. I'll write tomorrow confirming all the details. I only hope I don't pester you too much between now and September, but I'm so very excited."

"You pester us as much as you like Roger," said Ethel. "We're happy for you and for ourselves as well."

"I'll run you to the station," said Mr Hill.

"No there's no need for that. The walk will help me calm down a little bit even though it's so short. Tell Roy I shall look forward to working with him, and thank you for giving me the chance to carry your work forward."

Mr Hill was a little embarrassed by that. He hadn't actually done much work for the last two years. The two men shook hands and Roger set off for the station and the long journey back to Plymouth. It was a long and tedious journey. His head was in such a whirl. He longed to be able to tell someone, someone close to him. He wanted to share his excitement. In the end he had to settle for calling in to Michael's taxi firm but when he got there he said nothing. There was no one there except one of the drivers who was manning the phone. Roger's news was too immense. It would have to wait for Michael.

"Had a good week-end scribes?"

"Yes very good thanks."

"How'd the wedding go?"

The wedding. Crumbs, Roger had forgotten all about the wedding. "Oh," he said. "That's quite a story. The vicar fell ill half way through and I ended up reading the service."

"Getaway?"

"Straight up, I did."

"Cor you wait till I tell the rest of the lads we've got a vicar working with us."

"Bit of a laugh isn't it, but it was a pity for my pal James and his wife."

"Oh, I don't know. They'll never forget that will they?"

"No I don't suppose they will. Nor will I come to that. Anyway, I'd best be off back on board. Good-night."

Strangely enough that conversation did the trick. For almost the first time that long, long week-end he felt as if his feet were firmly on the ground again – or on deck, to be rather more accurate.

32

A Lot to Do

The journey on the liberty boat out to *Defiance* seemed even lovelier than usual. Was it because his life had a new dimension of excitement, or was it just that he was already beginning to feel demob-happy months before the event?

Roger made his way down to the mess. Mick was there.

"Hello scribes. You're back early. Had a good week-end?"

"Yes, very good thanks."

"How'd the wedding go?"

They repeated the conversation he had had with Tom at Michael's taxi office.

"So why have you come back so early? It's not like you to be early scribes."

"No." It was true. He usually came back on the last possible boat. "I've got quite a lot of work to do."

"Blimey. Who'd have thought you'd be early because of work? You wait 'til I tell the lads."

They laughed and Roger put his things away before going up to the CRO, taking the *Surrey Herald* with him. He was going to have to get cracking. July would be dominated by the ship's company annual leave. He hadn't any time to spare. He wrote to all the estate agents listed in the *Surrey Herald* and asked for properties up to about one hundred and fifty pounds. Then he sat back and began to make plans.

He could forget July. He would take a week-end at the end of June and buy a house. He laughed. Just like that! Well why not? He had taken a week-end for a wedding and bought a business just like that so why not a house?

Then he would come back and do his last real stint of naval duty through July. A couple of week-ends in August should be enough for basic furnishing. It would certainly have to be basic. He wasn't going to have much money left. He'd better write to Roy. He was going to need his help. Oh and for goodness' sake, he hadn't written to Mr and Mrs Hill yet. In his excitement he had forgotten the most important letter of all.

He turned back to his typewriter and hammered out the details of his offer. It struck him that it might be useful to get hold of the registration book of the older car so that he could replace it as quickly as possible after he took over. Would the Hills be upset if he asked for it? What was the hurry anyway? No he would wait. He wrote a warm and grateful covering letter and then sat down to write to Roy.

Dear Roy, I expect you have heard that I am buying the business from Mr Hill. One of the things that decided me was the fact that you said you wanted to carry on in the business. I shall need your help a lot and there are one or two things you can start doing as soon as you like.

First of all, keep your eyes open for good second-hand Rovers. We are going to have to replace the older one as soon as we can. My plan is that you will drive the one we buy because you know the customers and will be the first choice driver with me backing up in the car Mr Hill drives now.

I'm also going to need a telephonist. Mrs Hill answers the phone now, but there isn't a Mrs Wallace. What I thought was, if you know of someone who doesn't get out much and who could be relied on with telephones, we could transfer the business number to them and add my number as a second. It will look as though the business is growing!

The trouble is, I don't really know what I shall be able to pay a telephonist – not much I shouldn't think, but they would get their telephone bills paid for by us. See if you can find someone.

I shall be up before September to look for a house. If you are willing, I may need your help with things like getting telephones installed and so on. Keep a note of all your expenses and of the time you spend on my affairs. I don't want you out of pocket.

Roger sat back. He couldn't think of anything else he had to do. It had been a good evening's work. He slept well in his hammock that night. The following morning he was back in the CRO.

"Had a good week-end scribes?"

"Yes thanks."

"How did the wedding go?"

How many times was he going to have to answer that question? Certainly once more when Lieutenant Trelawney arrived. He told the story all over again, and then again when he went down to the mess deck for lunch. It was a bit unkind to the vicar, he thought, but by now he was playing the story for laughs.

In the evening he was back at work at Michael's Taxis and told the story one last time. He also told Michael about his purchase of Hill and Co.

"Pity," said Michael. "I was half hoping we could persuade you to stay down here and work for me full time. But there's nothing like having your own business. It's hell sometimes but I reckon you'll do all right. How much longer will you be able to help us out?"

"Not much longer I'm afraid. I shall go up to Surrey some week-ends and as you know, I'm tied up through July with annual leave."

"But you can give us some help in June and August?"

"Yes, and then I'd better stop. I'm demobbed in the middle of September."

"Don't stop until you have to. Carry on in September to the last minute."

"Thanks."

"And I've got a proposition for you."

"How do you mean?"

"You know the mess our books were in when you came?"

"Yes."

"If I sent everything to you once a month, how would you like to go on doing the books for me? You'll need every penny you can earn while you get started."

"Do you mean it?"

"Of course I do."

"I'd love to. Gosh, everything seems to be going my way at the moment."

"Then make the most of it. It won't always. You can be sure of that."

At the end of that week Roger began receiving details of houses for sale. Quite a lot of them went straight into the waste paper basket. He had specified up to one hundred and fifty pounds but a lot of the houses were two hundred pounds or more. He ditched those. And there were some that were pretty grotty. He ditched those. He wished he knew the area better. He was sure there would be places he wouldn't want to live.

Gradually he whittled the list down to ten houses he would go and see. He had told Lieutenant Trelawney all about his business and his plans. With his permission he now telephoned and made arrangements to visit all the properties on his list. Yet he had a funny feeling that he already knew which house he would buy – no particular reason, just a feeling.

At the end of June he set off for Surrey once more. Mr Hill had made one of the Rovers available for him. When he arrived to pick it up he noticed a brand new Morris Minor in the Hills' drive. They had bought a car for their retirement.

He drove from house to house, met estate agent after estate agent, became accustomed to their sales patter and eventually returned to the third house on his list. It was the one his instinct had told him he would buy.

It was a two up, two down end of terrace house on Green Lane in Hersham. It had been empty for some time and showed it. The long garden was a wilderness and neighbours had dumped some of their rubbish in it, but the house was dry as a bone and the area was pleasant.

The estate agent agreed to one hundred and forty pounds and asked the name of Roger's solicitor. Roger hesitated. He hadn't got one. That would be additional expense. Did he need one?

"It is customary sir. And I suppose you will be having a survey done?"

More expense. And wasn't there something about some tax you had to pay when you bought a house?

"Can you recommend a solicitor?"

The estate agent looked surprised. "Yes if you wish."

"Look," said Roger, "this is a house you want to sell. I suspect it's been on your hands for a bit. It's a house I want to buy with as little fuss as possible. If you will find a solicitor for me and pay his fees, I'll give you a cheque for one hundred and forty pounds now."

"Oh I don't think . . ."

And I shall want access to the house in August to get it fixed up and ready for when I move in in September."

"Sir, that's not the way these things work."

Roger took out the details of the other nine properties he had been to look at. He laid them on the desk, fanned out for maximum effect. "No I don't suppose it is, but somewhere along the line I'm sure I shall find someone who is willing to work with me on this. I'll wait while you give your boss a ring."

The estate agent was irritated. This jumped up sailor was treating him like a clerk. He WAS the boss for goodness' sake. But his firm was still very small and he needed every sale he could get. Besides, the sailor hadn't haggled too much over the price.

"Just give me a moment or two sir," he said and disappeared into an inner office. He rang a solicitor he often did business with – pity he couldn't use his own solicitor, he thought. He explained the situation, the two men did a deal and he came back to Roger.

"One hundred and fifty pounds and I'll agree to your terms."

"One hundred and fifty to cover ALL my expenses to do with the purchase?"

"You're a hard man sir."

"Probably not hard enough." Roger hesitated. If he haggled he could probably bring the man back down to one hundred and forty pounds again. Was it worth the aggravation?

The estate agent looked at Roger and thought he saw the sale slipping through his fingers. "Oh, very well sir, have it for one hundred and forty pounds."

Roger grinned. "Done," he said and took out his cheque book.

"I shouldn't allow you access until contracts have been signed and all the legal stuff completed but as you have paid in full and the house is empty I can probably make an exception." He went to a board covered in house keys and handed Roger a large one. "I'll keep the other two keys until we actually complete the deal."

"That's fine. Thank you for all your help," said Roger. "I'll be at the house once or twice in August and my colleague Roy Mays will probably also be at the house a few times letting in telephone engineers and so on."

The two shook hands and said their farewells and then Roger drove across Surrey to see his parents. It was high time that he put them in the picture and faced the music.

33
So Insignificant

Driving across the Surrey hills in that Rover was a new experience for Roger. He had done some driving for Michael in the Plymouth area and out as far as Yelverton once or twice. But this Rover, old though it was, was something special. He began to use the free-wheel, a feature that was only to be found on Rovers.

Gliding downhill in free-wheel was almost like riding a bike downhill. It was so exhilarating swishing through the stillness of the evening. Must be good for petrol consumption too, Roger thought. He felt like a man in love – in love with the car, the open road with its freedom, and the sheer pleasure of driving. He began to understand old toad of toad hall. What had he said?

'The poetry of motion! The real way to travel! The only way to travel! Here today – in next week tomorrow! Villages skipped, towns and cities jumped – always somebody else's horizon! O bliss! O poop-poop! O my! O my!'

Roger laughed happily. Toad was right. This was sheer bliss. It struck him that he didn't know where the 'poop-poop' was on his Rover. He hardly ever used one. He felt like singing. He did sing. Far too soon he had arrived at his parents' house. He pulled into the crescent drive and stopped behind his father's old Austin 16.

Gosh, his dad's car was as old as his, he thought. It's time he changed it he should think.

He rang the door bell and Gerry let him in. He didn't even notice that there was a second car on the drive. In the lounge Gerry was playing cards with his mother and Margaret. His father was listening to music and reading the paper. It was all so familiar. At once Roger felt at home and at ease in spite of the news he was bottling up.

Strange that: he didn't always feel at home when he was there. No, that wasn't true. He always felt at home but he often also wanted to be somewhere else. He grew bored at home. But now, in those moments, he felt warm and comfortable. He kissed his mother. When they had finished their game, he would make a fourth even though he wasn't much of a one for cards.

His dad put his papers down in a heap beside him, stood up and shook his son by the hand. "Well son, how are things in the Navy?"

"Oh, they're all right. But I've got some other news."

His mother looked up. News of a romance perhaps?

"I've . . . I've bought a business – a small chauffeur driven car hire business."

"But you're still in the Navy. How can you run a business while you are in the Navy? Is this firm down in Plymouth?"

"No Dad, it's in . . ." (it was no use telling his Dad it was in Hersham. No one had ever heard of Hersham). "It's in Walton on Thames."

"So how do you propose to look after it while you are in the Navy?"

"The present owner is going to keep things going until I'm out."

"That doesn't sound very wise to me. He's not going to bother with the business is he?"

"I don't think he's been bothering much for some time. The firm's a bit run-down. That's how I've managed to buy it but it's earning enough to give me a living and I'm sure I can turn things round."

Just like his father, thought his mother, the eternal optimist. "So where do you plan to live?" she asked. "Walton is rather a long way from here."

"I've bought a house," said Roger.

They all looked at him in astonishment.

"Oh it isn't much of a house, just a two up, two down end of terrace place a bit like Miss Holly's cottage in Beddingford."

"What, no bath and an outside toilet?" said Margaret.

"That's right."

"I wouldn't like that."

189

"No I don't expect you would. You're too used to the luxury here. But it's a start for me. It'll do until I can afford something better."

"So you've bought a business and a house?" asked his father, not too sure that he could believe what he was hearing.

"Yes Dad."

His father's heart sank. He was almost overwhelmed with his own business affairs, trying to move from his old premises in Croydon to Crawley New Town. Now his son would be wanting financial help just at the wrong time.

"So you are going to need some help?"

Roger was puzzled. "No," he said. "Everything is all organised."

"Financial help?"

"Oh. No, not that either. You gave me some help. Don't you remember? You gave me a one hundred pounds. With the money I've saved that was enough."

"So how much do you owe?"

"I don't actually owe anything. I have committed myself to paying the owner of the business a bit over the next three years, but that won't be a problem."

"I hope you know what you are doing."

Roger decided to spin a bit of a yarn. It would help to satisfy his dad. "You know the taxi firm I work for in my spare time down in Plymouth?"

"Yes."

"Well I've checked all my figures with the owner and he is sure I can make a go of things. He's also asked me to go on doing the books for his firm after I leave the Navy."

That really did impress his father. He had never really understood figures and the costs of his own business move had spiralled almost out of control.

"Well just be very careful and don't get too cocky."

"No Dad."

His father went back to his paper and Roger joined the others at the card table. They played until supper time and then went to bed. Roger went back to his old bed, sharing a room with Gerry.

"I hope you didn't feel that Dad was being too negative this evening. He's got a lot on his plate with this move to Crawley. It's all been a bit of a mess."

"I didn't think Dad was too bad. I expected him to be much worse. He never really believes that any of us can do anything ourselves does he? He's never even allowed me to use the motor mower yet."

They both laughed.

"*I* don't want to use the motor mower thank you very much," Gerry said. "Seriously though, have you really got this business and your house?"

"Yes," said Roger, "but don't imagine any of it is very good. The house is primitive and the business is only a two car affair, and one of those cars needs replacing. It's as old as Dad's Austin."

"That still goes OK."

"Yes, but it's no good for the kind of work I want to do. I'm aiming to drive wealthy people, people with money to spare. There are lots of them around Walton and Weybridge. But they won't be satisfied with old cars."

"No I don't suppose they will. Oh well, it's time we went to sleep. I hope it all works out."

They drifted through a little more conversation into sleep. The following morning they all went to church in the Austin and in the afternoon they went for a walk together.

"Let's hear some more about this business," said Roger's dad.

The two of them walked ahead of the rest and Roger wondered how to begin, what to say.

"Business isn't all a bed of roses you know."

"No I don't suppose it is. Your move to Crawley must have been an absolute nightmare."

Without realising it, he had done the trick. He had switched attention from his own tiny concerns to his dad's. He began to hear all about the post-war problems with new buildings: interviews, Board of Trade certificates, bureaucracy, shortage of materials, shortage of workers, delayed completion because of rules about what you could spend in one year, spiralling costs, solicitors, banks, it all poured out. How trivial his own concerns appeared. He was going to employ one, perhaps two people. His Dad was struggling to do his best for a hundred or more.

"So when do you hope to complete the move Dad?"

"Pretty soon now. Our's will be the first factory to open in Crawley," his Dad said proudly, "and it will have wonderful facilities for the staff working there. Over eighty of my old staff are coming down with us and there are new homes and flats for all of them. It really is a wonderful opportunity for them all.

"I just hope we shall be able to earn enough to pay off the debts we've incurred. It has all cost far more than I ever dreamed. If I had known, I don't think I'd have started."

It was a very sober Roger who drove back to Hersham. When he had taken the car, the petrol tank had been full. He filled up again before he returned it. Blimey, he had spent nearly *five bob in petrol. It had been an expensive week-end. He drove past his new house and returned the car, stopping for a chat with the Hills.

He was so late in London that he had to travel down on the mail train. He dozed a good deal until he heard:

"This is Plymouth North Road, Plymouth North Road, Plymouth North Road."

He walked to Devonport Park and found an empty bench to sleep on until the usual copper moved him on in the morning. As he travelled out on the liberty boat he found himself thinking about Plymouth's weather. It was strange: Plymouth was so wet but at that time of morning it hardly ever rained. It often had been raining, so everything was fresh and clean. Nor would it be long before it was raining again, but at seven in the morning it was almost always dry and clear. He loved that trip out on the boat.

*Five bob = five shillings: 25p but worth a great deal more.

34

Frantic Work
and Sheer Boredom

Roger hadn't been back on board more than a few days before he was immersed in the arrangements for annual leave. For two weeks he worked flat out. Every evening he collapsed exhausted into his hammock. He had no time or energy to think about anything else.

And then it was over. The men were gone and he was stuck on board, part of the skeleton crew that always remained. As always, he was bored and lonely. It dawned on him that he had made no real friends in the Navy apart from James. There had been Dave when he was in training, but no one since. He was on good terms with everyone in the mess and in the office, but he had no close friends, not like school. Curiously enough he felt closest to Lieutenant Trelawney. But that could never become close friendship. Officers and ratings didn't mix like that – besides they were of different generations. But the craggy Cornishman had come to mean a great deal to Roger and had been very good to him, incredibly good come to think of it. And Roger had liked his wife too. She would be worth getting to know better.

But he never would get to know them better. Fairly soon he would be gone and another 'scribes' would take his place. It was barmy. He found himself getting sentimental about his job and the Navy. What about afterwards, he thought? What friends would he make afterwards? He'd chosen his new job but it was not exactly the kind of job where you made friends was it? Clients, customers, colleagues, but not friends. And not wives either, he

j

thought. Immediately his mind flew away to Gladys.

It must be just about time for her wedding. Should he write and wish her well? No. He didn't think so. If she had a scrap of feeling left for him a letter would only cause a ripple she could do without. Ironic wasn't it? He had let her go so easily because he had nothing to offer. Now he had a thriving business and a beautiful home! Just see what she was missing!

He laughed bitterly. It was no use thinking like that. He must just wish her well in his heart – and deep down he did wish her well – and get on with his life. There were plenty of other fish in the sea. What was it his brother had written in his autograph book?

'Never run after a bus or a woman. There will always be another one coming along soon.'

Did he want another one soon? He was only twenty for goodness' sake. He paced the deck outside the CRO, head down, hands clasped behind his back just as old seamen did. He found himself thinking about the nature of love. He went back into the office and began to scribble:

> *It is not enough to love.*
> *We need also to be loved.*
>
> *It is not sufficient to give.*
> *We need the joy of giving,*
> *giving to someone who receives*
> *with gladness and warmth.*
>
> *It is not enough even to be loved.*
> *We need to be loved as we are,*
> *for ourselves,*
> *and in ways that bring us joy.*
>
> *How wonderful life would be*
> *if all these needs were met.*

Perhaps one day he would be able to change that last couplet and write:

> *How wonderful life becomes*
> *when all these needs are met.*

The poem wasn't about Gladys. Well it wasn't, was it . . . Was it . . ? He added it to the poems in her exercise book. She would never see that exercise book now. He wondered how long he would keep it.

The two weeks with the ship's company away dragged by dreadfully slowly. And then life went back to normal for a little while: nine to five in the CRO and off ashore to work for Michael's taxis.

35

Tom

One evening he walked cheerfully into the taxi office only to find an atmosphere heavy with misery. The men were silent, dragging at their fags and looking at the floor. Roger curbed his instinct to say something bright. This was not the time.

He tapped at the door of the inner office and walked in. Michael was standing by the window, gazing out but obviously seeing nothing – nothing except what was in his mind and that looked pretty bleak.

"Michael, what on earth is the matter with everyone?"

"It's Tom. He's dead . . . killed in a road accident."

"Oh no . . . How did it happen?"

"A little girl ran out into the road after her ball. Tom swerved to avoid her and went straight into a wall. He went through the windscreen into the wall and was killed outright."

"And the girl?"

"Oh she was all right. He managed to miss her completely."

"Poor Tom."

The death put a blight on the whole evening.

Two evenings later Michael said to Roger, "You're an atheist aren't you?"

Roger had never thought about it quite in those terms. A lot of people didn't like the word 'atheist'. They were superstitious about it perhaps because the church had always demonised atheists. But yes, he supposed he was. He certainly didn't have any religious beliefs any more and if that made him an atheist, that's what he was. So he answered, "Yes".

"Tom was an atheist."

"Yes I know." Tom was sometimes a bit belligerent about it. If he wasn't sounding off about the government or Plymouth Argyle, he was often sounding off about the church.

"I want you to come with me to see Tom's wife."

"Me! But I hardly knew Tom."

"That doesn't matter. It might even help a bit, and you are an atheist. You've just said so."

So the two of them drove off to see Tom's wife. They sat in her lounge with her two adult daughters.

"What's happening about Tom's funeral?" asked Michael.

"It's on Friday at the new crematorium at 3 o'clock."

"Who's taking it?" asked Michael gently.

"Why nobody's taking it," the widow answered. "Tom was an atheist. You know that Michael."

"So what happens?"

"Well we all go there and sit for a little while and then someone presses a button or something and the coffin is taken away from us." She began to sob and her daughters moved to comfort her.

"That won't do," said Michael. "That won't do at all. Tom deserves better than that. Look Emily, would you mind if I stood up and said something about how we felt about Tom at work?"

She looked at him through her tears. "Would you? Oh Michael would you? Yes, I'd like that."

"And why don't you ask George to say something about their life at sea together and about Tom's sailing?"

"Do you think he would?"

"Of course he would. He and Tom have always been such good friends."

"I'll ask him," said one of the daughters.

"Good. Now what we need is someone to put together a little service, something with no religion in it, but something respectful and decent, and in the middle of it George and I can speak about Tom."

"Something like that would be wonderful but . . ."

Michael interrupted her. "That's why I've brought this young man with me."

Roger was shaken to the core. What on earth did Michael mean?

"You see Roger here is an atheist and although he's a bit

young, he's begun taking services recently, weddings and funerals like. He could put something suitable together for us I'm sure."

Roger was staggered but he had no chance to protest. Emily was so grateful that he just caved in until they were back in the car and then his fear and anger took over.

"What the hell do you think you are doing? I haven't a clue. I've never even been to a funeral. God what a mess you've got us into."

Michael pulled up outside a church. He walked in, knelt in a pew for a moment or two and walked out. Back in the car he drew a 'Book of Common Prayer' out from under his coat.

"There," he said, "it can't be all that difficult. Just read the funeral service and work out how it all goes. Then do something similar but knock all the religious stuff out of it. Whatever you do will be better than what they would have had."

"But I shall be on board ship on Friday."

"No you won't. You tell Lieutenant Trelawney what's on and he'll give you the afternoon ashore. Tell him I got you into it if you like."

"Why? Do you know him?"

" 'Course I do. Everybody knows old . . . Lieutenant Trelawney."

So Roger got down to work. Michael was right. The boss didn't hesitate. He gave him Friday afternoon off, and he also told him he could work at the funeral in office hours.

Roger studied the prayer book and thought about services he had been to in chapel. It was a pity they didn't have hymns to fill up the time. After all, nobody thought about the words when they sang a hymn. But he would have to do without. He planned out an outline structure. If he wasn't reading from the Bible what would he read? He would need to read something. He began to skim through his old school Palgrave's treasury for a suitable poem or two. He also began scribbling down what he thought Tom's funeral was all about.

It wasn't about sin and forgiveness or about heaven or any of that stuff. It was just about Tom wasn't it, about his life and the sort of chap he had been? And it was about trying to find something comforting to say to Emily and her daughters.

Of course, what would really give them comfort was hearing

about the friendship and respect everyone had for Tom. Michael and this George chap would do that. But was there anything he could say?

He found that he was quite enjoying this. It was something worthwhile. It was all wrong that atheists should be treated without respect when they died. They deserved just as much attention as anyone else.

And so at last Friday came. He went ashore at lunch-time and walked to Michael's taxis. There he put on his forbidden black Naval suit with the gold badges. It was the only respectable dark suit that he owned. He had thought about taking the badges off but reckoned that there would be marks from his sewing.

He had told Michael about the suit. "I won't wear my cap. If I cover it all over with a raincoat outside, I shall be in one of your cars both going and coming away so it should be OK."

Michael assured him that it would be OK, but privately he wasn't so sure. Oh well, if Roger got into trouble it wouldn't be serious and it was worth it for Tom.

36
Tom's Funeral

Michael drove Roger himself. They arrived at the crematorium early and were lucky to find it empty except for an attendant. There was no funeral in the slot before Tom's.

Michael introduced Roger as the man taking the ceremony. The attendant looked at him in some surprise. He was only a kid. "Never been here before?"

"No," said Roger. "I'd be grateful if you could show me what I have to do."

The attendant wondered how many funerals this lad had taken. He decided to take him right through from beginning to end. "Usually," he said, "you lead the procession in, walking in front of the coffin. If there are people already here I shall ask them to stand.

"You take the service from that lectern there. That's important because our microphone is there and the buttons."

"The buttons?"

"Yes," said the attendant leading Roger to the lectern. "At the committal you press that green one. And at the end of the service you press that red one. Then you go out of that door – in one door and out of another. It makes it easier to get the next congregation in."

Roger knew from the prayer book what the committal was but he didn't actually know what would happen when he pressed the green button. How could he ask without showing his ignorance?

"Is the committal the same here as at other crematoria?" he asked.

"I don't know what you're used to? Some places have doors which open and the coffin goes through; some have gates or curtains which shut. And some are like us, the coffin goes down on a lift and stops just below the top of the catafalque."

"Thanks. I suppose I should have guessed," he said. He prepared his papers on the lectern and then asked, "Is there somewhere I can go to the toilet and tidy up?"

The attendant looked at his tense white face and grinned to himself. The lad had got the shits he shouldn't wonder. "Yes sir, I'll take you to the vestry."

The attendant was right about Roger. His stomach was churning. After he had made himself comfortable he struggled to get his hair to sit down tidily and then he went and stood by the entrance door.

The hearse arrived with the undertaker walking in front carrying his top hat. Quite a crowd of people had come. The chapel was soon filled to capacity and after the coffin was in place, people lined the aisle and filled the entrance. Roger looked at all the people and then at Emily standing there with her two daughters.

"Please sit down," he said, "if you can . . ." And then he spoke to Emily. "You must be thrilled that so many people have come. This congregation speaks for itself. It's obvious that Tom has been greatly loved and respected. . ." He paused. He had lost his place. That wasn't part of his script. He looked down and picked up the first sheet of paper. "I'm going to begin by reading two poems," he said and the ceremony proper commenced.

Then he said, "We all come to a funeral with our own beliefs about life and death. You all know that Tom was not a religious man so this won't be a religious ceremony.

"We don't want to cause offence but we do want to celebrate Tom's life openly and honestly and without hypocrisy."

He could almost feel the congregation supporting him, urging him on. Suddenly he knew that even if he wasn't speaking for all of them, he was certainly speaking for most of them. It was a good feeling.

"And we want to bring what comfort and support and love we can to Tom's family. Our families and our friends are far and away the most important people in the world to us. At a time like this, they are the only people who matter."

201

Oh golly. He was getting carried away. He reined himself in.

"There are two people here who are going to talk about Tom. They both knew him well. I'm going to ask Michael of Michael's Taxis to speak first and then George will speak to us. George is one of Tom's oldest friends going right back to when they joined the Navy together."

He took his script and moved away from the lectern to a side wall. Michael spoke generously of Tom's value as a colleague and as a driver but most of all as a friend. As he returned to his place a man in a dark suit pushed through the crush at the entrance of the chapel and stepped forward. Roger looked at him in amazement and in growing embarrassment.

Oh golly. He was in for it now. There he had been standing like an atheist vicar if you could have such a thing, spouting his stuff, putting out his ideas as if they mattered . . . oh crikey, and wearing his illegal uniform . . . Oh hell . . . and here was the boss. And he had called him 'George'!

He hadn't heard a word Lieutenant Trelawney was saying but he dragged himself back to the funeral. Whatever happened afterwards it was Tom and his family who mattered now. He forced himself to pay attention as the boss spoke of his old ship-mate, told a couple of stories that made people laugh and lifted the atmosphere, and then spoke of Tom's more recent passion for sailing, a passion they shared.

"Some time ago," the boss said, "the young man who is conducting this ceremony for us sent me a poem. I told my Martha I'd like it read at my funeral. So I'm going to ask young Mr Wallace here to read it for us now."

Roger stepped back to the lectern and only just heard the boss mutter, "Well done boy. You'm doing fine." He went back to his wife in the crush by the door. Roger looked at the sheet of paper which he had typed himself all those months ago. He didn't need to read. He knew the poem off by heart. But he was feeling choked by the boss's encouragement. He cleared his throat.

"I'm going to read John Masefield's poem *Sea Fever.*"

When Roger finished reading there was a long silence and he suddenly felt very tired as if his strength had gone out of him. Then he asked the congregation to stand for the committal. He had scribbled 'Green button' across his script. He spoke briefly of ourselves as creatures of nature, of death as being a return to stillness. As he pressed the button he said, "We commit Tom in these moments with the familiar words 'dust to dust, ashes to ashes.' And now," he added, "I'm going to surprise you all. by quoting Jesus.

"Michael has spoken of the way Tom died, saving the life of a young child. It seemed to me that there are some well known words of Jesus we can alter slightly to end this ceremony: Greater love hath no man than this, that a man lay down his life for a complete stranger, a child with her life still to come."

And then he spoke brief words of peace and they all filed out to music which Michael had provided.

Emily was so grateful. It was difficult. Roger didn't know how to respond. He was embarrassed but pleased too. He felt humbled by their gratitude, satisfied too. He felt that he had never done anything so worthwhile in his life. People shook him by the hand, thanked him, and their thanks were genuine. He could feel it, sense it. He was moved by them all. Michael shook his hand but the two couldn't look at each other. Emotion was too strong in them. At last Lieutenant Trelawney and Martha stood before him. Martha gave him a hug and tears filled his eyes. Lieutenant Trelawney gripped his hand firmly.

"Well done boy. You've done us all proud." And then he smiled and said, "You'd better get rid of they badges. Us wouldn't want nobody to notice would us?"

It was all Roger could do to speak. "Sir," he said and fled to the vestry. The tears poured down his face. People had been so kind. Hell, it was as bad as if it had been his own father who had died. He pulled himself together and washed his face before stepping out onto the fringes of the crowd outside.

The undertaker made his way across to him and slipped an envelope into his hand. Roger didn't know what it was but put it in his pocket as the undertaker said to him, "I was worried about this one. I didn't know what to expect. But it was good, as good as any funeral I've ever been to. We could do with more funerals like that for people without religion."

All Roger felt was utter exhaustion and yet in contradictory fashion he was on a high. Michael came across to him. "We're all going to the Anchor for a drink and a sandwich."

"Do you mind if I don't come?" Roger answered. "I'd like just to walk quietly back to the office and then go back on board."

"You'll need an office key," Michael said. "We closed the business as a mark of respect." He gave Roger a key. "Let me have it back tomorrow."

Roger put it in his pocket and felt the undertaker's envelope. He pulled it out and looked at it. On the outside it said, 'Minister's fee'.

Roger gave it to Michael. "I can't take this," he said. "Will you give it to Tom's wife for me?"

Michael took it. "If you're not coming to the pub you'd better come and say good-bye to Emily again." He took Roger over, realised the lad was lost now for words and eased his path through. He shook Roger's hand again and let him go.

Slowly Roger walked out of the crematorium grounds. He felt washed out but there was a deep contentment too.

Back at Michael's taxis he changed into his proper uniform, sat down and quietly cut off the badges on his illegal suit. There were marks where the badges had been. He had been right. Then he cut off the naval buttons and drew the old buttons out of the inside pocket where he had kept them. But he had no needle and thread. He must remember to bring his 'housewife' ashore next time he came.

He was winding down nicely. He sailed on an almost empty liberty boat back to *Defiance* and felt at peace as he looked at the wake shining in the evening sunlight. Back on board he went to see if James was on duty or ashore. He needed company and was lucky. The two of them strode up and down on deck, heads bowed, hands clasped behind them and Roger talked until he had emptied himself of all his conflicting emotions.

James listened but said nothing. He hadn't realised Roger was an atheist now and it troubled him. He would have to pray for him. Did it mean that they could no longer be friends? Surely not. When Roger had fallen silent and it was time to go their separate ways he just said, "What you need is a wife like my Susan."

Roger's hammock called, but it was still a while before he slept.

Footnote:
When the author conducted his first non-religious ceremony for the British Humanist Association he little dreamed that he would become one of the first of a new network of celebrants trained,

authorised and supervised by the BHA to serve those with no religious beliefs. Nor did he dream that the day would come when this, his true vocation, took over his life completely but that is the way things have worked out.

37

Preparation for Civvy Street

During August Roger spent a couple of weeks in Surrey. He had a lot to do. He fetched his push bike from his parents home and rode around buying the basic necessities for his new home. They were very basic indeed. Anything he felt he could do without never appeared on his list.

He spent some time with Roy to make sure that there would be gas, electricity and water when he needed them, and he showed Roy where he wanted his telephone – on top of a stand of cardboard boxes that made a primitive filing cabinet.

Roy also took him to see a few cars. He had been looking at a range of second-hand cars. Armstrong-Siddeley, Humber and Lanchester all featured among his favourites but because Roger had asked him to, he had looked out one or two Rovers as well.

It was the Rovers Roger looked at. The business had always used Rovers. He felt that he had a tradition to maintain. He had also seen one or two of the new Rovers which had only been on the market for a couple of years. They were way beyond his pocket of course but he felt that they would make an excellent future buy. The older Rovers were superb cars but these new ones would really justify the firm's claim to being 'Luxury Car Hire'. Perhaps in another two or three years . . . But for now he must concentrate on the older models that had been in production since the mid-1930s. There was one post-war one which particularly attracted him. But he was shaken by the price. He had been too optimistic. He hadn't fully taken into account the way prices had risen. Back in 1939 a new 12 horse power 4-light Rover Saloon only cost three hundred and ten pounds. But, what with purchase tax and everything, the equivalent car had risen in price to almost eight hundred pounds.

He had realised that he would have to go for something second-hand but he hadn't realised that they were holding their price so well. The car Roy had found was one of the 16 horse power saloons from 1946. She was a real beauty but the price was three hundred and twenty pounds, a good deal more than he really wanted to pay. It would mean going into debt with an HP arrangement. But as he looked at the car he knew that if it was still available when he was ready he would take the risk. She really was superb. Blimey! Fancy paying more than twice as much for a car as he had paid for his house! The world had gone mad.

Roy also took Roger to see a mate of his. They had been in the Army together fighting Rommel in the western desert. Roger was shocked when he first met George. He had been blown up by a land-mine and lost a leg and an eye. Roy left the two of them together. George lived in a small flat with his wife. He had an artificial leg but didn't really get on with it. At home he preferred to swing himself about using crutches.

Roger's sense of shock soon turned to admiration. The man was so positive. When Roger asked about his disability George told him how lucky he was to have avoided D Day and the western front; how lucky he was to be alive and to have a small pension. But he didn't get out much. He didn't like people to see him as he was.

They talked about Hill and Company and Roger spoke of his need for a telephonist who would be more or less always there.

"The trouble is," said Roger, "I haven't a clue how much I can afford to pay."

"Look guv'nor," George said, "let's trust one another shall we? You pay my telephone bills for a while until you see how things are going and then work out what you think is fair. When you feel you are ready we can have a talk about things and agree a wage for me."

"OK," replied Roger. "You've got a deal except that I think you have been too generous to me. I'll try to set something aside from the start. Then when we do have our chat, there should be a bit of back pay to come as well."

On that simple basis Roger took on his first employee. He

arranged with Mr Hill and with the post office telephones that the Hill and Co. number should be transferred to George and felt that he had done all that he could except for cleaning work on his house.

His house!

On his first visit, the house still wasn't technically his. But he went to see the estate agent on his second visit to collect the rest of the keys. Everything was now complete and the house actually belonged to him. He felt so proud.

Never mind the fact that it was virtually empty. Never mind the fact that it was primitive. Bit by bit he could change all that. The only thing that really mattered was the fact that it was his own, his very own house.

Who'd have thought it? Two years ago he had been a school-boy and now, after his two years in the Navy, he was a businessman and a property owner. He laughed at himself but even more, he laughed for sheer joy. He began to sing:

"I know where I'm going . . ." and then he stopped short. Oh damn. Why had he begun that song of all songs. The next line was the one he couldn't sing and all because of that bloody farmer.

'I know where I'm going and I know who's going with me.'

No he didn't. It was the one fly in the ointment. Oh if only . . ? but it was no use thinking like that. It was certainly no good moping around on a day like this. It was time to get on with some work. He must clean his house. It wasn't THAT dirty but it had been empty for some time. He scrubbed it through from top to bottom and he ordered a ton of coal. He might not have any luxuries but he didn't intend to be cold.

Back on *Defiance* his duties were coming to an end. He had thought that when the day came for him to leave he would feel that he couldn't get away quickly enough, but it wasn't so.

He had grown accustomed to the old ship, fond of it even. He loved the journeys to and fro on the liberty boat. He even liked his corner in the office and he had immense respect and affection for Lieutenant Trelawney, and gratitude too. He sat at his typewriter one day and wrote:

> *I shall be using you no more*
> *Mr Typewriter.*
> *You have helped me much of yore*
> *Mr Typewriter.*

As I leave you now dear friend
I feel I HAVE come to the end
as a 'writer'.

It's been a long, long time
Mr Typewriter.
You've typed my essays,
screeds and rhyme,
Mr Typewriter.
As I leave you now old chap
I'm no longer in a flap
as a 'writer'.

The future will be bright
Mr Typewriter.
There'll be other keys to smite
Mr Typewriter.
To forget you'd be a crime
after the way you've passed my time
as a 'writer'.

*1"2/3@4£5_6&7'8(9)0?-¹/₄³/₄
Mr Typewriter,
QqWwEeRrTtYyUuIiOoPp¹/₃²/₃
Mr Typewriter,
AaSsDdFfGgHhJjKkLl:;=,
ZzXxCcVvBbNnMm,.%¹/₂,
as a 'writer'.

The boss read it and took it into the main office where he pinned it up on the bulkhead. Something of Roger would remain after he had gone, but not much.

As he was pinning it up Roger noticed the extra half ring on his sleeve.

"Sir," he said excitedly, "you've been promoted sir! Congratulations sir."

The chiefs hadn't noticed either. As they crowded round, Lieutenant Commander Trelawney's craggy face cracked into an embarrassed but highly delighted broad beam.

"Bliddy well deserve it after putting up with you for so long

k

scribes. Go and get us a last cup of coffee."

A week before he was due to be demobbed, he was transferred back to HMS *Drake*, Devonport barracks. As he sailed away from *Defiance* for the last time there was an unexpected lump in his throat. He had expected to feel nothing but excitement over the future. He had been such a reluctant seaman and yet now that it came to it he realised that even his naval career, pathetic though it had been, had managed to get under his skin.

James was also due for demob and sailed with him. He felt nothing of Roger's sentiment. He couldn't wait to get out, and once they were back in *Drake*, Roger shared his feelings to the full. For a week they went about collecting stamps as they completed each of the requirements of their demob. They handed in their hammocks but kept their kit. They still had to serve for five years in the Royal Naval Special Reserve. For five years the possibility of call up would always be there in the background and there would be three three week periods of service too. The Navy had not quite finished with them yet.

Roger went with James to Central Hall that Sunday and said his good-byes and then at last it was all over. He marched out of the gates with his kit-bag over his shoulder and made his way to Michael's taxis. He said his good-byes there and Michael himself drove him to Plymouth North Road station.

He caught the train to Exeter. At Exeter he got off the train, left his kit-bag in the left luggage office and caught another train. Before setting off for Surrey and a new life he must make one more trip back to school to see Mr Emerson and he must go to Beddingford too. The way he felt about Gladys, he couldn't see himself coming to that part of the country again in a hurry, so he must take one last opportunity to say good-bye and thank you to Miss Holly and to Barbara and to the Guthries who had all looked after him so well when he was an evacuee.

38

Awkward Moments.
New Beginnings?

He left Miss Holly to the last. After seeing her he walked down the High Street from her tiny cottage and strolled along the river. He looked across at the Riverside Hotel.

Should he call in and ask after Gladys?

No. He'd better not. He walked on and round the park, then back along the river.

Surely it wouldn't do any harm just to ask. Then that would be it, finished. She'd be out of his life for ever.

He felt sticky and uncomfortable and hopelessly indecisive but at last he pushed his way through the main door and made his way to the desk.

"Can I help you?"

He looked at the girl's bangle. This must be Sally.

"You must be Sally," he said.

Her eyebrows shot up. "Who wants to know?" she asked haughtily.

"My name's Roger – Roger Wallace."

"Roger Wallace! Oh!" She sounded disapproving. "And what are YOU doing here? What do you want?"

"I've just been demobbed and I'm leaving the area for the last time. So I thought I'd like to find out about Gladys before I went. Did her wedding go all right? Is she happy? That sort of thing." He blurted it all out.

Sally looked at him, tense and white before her. Had she been wrong about this man?

"What's it to you?" she asked.

"What's it to me? What do you think it is to me? It's everything to me. I want to know that she is happy, that's all."

"There's no need to shout. I'm not deaf you know." She paused for what seemed an age. "You really cared about her then did you?"

"Of course I did."

Still Sally hesitated. And then she said, "Gladys couldn't go through with the wedding. She broke her engagement off. It was all, well it was horrible really and her parents are still furious with her."

"So where is she, how is she, what's she doing?"

"She's got a job in London."

"LONDON! I'm going to London now. Can you give me her address so that I can look her up?"

Again Sally paused, uncertain, troubled, and then she said, "Perhaps you'd better ask her herself. She's sitting in the flat waiting for her taxi."

"WHAT!" He ran to the hotel door.

"Don't forget your suitcase."

He did a circle, ran back to the desk, leaned over and grabbed Sally and kissed her full on the lips. "Thanks," and he was gone.

So she had been wrong. Oh dear. She wondered how Gladys would receive him.

He raced round to the flat, tapped on the door and walked in. Gladys was sitting on the sofa beside two large suitcases. She looked pretty dejected. When she saw who it was she looked no happier. Her eyes were cold and hostile. They brought him up short.

"What are you doing here?"

How on earth was he to answer her? How was he to handle this situation. Her greeting was not what he had expected.

"I . . . I wondered if I could share your taxi?"

She took her time answering. "I don't see why not." And then she added, "You'd better sit down while we are waiting."

There was nowhere to sit except beside her on the sofa. Gingerly he sat, as far from her as he could manage.

"Sally told me . . ."

"I suppose Sally said . . ."

They both spoke at once.

212

"Sorry, after you."

"No, you go first."

It was all so awkward. What on earth was the matter. They had never been awkward with one another, never.

"I'm surprised Sally sent you after the way you've behaved."

"Why? What have I done?" His astonishment was genuine. His dismay was obvious and then a car horn sounded twice.

"That'll be the taxi," she said.

He picked up her suitcases. She took his little one and a small hold-all. She locked the door of the flat and dropped the key through the letter box. They were silent on the way to the station. The driver turned to Roger for his money but Gladys pushed Roger out of the way. This was her taxi and she was paying.

She bought her ticket and the two of them sat silently until the train came. They found an empty compartment and climbed aboard with the suitcases. Roger hoisted them onto the luggage rack and they sat facing one another. For a while they were still silent and then Roger said, "You were going to tell me what I've done wrong."

"As if you don't know," she said. "You went to Perspins didn't you but you never came to see me? And you promised to come and spend the week-end with me and then came up with that cock and bull story about someone stealing your pay book and YOU being put on a charge. I asks you. Do you think I'm simple?"

He was all set to interrupt but she wouldn't let him.

The accusations and the hostility were all coming thick and fast.

"And then when I wrote to tell you I was going out with my farmer and we was going to get married, all you could do was to send a pathetic letter wishing me every happiness. It was obvious you didn't think much of me. You didn't think I was worth fighting for did you? Just let me go. 'Good-bye Gladys. Be happy.' What sort of a man would behave like that to someone he really loved?"

She was spent at last. It had all built up inside her for months and now it had all poured out until she was empty.

They were drawing near to Exeter by the time she had finished. Roger sat quietly for a while. His dismay had gone. His anxiety had gone too. He felt very calm. At last he said, "One day if you want me to, I'll answer all the things you have said to me and you'll see that, however wrong I may have been, I've always told

213

you the truth and always been trying to do what I thought a man who really loved you should do. But I can see now how things must have looked to you."

They had no time for more. Exeter meant a change of trains and Roger had to get his kit-bag. The London train, when it came, was packed. They forced their way into the corridor, up-ended Gladys's two large cases and sat on them. It wasn't conducive to conversation. All the way to London they said very little.

"Sally said you were going to work in London. I shan't be far away. Could I have your address and could we start again?"

"I'm not going to be in London itself," she answered. "I'm going to be an under-manager at a big hotel called Oatlands Park in a place called Weybridge."

WEYBRIDGE! There was hope yet.

"And are you Gladys Hill or Laura Hilliard?"

For the first time her face broke into a smile. "Oh I'm just old Gladys. I decided that if they couldn't employ Gladys Hill they weren't fit people to work for."

"That's true."

As their journey neared its end at Waterloo Roger said, "I'm coming out in your direction but I've got a telephone call to make first. If you can hang on, I can come out to Weybridge with you."

"I'm not going to Weybridge. They told me to get off at Walton on Thames. It's nearer."

While she bought her ticket, Roger ran and made his telephone call. They caught the train out to Walton. As they left the intensity of London's housing behind and began to see little bits of green their spirits rose. They got off the train at Walton.

"You don't have to come with me," she said, but by now she already knew that she wanted him with her.

"Yes I do. I need to know where I can find you."

"We have to go under the underpass. There are taxis the other side."

"No we don't," said Roger as Roy stepped forward. "That's why I had to make a telephone call. Roy, this is Gladys. Gladys – Roy."

"Miss," said Roy. To her amusement he touched his cap before taking the cases she was carrying. They came to the car and loaded up.

"Oatlands Park Hotel please Roy." He opened the back

passenger door for Gladys and then jumped in the other side.

"Had a good journey guv'nor?"

"Not bad thanks. The train was a bit crowded though."

"No more trains for you now guv'nor," laughed Roy. "That Rover you liked is still there."

"Oh good. We'll go and see about that next week."

By the time that conversation was complete they were at the Oatlands Park Hotel. It stood way back off the road like a very grand mansion house with its own splendid drive.

"Don't you dare move," Roger whispered to Gladys. He got out of the car, walked around it and opened the door for her. He and Roy carried her cases into the hotel and Roy made himself scarce.

"When do you actually begin work?" asked Roger.

"Monday," she said.

"Would you come out with me tomorrow so that I can show you my home?"

"Oh no," she said. "I'm not ready for that yet. In fact I doubt if I ever will be. We've a very long way to go before you will persuade me to meet your parents."

"I'm not asking you to meet my parents." Roger was puzzled and then light dawned. "Oh I see . . . No . . . I don't want to show you my parents' home. I want to show you MY home."

"YOUR home?"

"Yes."

There was a long silence. Ever since he had introduced her to Roy she had felt bemused. Roy had called him 'guv'nor'. And what was all this about a Rover? And what did he mean by his home? She had so many questions that needed answering.

"So can I pick you up tomorrow and take you out for the day?"

"Well I was going to . . . Oh why not? Yes, all right. Pick me up at eight o'clock." There, that would test him.

"Lovely," he said. He turned to go. Then he turned back, grabbed her, held her tight and kissed her forcefully before turning once more and striding out to where Roy was waiting with the back passenger door open.

"No," said Roger. "Front please."

He jumped in and Roy began to drive away as Gladys came out onto the drive to wave.

"Things are working out very nicely Roy," said Roger. "Take me to the Hills next please."

39

The Beginning of a Dream

Roy drove him to the Hills'. They went into the house together and Mr Hill gave Roy his Sunday work for the last time. They transferred Roger's kit to the other Rover and Roy went on his way.

It didn't take long for the hand over of the business. Roger had brought his second payment in cash so that the business would become his own at once with no bank delays.

"I expect you've got mixed feelings about handing over your business to someone else."

"No," said Mr Hill. "The hard bit is over. I have hated these months waiting for you to be ready. I've dreaded something going wrong. It has been the longest few weeks of my life. And now I can't wait to be shot of it all."

"Well I can't tell you how grateful I am. I'll pop in once a month with the 'goodwill' payments so you'll know how things are working out."

"And don't forget to bring that Gladys with you," said Mrs Hill.

Roger laughed. "I might just do that," he replied. Oh yes. He might just do that.

He drove home and parked on the concrete forecourt. He went inside and fussed around like an old hen. What on earth would Gladys make of this? At last he went to bed but he had a pretty awful night.

At a few minutes before eight the following morning he drew up outside the Oatlands Park Hotel. Gladys was already waiting.

She walked across to the car.

"Front or back madam?" asked Roger.

"Front of course, you ninny."

He opened the door, she jumped in and he closed it. As they drew away she asked, "Nice car. Whose is it?"

"Mine," Roger answered.

"Why did that Roy call you guv'nor?"

"I expect he calls everyone 'guv'nor'."

She was quiet for a moment or two. "Yes I expect he does," she said, "but that's not it is it?"

"No," he said. "I'm his boss now and the car he was driving is my car too."

"Tell me about it."

"I will later on today, but it's a long story. The short of it is that I've bought a run-down firm, a sort of luxury taxi firm called 'Hill and Co.' "

The name of the firm was not lost on her.

"But I haven't time to tell you any more because this is my house."

He drove onto the concrete forecourt and they got out of the car. Curtains twitched across the road and Gladys grinned. So people were just as nosey in Surrey as they were back in Devon.

Roger gave her the long front door key. She climbed two steps, opened the door and stepped inside straight into the front room.

"This is the lounge," said Roger unnecessarily.

It was empty, not just fairly empty but completely empty. There was literally nothing in the room, not even curtains.

As Roger closed the door Gladys noticed three hooks on the back of the door and they hung their coats on the hooks.

After she had recovered from the shock of its emptiness she looked around again. It was a decent sized, light room with a fairly high ceiling. Yes, she thought, this could be made very nice. But she said nothing.

A door led past central stairs into the back room. This was darker and not as large.

"The dining-room," said Roger, "but I'm afraid that at the moment it doubles up as my living-room and office."

She looked at the way he had organised it. The 'office' was under the stairs. She guessed there had been cupboards there and felt that it was a pity to have lost them. Cupboards are always so useful in a house. There was a small table with a portable typewriter on it. On either side of the table were cardboard boxes containing all the paper, envelopes and files and so on that his office needed. On top of one pile of boxes was a telephone.

She looked at the rest of the room. There was an old card table with two chairs he must have picked up cheap. On either side of the fire were two deck-chairs. A wireless stood on the mantelpiece. She looked at it all, took it all in but still she said nothing.

They passed through to the kitchen. It was small. Against the wall adjoining the neighbours, there was a trestle table for a work top, and there were a couple of cupboards on the wall. She opened them. Two cups and saucers, two side plates and two dinner plates and two cereal bowls – decent china too.

"Would you like a cup of tea or coffee?"

"Not yet," she said.

Inwardly he was hopping about like a mad thing but outwardly he managed to look reasonably calm. Gladys simply went on with her inspection.

A couple of saucepans and a frying pan hung from nails on the wall. A cupboard under the trestle table held vegetables and a small free-standing cupboard held all the rest of his foodstuffs – cereals, coffee, tea, butter, jam, not much else. Beside it in the corner was a broom cupboard.

On the other side of the kitchen beneath the window there was a sink and draining board. Only a cold water tap, she noticed. Next to it was a gas cooker with a kettle standing on it and next to that, the door to the garden. A bath hung on the back of it. It was pretty much the same as her mother's kitchen, but her mother had a range in the dining-room and a wash-boiler in the kitchen.

Gladys unlocked the kitchen door and stepped out onto the yard. Flagstones covered a small area that led to 'the little house' and a clothes line ran from the corner of the house to the little house.

"I'll just use your toilet," she said. It was only an excuse to look inside. It was spotless. When she came out she said, "You'll need to lag that piping before winter sets in. You don't want a burst out there."

"Yes," he said, "and I thought I'd get a paraffin heater."

"Good idea."

She looked over the wilderness that was his garden. It was quite a decent size, long too. She would see it better from the bedroom.

"Are you going to show me upstairs?"

"Yes if you like."

They went back through the house to the steep, narrow stairs and climbed. At the top she turned right into the front bedroom. Like the lounge, it was completely empty.

She crossed into the back bedroom. His clothes were lined up in neat piles along one wall as if he had prepared them for a kit inspection. She looked at his bed. He had placed his kit-bag on the floor and simply made up a bed of sheets and blankets on top of it. He didn't even have a mattress.

In the corner, over the stairs, there was an extra space which would make a good wardrobe. His suit and naval uniforms hung there.

"Why have you still got your uniforms? I thought you were demobbed?"

"Yes I am, but we have to do five years in the Special Reserve, and I shall have to go back three times for three week refresher courses."

It was as she stepped over to the window that she noticed that the electric light had no shade. She guessed that none of the lights had shades. A large piece of cloth hung from one side of the window – his curtain. She smiled to herself. How modest!

She lowered the sash window and looked out across the wilderness of brambles and nettles and other people's rubbish. And all the while she said nothing and all the while he waited, curbing his impatience, struggling with feelings that were part excitement, part foreboding. At long last she said:

"Is this your dream then, an empty house and a wilderness and a run down taxi firm?"

"No," he said, "that's my reality, the beginning of my dream if you like."

"What will you do with the wilderness?"

He stood behind her and put his arms around her, half expecting her to push him away, but she didn't.

"I could do with the help of an expert," he replied, "but I thought I'd try to turn it into a kind of cottage garden with lots of

219

flowers at this end and a vegetable garden at the far end. A long time ago someone told me about her dream garden and I liked the picture she painted."

Still looking at the garden, she asked, "And what will you do with the house?"

"Not a lot until I can find someone to share it."

She laughed. "You certainly know how to tempt a girl don't you?" She pulled herself out of his arms, turned round and with a sweep of her hand added, "Offering her all this."

He laughed too. "Yes, it would have to be someone very special who would be willing to come and share this, you're right."

"Special or foolish?" she asked.

"Foolish I suppose, but she would be very special to me."

"And do you think you'll find someone?"

"Who knows? Of course, she wouldn't have to live in the house while it is like this. She could wait until I had made it the way she wanted."

"But that would take ages."

"Yes I suppose. Anyway, it's academic isn't it. The only girl I ever wanted never gave me any encouragement."

She backed off from this conversation. They were like a pair of boxers circling the ring, eyeing each other up, unsure of themselves and she was not sure where she wanted this to go.

"I think it's time for a cup of coffee," she said. "You can bring it up here if you like."

"Right." When he returned she was back by the window looking out over the wilderness with unseeing eyes. She seemed far away.

"How long ago was it when you had this girlfriend?"

She was still playing games with him. Well if that was the way she wanted it, he could play games too.

"It all finished last year," he said. "I first knew her when I was at school."

"Last year," she replied. "That's a long time ago. I don't suppose you've given this girl a moment's thought since."

He turned away . . . walked out of the room.

Oh damn! What had she done? She was scared. She listened to him run down the stairs. She knew how sensitive he was. Blast it. She had pushed him too hard. Anxiety took hold of her. Then she heard him coming back up the stairs. Tense and worried she stood facing the door, ready to apologise.

But when he came back into the room he simply gave her an exercise book with her name on it. He never said a word.

She sat cross-legged on the bottom of his bed, sipped her coffee and skimmed through the book.

There were a lot of poems, all dated, and each one written for her. She closed the book and opened it again at random. The poem facing her had been inspired by Keats it said. She didn't know anything about Keats except that he had been a poet. She felt ignorant. She hadn't had his schooling. Did that matter?

It didn't seem to matter to him. They had been through all that hadn't they. He had pooh-poohed her when she talked to him about class, and money and all that and he hadn't liked it when she called herself a mere chambermaid – not that she was any more. But he had told her about his grandmother who had been an illiterate scullery-maid. Yet Roger had obviously loved her best of all his grandparents and been proud of her too. Gladys wished she had met her. Roger might just as well not have been there, she was so wrapped up in her own thoughts but he was content to let her be. He stood by the window and allowed her the peace and quiet she needed.

She was thinking about the house – Roger's empty house. They could really make something of this house and its wilderness. They really could, and she could be in on it from the start, share all of it with him, the work, the fun and the sense of achievement. She could give up her room at the hotel and live here, going in to work each day. She began to dream. Perhaps in a while they would have a couple of kids . . .

Whoops!

It was no use thinking along those lines, not yet. She turned back to the exercise book and read a few lines:

> *There is a marvel in the gifts you bring,*
> *they give my heart fresh cause to sing.*
> *The beauty of your life flows into mine*
> *and gives my heart a hint of the divine.*
> *The warmth I feel I all derive from you*
> *and gladly give it back as is your due.*
> *So take my gifts, for each one is your own,*
> *each rivulet of love is to a river grown.*

She closed the book. So he had been thinking of her right through the year just as she had been thinking of him – unable to get him out of her mind. She thought about his words. Dear Roger, he was so serious. Well yes he was! But he was always good for a laugh too. Perhaps she would be good for him, lighten him up a bit.

She mused for a while longer. It was only because he was serious that he had written those poems. Of course, half the stuff he said about her was rubbish but it was nice to have it said all the same especially as he meant it. And what if he was serious? Real love was a serious business wasn't it? It was when it was the sort of love that's for life, that's for sure. She clasped the book to her.

"Can I keep this book?" she asked.

"Of course. It's all for you."

"And I might never have seen it." She was silent again for a while and then right out of the blue she asked, "Do you want to make love to me?"

Be looked at her in amazement. "What NOW? Well yes, of course I do. But . . . oh hell . . . I haven't . . . well, you know, I haven't been shopping."

She hooted with laughter. "Don't worry about that. If we're going to get married it doesn't matter does it?"

She started to strip and in no time the two of them were snuggled up together in Roger's bed.

"Gyaw," she said, "you don't half believe in giving a girl luxury. The floor of the cricket pavilion and now this!"

She had slipped back into broad Devonshire. Until that moment Roger hadn't noticed throughout the whole week-end that over the course of their year apart her accent had softened to no more than a gentle and lovely burr.

"Why don't you lie on top of me?" he said.

"Durned good idea."

She moved over and they lay still for a little while. He began to caress her firm, soft body. He was so happy. He hadn't felt happy like this since the holiday in Lynton and Lynmouth. She was his and he was hers. It was paradise. She felt so beautiful.

And then she took him. He began to move. "No," she said, "leave it all to me." He lay back in ecstasy. He came far too soon. She continued to lay on top of him for a while. Lazily, almost casually, he continued to make love to her body and the two of

222

them dozed a bit.

"It's time you did a bit of work," she said and slipped off him inviting him to take his turn on top. There was no hurry. He kissed her lips, her face, her neck. Soon the tides of passion began to rise in him again and he took her. She preferred it this way. He gave her the excitement she craved, stirred her with his power and brought her to a marvellous fulfilment.

Once more they lay quietly, gripped in a deep contentment bordering on sleep. At last she broke the peace of their silence.

"I'm starving," she said and they both had a fit of the giggles. They ran downstairs and washed in cold water at the sink. Roger put the kettle on for more coffee.

"We'd better go out to eat," he said. "There isn't much food in the house."

"So I shall have another ride in that posh car?"

"Yes, and after we've eaten we can have a walk in Bushy Park."

Fully dressed again, they had just put their coats on when Roger took her by the arms and asked, "Did you mean what you said when we went to bed?"

"What did I say?"

"You said that if we're going to get married it doesn't matter about being protected."

"Well it doesn't does it?"

"Are we going to get married then?"

"We are if you've made me pregnant."

"But what if I haven't?"

Her eyes sparkled with delight and merriment and once again she dropped into broad Devonshire:

"Us'll 'ave to zee won' us? Besides, you haven't asked me yet."

As Roger dropped to one knee and began, "Gladys Laura Hill, will you marry me?" she opened the door, skipped down the steps to the car and answered:

"Come on Roger Wallace. Don' ee keep a maid waiting. I'm hungry."